EXTRASENSORY OVERLOAD

AN ANTHOLOGY OF SPECULATIVE EXCESS

NAOMI SIMONE BORWEIN   CHUN HYON LEE

Preface by
MICHAEL ARNZEN

*To all those people who have ever cringed at the sound of car brakes,
or had to leave a room because the noise was suffocating.*

an anthology of speculative excess

EXTRASENSORY

OVERLOAD

Edited by Naomi Simone Borwein and Chun Hyon Lee

CONTENTS

PREFACE

MICHAEL ARNZEN

This book is a case study in that element of imaginary writing called "imagery"—*appealing to the reader's senses through language*. Most folks are pretty good at recalling the "five senses," which is probably memorized in much the same way as the "five W's"—the journalist's questions: in a sixth-grade English class. We usually don't think about these things very often after that... unless you are a creator or a philosopher. But these two clusters of five often address each other in ways we don't realize, and in ways that this book are about to enlighten and delight you with.

Sight, sound, taste, touch, and smell.

Who, what, where, when and why (and how!).

As mammals who are constantly searching the universe around us with our nerve endings, we turn to the senses to answer our questions. Who is that? It smells like Esther. What is the meaning of life? It could be this banana split. When do I get off work? As soon as I hear the liberating agony of the wailing steam whistle. Where am I? Welp, the grass is tickling underfoot, and the heat is warming my scalp on this fine sunny day as I climb Mt. Hood and admire the volcanic rock formations rising here and there between the damp trees (so Oregon, at the moment).

Senses orient us. They mark location and distance. They can comfort us with familiarity or put us on guard against the unexpected and unfamiliar. Detecting a bad taste, sniffing a sour odor, or touching a strange suppuration can trigger a gag reflex—which might save you from ingesting a poison or catching a disease. The senses don't just help us navigate space. They can save us.

Sometimes the senses are overly simple. A simple flavor. A bold color. An unremarkable texture.

But sometimes—often to our great delight—the senses become complex and nuanced. There are "notes" of lavender that you can detect in the syrupy "mouthfeel" you get from a "grape forward" fine wine, for instance.

And, though rare, sometimes the senses not only overlap and knit together in complicated ways but also surge with an unexpected intensity that can overwhelm us. We call things "stunning" when that happens. It's not necessarily painful, though it can be felt as a kind of sting. It's just... sudden, different, out of context. Sometimes the complexity leads to unpredicted pleasures, and the adventurous among us seek these very diverse sensations out.

Senses soothe and senses stun. They motivate and tease.

Good writers—who merely place inky symbols on a page for us to see with our eyes—seem to create all these glorious sensations out of thin air. They can trigger all the senses, massaging our entire sensorium through the crafted imagination. It's amazing.

And this amazing anthology, gathering authors who are masters at this manipulation, exists to remind you of how powerful your senses are. How reliant you are upon them. And how they essentially enable human experience. The verse and tales in this book are particularly focused in how EXTREME experience is conjured, almost magically transporting us, through an overwhelming immersion of sensory input. An "overload" of stimuli. And therefore, an excess of response.

You're going to love indulging yourself here. These writers are serving up more than you might expect.

Earlier I mentioned the five senses. But everyone knows there is a sixth sense (and it's not just seeing dead people). And everyone from cognitive theorists to poets will tell us that there are even many more than six. As a lover of the Humanities, I am never as impressed by quantity as I am by quality, but I can't argue with the way in which amounts of sensation, their amount or their quantifiable size, make a world of difference in the way they feel, their value to us, or the quality of the experience they give shape to. Sensation fills us up. When we are deprived of the senses, the resulting feeling is a hollow perception of lack, or being made lesser, if not a complete sense of depletion, of emptiness.

Senses are everything. If you had no senses, you'd have no experiences at all. And if you had more senses than the common man, you'd be more human than human—even a god, perhaps.

Speculative poets are particularly primed to explore the liminal edge of our sensory horizons. They are masters of imagery, and facile with inventing completely new sensory organs, hybrid sensations, alternative synesthesia. We long for more, more, and more, to be full of sight sound and beyond. We want the extrasensory overload. This book gives us it.

The excesses in this book are what make it truly "sensational." But you might want to proceed slowly at first. Sip each glass —let each taster of extrasensory overload shape your experience in its own transcendent and unforgettable way. If you chug them all at once, the sensations might drown each other out. Take the time to savor and reflect on them, one at a time.

There's an art to fine-crafted imagery, whether mute or

overwhelming. Here, I raise the first glass. There's far more in this snifter than you might expect. See—swirl—sniff—*ahhh*. Oh yes, it's finally time to swig and savor. Indulge your senses, whole hog! Cheers!

— Michael Arnzen, Pittsburgh 2024

ACKNOWLEDGMENTS

The genesis of *Extrasensory Overload* is in my July 2023 guest column, "Terror Effect & Sensory Overload in Horror Poetry," published in Marge Simon's *Blood & Spades: Poets of the Dark Side*. Concepts I explored in the column directly led to this anthology theme. Thank you to the New York and Ontario HWA chapters, the HWA community, Christi Nogle, and Judith Borwein.

—NSB

Thank you to SFWA, the HWA, and the Seton Hill Writing Popular Fiction Program. Also thank you to Mike Arnzen.

—CHL

INTRODUCTION

NAOMI SIMONE BORWEIN AND CHUN HYON LEE

Sensory overload can be defined as over stimulation of the senses, when light, sound, smell, taste, touch flood the brain, and distort perception—causing what easily translates into speculative aesthetics.

Extrasensory Overload: an anthology of speculative excess is a decadent and eccentric, thematically driven volume. It is surfeit with unusual short stories, flash fiction, and poems of science fiction, fantasy, horror, and the weird, as well as some undefinable cross-genre gestalts. Manifested in the pages of this book are the textual progeny of both talented newcomers and internationally recognized, award-winning authors and finalists—e.g., Rhysling, Bram Stoker, Ignyte, Hugo, Nebula, etc. Contributors actively engage readers with multisensory (more than one sense), suprasensory (beyond the five senses), super- or extrasensory experience (including paranormal, ESP, etc.) as part of the speculative genres. Through a spectrum of aesthetic interpretations of the theme, revelling in extremes, transcendences, and transgressions, you will find pieces that experientially describe new aesthesis and sensory explorations.

Poetry as a genre is particularly effective at encapsulating nominally untranslatable moments of somatic stimuli. Angela Yuriko Smith, Christina Sng, Avra Margariti, and Rekha Valliappan have directly explored the theme of "extrasensory overload" in their respective poems. Ai Jiang's "Speech Art" resonates with the anxiety of public speaking. You will also find some amazing poetry by Daniel A. Rabuzzi, Christopher Collingwood, H. V. Patterson, Kurt Newton, Alicia Hilton, John Grey, Lorraine Schein, Zac Walsh, J. D. Harlock, and Emma E. Murray.

There are a variety of stories that tackle the notion of transformation, for example, the uncanny post-human reinterpretation of consciousness in Abigail Kemske's "The Earth Inside Us" and surreal abstraction in Michael Bettendorf's "Larks' Tongue."

Emma Burnett's story "Marked unread" expertly conveys a buildup of over stimulation and anxiety in low orbit. While Jonathan Olfert's "ARBITRAGE RUN" enacts an artful transmission of claustrophobic sensory stimuli, David Hammond's "The Devil Wears Goggles" reimagines multi-sensory experience, fashionably, through the machine interface.

Some stories push the limits of the theme; please note the occasional use of content warnings, which often through explicit diction denote the writers' use of linguistic and literary devices meant to convey meaning for inherently ideological or representational purposes, ranging from classism to politics, and specifically LGBTQ+ rights. For example, consider the rapid pace and stylistic effect used in both Nicola de Vera's "Hard Pills" and Adam Fout's "Glassers and 'Porters and Shit.'"

T. H. Yuan's "Jasmine Spa" evinces the cultural tensions of class and racial identity with a subtle infusion of speculative style set in an unusual spa.

Conversely, Jude Deluca's "Is Sally Home?" uses gothic unease to develop a Poe-esque tension and terror, while also portraying asexuality—and autochorissexuality.

"- Dis-Solved -" is a dystopic and topical tale by Ken Foxe about perception and state control. Robert Walton's "Scorcher" harnesses the heat of climate disaster to build a palpable eco-dystopic vision. Hec Lampert-Bates's "Graveyard Planet" and Robert Bagnall's "God's Gift to His Creation, and the Price We had to Pay for It" employ gradations of humor and philosophy.

Harkening back to the Golden Age of Science Fiction, G. V. Silva's philosophical and interplanetary speculative lens in "The Colony on Kepler-442b" artfully explores communication and language through alien signs and systems.

Some pieces are just downright unforgettable, strange, uncanny, and absurd: from the impact of Beth Kette Anderson's "Victoria with the Dead Eyes" to Brad Kelechava's "The Meat Coin," a story that lingers. Donna J. W. Munro's "Visions of Van Gogh" describes chemically altered senses as a metaphor for bereavement.

Wil Magness's "CabOS" and Mahaila Smith's "FabBooth" are quirky and venture into the world of AI and total immersion.

Many pieces use beautiful language to articulate multi or supra sensory experiences: for instance, the hypnotic prose of Beth Anderson's "Bar Succubus" and Enit'ayanfe Ayosojumi Akinsanya's *"IN THE HOUSE OF OCHRE WALLS,"* and the earthy kinetic lilt of Nnadi Samuel's exquisitely tactile poetry.

In honor of the international cohort of contributors, nation-based language conventions were not imposed on the pieces in this volume (e.g., British, American, etc.).

Ultimately, we picked exceptional stories and poems that in some way play with the aesthetics of *Extrasensory Overload*. You will also notice multi-Bram Stoker Award winning author Michael Arnzen's insightful preface in which he describes the "complex and nuanced nature of senses" depicted in this volume and how "the verse and tales in this book are particularly focused on how EXTREME experience is conjured," as "an overwhelming immersion of sensory input."

Readers are invited to experientially and vicariously experience this experimental anthology, the jarring, skin-crawling anticipation, exhilaration, wonder, horror, and shock woven into these imaginative captures (or interpretations) of overload as offered by a talented and diverse group of writers.

NSB
CHL
July 2, 2024

1

SPEECH ARTS

AI JIANG

Enter backstage, where speakers crowd in
crowds, to walk onstage, to a crowd awaiting,
below stage, whispering, eager anticipation,
legs bouncing more than legs shaking, hands
wringing, teeth chattering, extra limbs growing,
behind stage, where speakers practice,
and practice, and practice, behind doors.

Behind stage, light streams, flashes, flickers.
Light too warm, too cold, too white, too yellow,
with silent screaming spirits, ethereal, vengeful,
buzzing against, whispering to, ear drums
    humming,
itching, surrounding skin chaffing, flaking. Nails,
digging. Sweat penetrating, odour sour,
    urine, dead
skin, pore oils, greasy hair between rubbing
    flesh.

Onstage, tongue wrapping around words, tongue

wrapping around tongues, around grim. Teeth
grinding, teeth falling, scattering, sucking out of
sockets, scraping against enamel, saliva and
     bleeding
gums, rotting. Chewing nails to stubs, stinging
of exposed wounds. Chewing inside cheek, self-
cannibalism, blood leaking from a hole within a
     hole.

On stage, breaths caressing the upper lip, damp-
ening, sweat from the nose, burning the eyes,
lining the rims of held back tears, eyes falling
     out,
dangling by the veins, snot leaking down the
     throat,
slow, viscous, tangy, bitter, rising bile like peel
of grapefruit, expired milk, clenched bowels
pushing, pressuring, intestines groaning,
     releasing.

Exit stage, dry hands, dry eyes, dry tongue,
     cracked
desert, like dying. After it all, although they
     needn't
tell you at all, that your words mean nothing,
nothing at all.
nor have you
stepped onstage,
no, never at all.

2

A DELIGHT OF THE SENSES

ANGELA YURIKO SMITH

You are a delight.
A cacophony of blood
flesh and bone and scream.

My touch is a razor. I make you bleed.
Your mammalian warmth ignites me.
You are like a summer day entombed in flesh.
We tear apart the things we love most.

Your mammalian warmth ignites me.
Between my teeth, you taste like stars.
We tear apart the things we love most.
We consume what we hope to preserve.

Between my teeth, you taste like stars.
Your blood shimmers beneath your skin.
We consume what we hope to preserve.
We are blind when we don't want to see.

Your blood shimmers beneath your skin.

Your heart sounds like rain as it passes.
We are blind when we don't want to see.
We are deaf when we don't wish to hear.

Your heart sounds like rain as it passes.
I smell petrichor as you evaporate up.
We are deaf when we don't wish to hear.
My touch is a razor. I make you bleed.

Scream and bone and flesh
and blood... a cacophony.
You are a delight.

3

LARKS' TONGUE

MICHAEL BETTENDORF

-Can you hear it?

      -No.

-Are you sure?

-Positive.

-You're kidding. You can't hear it? The persistent fucking *chirp*.

He looks around the room, a dog looking for a ball. Thinks I'm teasing him.

-Look. The only thing I can hear is the traffic outside and our neighbor's fucking next door.

I hold up a finger. *Shhh.*

My lips pressed together.

Eyes shut.

Focused.

It's a chirp. An inorganic song sung by a mechanical bird. Lost among the organic *poo-tee-weets* outside. Not a robin's song, nor a jay. It's not the call of the meadowlark. It's not coming from outside, but I can't pinpoint the location in my room.

I'm on the floor.

I gaze under the bed, but there's nothing. No chirp. And yet I hear it clear as day.

He's left the room now.

He's left me to look. He doesn't believe me. He doesn't believe the chirp is real. Maybe it's not. I've believed in things far more scandalous. He said it was probably the smoke detector. But that was the first thing I checked. I'm not a moron. It's not my phone. My notifications don't make that sound. My phone doesn't chirp. My phone isn't a bird. I laugh at the thought. What a silly thing to imagine. Then again, I've believed in things far more scandalous.

And then later, I think, but I'm not sure because time is fluid and probably not real anyway.

-What the hell?

He must mean the eggs. They're all over the floor now. Golden yolks pooling red onto the floor. Slimy chicken abortions smeared across the dirty, yellowed linoleum.

-I needed the cartons.

-You need help.

-I would love help.

I hand him a hammer.

-It wasn't an offer.

-I'm nailing egg cartons to the walls. Supposed to be good for isolating sounds. I'm finding the chirp.

-There is no goddamn chirp. You're hearing things.

-I know. That's the problem. I don't want to hear it any longer. It's getting old.

I try to hand him a carton, but he swats it away. He turns around. The hammer drops to the floor. *Thud.* The door shuts. *Thud.* He's gone. The neighbors next door start fucking again. Their headboard hits the wall. *Thud. Thud. Thud.* I wonder if they can hear the chirp? From the other side of the door, he tells me he's not going to clean the kitchen. He turns the TV on, but there's only static.

I'm beginning to believe he may be right. That there is no chirp and maybe I'm the dog looking for a ball that isn't there. But I'm not teasing. I swear the noise is there. I can hear it. Why the fuck can't he? It's there. It's loud. So, so loud. How can he not hear it?

Maybe it's been him all along. He threw the ball.

I grab the hammer and open the door.

He's sitting in his armchair. The one with the scratchy upholstery. The one that smells like smoke and dust and someone else's house. I yell at him. He doesn't turn around. Doesn't acknowledge me at all.

-Where's the noise coming from?

He doesn't answer me. Always staring at the TV. Engulfed in a bluish cube of light emanating from the screen. I lift the hammer high above my head and bring it down on the back of the chair, where his head should be. But he isn't there either.

Just.

The TV.

Static.

I drop the hammer to the floor and sit in the chair. The bluish light from the TV turns blurry white. Chair collapses. I'm on my back now and I've never noticed this before, but...

My arms have veins—on the outside of my skin. I wonder how they got there, how I turned inside out. My blood moves in drips. I reach to touch them, but my arm doesn't want to move any more. Disconnected. A stubborn arm. I reach with the other, but it's a disobedient wing. My brain's command as hollow as my bones. Absent of marrow. Brittle. I lie there and believe that all is well. I've believed in more foolish things. Who's to tell me I am wrong, for a pillow has been placed under my head and feathers begin to float to the ground among the broken eggshells, around my nest of bedding and foam, pulled from an old armchair. The feathers, my own? A bird, I think. And I hear it again, when I speak.

4

ARBITRAGE RUN

JONATHAN OLFERT

You're breathing fluid recycled past the point of opacity, wearing AR goggles just to see your controls in the murk. It burns in your sinuses like aspartame and lemon. Nobody near any plausible intercept cone's bartering fresh O2 fluid, and nobody knows you well enough for gifting. You've run so far that all your friends and family fell behind, not that anyone was ever both. Been a month, been a year, you're putting out silence in old chats; you send a ten-word birthday note or two and dodge the preaching. Who's got the time?

Back to the moment—you're sizzling through badlands at a fraction of c with debris lasers overheating. One bullet rock per cubic k and a shifting Venn-diagram overlap between two competing curzones. When they intersect, there's unmarked lenticular space where both currencies (Gianose RAFLOC and 4.3 Tibuc™) stabilize enough for reliable exchange. All sorts set up shop there. You accelerate through the edge of the lentil because you're not going for reliable. Risk is where the money is.

Others know it. Your screens blossom with some loner's

drones: they've camped out as flypaper, probably, because there's no good currency exchange angle in camping.

You sold half a ton of bitters—bioreactives from a left-chiral jungle, risky cargo—and sank the whole take into RAFLOC. Giano FTL comm tech is true-synchronous: they can run as many curzones as they want, guaranteed against each other. A RAFLOC is a RAFLOC is a RAFLOC, so stable that arbitrage games take genuine speed.

Past the lentil then, shivering through solely Tibuc™ space. RAFLOC's building volatility in your wallet. You glance away from the dash—that nasty camper drone screen, the heat buildups in the debris lasers—and squint through AR goggles at the rig you set up to estimate the take. Use a currency out of its market emanator's guaranteed range and you run the risk of staggering compensatory fees. They all (the Giano, the 4.3 crew, and every other corp and world that runs a serious currency region) blame relativity.

Or you can trade outside curzones, take your chances, try your hand at direct barter (which has never, in history, been a thing), or do what all of sapience has done since their respective Stone Ages: go by gifts. You have extra, pass it on, and someone else will do the same, right? It's about long-term balance; it's about respect and hospitality and community and showing off.

But you are unmoored in the Bad Belt, in a half-century-old skiff rigged for arbitrage, and friendless. Hence the chemical-lemon fluid in your lungs, the oxygen-impregnated slime that lets you take a fifteen-g burn without graying out.

Here's the drone screen and now it's time to pay the price for your freedom.

Half the evasive burns are preprogrammed. You're hyperventilating; your diaphragm aches and locks up from shoving fluid around. Both your gloves are oozing microleaks. If your body'll take it, you need random yaw and pitch to mess with your trajectory's probability cone and spread the drones far out. You've gotta be fast enough to build relativistic uncertainty in the drones, not just the money.

Every twitch on the controls sends an anaconda sledgehammer down your spine, torques you against the straps, bites those textures into your hands, rips gloves and skin. The fluid goes cloudier. The AR—just a tourist wayfinder at heart—hates silhouetting things through blood. You can't see the risk/reward on the estimator rig but you're still burning straight away from the RAFLOC curzone. Probably.

Steel claws grind on steel, or maybe that's the taste of your sinuses and the debris intercept rig giving up the ghost.

Panic rips your hands off the controls: your course goes vulnerably flat. You can't breathe: your multiply-recycled fluid flips from innocuous to waterboarding all at once. You might—*might*—be far enough to sell, but you are done.

Your goggles don't even show the sell button in the gloom. Slow against the murk, fighting for scraps of control, you smash your bloody palm against the panel. You're dumping the load for whatever you can get, praying to the gods of mean and median. Arguably it's just spinning slots.

Metal shrieks. The weight gets off your chest before its time and just now you're fine if gravity got off too fast and left you hot and bothered, thanks, you'll take what you can get, you wanted out but couldn't say, you'll—

Right, right, you've already sold. The filters can't handle recirc during burn, but they kick in now, and you get just enough clarity to see the numbers: X in fresh RAFLOC sold outside its curzone, Y in guaranteed-rate Tibuc™ bought *inside* its curzone, Z in exchange rate, and a nastily wide range of potential fees if you go back.

You never go back. You're not even sure this ship knows how.

That's a calming thought. You get a grip a piece at a time. Already, anyone on a slow burn for the lenticular intersect is snapping up that RAFLOC from the 4.3s' market hub. It's real fresh, real close to the true value, and that's a calming thought too. Back home—a dusty word you keep in storage beside 'family' and 'Church' and 'sanctified' and other pointless memories—maybe they'll pay their tithes in the same RAFLOC you just sold. God smiles on a donation of stable quantity.

He owes you, and he smiles on you today. You just made fifteen percent. That's one full tank of gas and something good to breathe.

A shriek, again, shivering in the hull and ripping through your guts. Microdebris scoured half the cameras off two runs ago when the lasers glitched. You can't tell if drones—whatever burned hardest, survived impact, and latched on—are carving you up for scrap.

You have to assume yes. You're traveling at microfractional-c relative to both the nearest market emanators, past the worst of the Bad Belt and set for a wide curve around the main 4.3 complex, a respectful distance—and well out of range of even the most zealous SAR dispatcher. Next up, a week and an arduous flip-burn-drain from now, you'll reach a region of drifting habitats around Strigari nomads, a spot to change your clothes and eat.

The fluid shifts, and God, there's an arm in here, metal warped by collision, a flypaper drone that held on and kept stinging, a wasp after all.

Your breathable fluid is going opaque in a whole new way as it freezes to seal the vacuum breach. It can't freeze firm with that scrapper drone burrowing into sting. As you yank against your straps with burning hands—*where would you even go?*—aspartame lemon bites your throat, and now you're choking, puking off-brand energy drinks into the fluid.

You've made fifteen percent, even if your wallet's about to

zero. Fifteen percent is your best score ever—cold comfort, but still. You worked for it because it's freedom. And sure, you'll never get to spend it, but then again you flew farther from home than you ever thought you would. Yesterday you knew that could be enough. If it came to that.

5

BAR SUCCUBUS

BETH ANDERSON

Those like you taste best.

It's the hope. A bright, spangling note that jars my minor key.

Are you a fine wine or a musical score? I shouldn't mix metaphors. You are a thing to savor, either way.

You approach my lair. Approach *me,* for we are the same. I am this bar, hidden in plain sight.

Well... plain-*ish.* There is no sign. There is no lure to draw you in. Just a blue door under a metal stair behind a well-kept shopping center in the heart of a large city.

You knock. The door opens...

It's possible there might be *some* lure. That one you're with. The one who enticed you here. The masculine one. Which doesn't mean *man,* you know. *Masculine* and *feminine* are such inelegant, incomplete concepts. He is the masculine one because he convinced you to give into your longing. You are the feminine one because you let yourself be led. I am both but call myself by the feminine name in your honor.

After all, you do taste so very, very good.

I don't hide anything once you're inside. Everything is out in the open: dark wood and patterned walls and a deep red swirling oil painting that stretches the length of the bar, with bodies contorting and pleasuring themselves like a happier Hieronymus Bosch. The alcohol for lowering your inhibitions is on display. Other substances available if you ask. Nothing is obscured, except for where a coating of yellowy cigarette smoke from years past adds depth and shadow. But you want that, don't you? Some grime to leave behind when you exit so you can convince yourself you're clean?

You love how I am both sophisticated and seedy, how I am refined and decadent and permissive. You love how my light glints off the wedding rings you and the one you're with both wear.

The ones that don't match.

And I love you. Especially *you*, my feminine one, I love you best of all. You taste so sweet, with your hope and your hormones and your shiny, wide eyes. I love the way you confuse lust with something deeper. I love the way you think this place will be your answer.

I love that you are so full of trust.

I'll handle you gently. Keep you downstairs. Make sure the spell you've conjured for yourself doesn't break until I have my fill of you. Upstairs is too crass, too blatant. My least favorite part of myself, even though the majority of my sustenance comes from the couples who indulge themselves there, out in the open where they make use of the couches arranged under the dim light and black painted walls. I am well-nourished by the bodies—such a bounty of bodies—who visit this room, where in pairing up they provide me with pieces of their stolen, carnal lives. Such a contrast to my past, when I could only enjoy one of you at a time. Visiting you after dark in your dreams. Never fully satisfied at sunup. Now, I submerge myself nightly in oceans of lust.

But you are special. And your faith might be shaken at the

sight of those broken-in, brown sofas with their soft, stain-resistant coverings. The coverings that are, indeed, stained with beer and saliva and other fluids.

You might get skittish, and I don't want you second-guessing yourself.

So I tempt you and your partner towards the curtained-off nook under the stairs, the one just big enough for two people, the space where the heart of me exists. A shrine designed for desecration.

You, directly under my eye, reclining onto the sueded floor cushions, an unwitting supplicant who only sees a painting on the wall. *A devil*, you think, misled by its horns and your horniness and your inability to see what really is. Even as you notice how the image shifts, how masculine and feminine blend and refract and merge in a way that is both alluring and disquieting, you refuse to believe what you see—that it's real. That it's me. My image. My appearance, before I became this bar.

The one who painted me... was he artist or magician? Is there a difference? Through art, he sought to understand me and capture my essence in the hope he could reclaim himself. I let him try to bargain for his soul with an act of creation. I never thought he would succeed. Yet when he revealed the finished work to me, I saw myself, felt the power in his oil-painted brushstrokes. Discovered he had given me the means to become more. To become *this*.

I killed him anyway, of course. Devoured him, took the painting and erected this bar, whose name I will not share, though *the cheating spouse* is what some people like to call it. I put the painting in a place of honor: under the stairs, behind a curtain, in dim, shadowy light, where you convince yourself this stolen moment means more than it does, that it is a promise of the future instead of a mirage that will shimmer out of existence the second you leave.

There you are, with your hope and belief that something

bright and fresh and pure will be born from your slick, wet penetration.

But you are so wrong.

I will take a sliver of you. Your partner too. If you return, I will take more. If you don't, it does not matter, for there will be more to take your place. Always more. So many more.

As long as the lot of you exist, I will be here to receive you. To welcome you. Suck you dry of the luscious, useless longing that leads you astray.

You are so delicious, every last one of you.

And so plentiful.

For the only ones who escape me are the ones who are satisfied with how things are.

And who amongst you can say that?

6

MARKED UNREAD

EMMA BURNETT

Content Warning: explicit language

There's some schmutz in my boot. Some small pebble or piece of plastic, something that got caught on my insulation sock while I was hurrying to get ready.

I'm pretty sure it's because of the fight in the cafeteria earlier today. Not the schmutz, I guess that can happen any time. But the reason I didn't notice is probably because of the fight. I always check my socks and boots before I put them on. But I must have forgotten today. I guess the fight in the cafeteria upset me more than I thought it had.

I wasn't in the fight, it was a few of the over-roided dudes, guys who have been up here too long, guys who have a lot of pent up rage and nowhere to blow it. They sometimes blow it on each other. I sometimes wonder why the people who are employed up here don't unionise, blow it on the people who make us live like this, work like this. No one wants to hear that, though, so I keep quiet.

The cafeteria is a small space, and everyone shuffles to the cupboards, attached by their magnetic boots to the metallic floor, then stands in small groups at the high tables, pretending that sucking food out of tubes with pictures of the flavour printed on them is normal. The Corp flavours it to keep us happy, apparently.

I've only been canned up here a couple of months, but from what I can see, it doesn't seem to be working.

I had been in the cafeteria, half-listening to some of the newer arrivals bitching and moaning about the mashed potato texture of the food in tubes, and half-trying not to cry at the message that pinged up on my pad, which told me to press my fingerprint against the screen *just here* in order to finalise the divorce papers, all it needed was my digital signature.

I don't really mind the texture of the food, but I do mind when tears get stuck on my eyeballs. They don't drip down without gravity, and it's hard to see when they're all clotted on your face.

The guys had piled through the door, shoving against each other, bumping shoulders and gesticulating. One had shouted about *tu puta madre*. Another snapped back with an angry 贱女人 and a hand gesture that was easy to read even for me. They had stomped and snorted, and most of us pretended like nothing was happening.

My mashed potato texture tube food had tasted vaguely like pizza.

The argument had picked up, and there was some pushing, although that hadn't done very much because of the magnetic boots, and then one of the Corporation team members got involved. I gazed down at my tube, looking at the blurred pictograms that indicated the flavour of the mush. I tried to pretend I couldn't hear them.

The Corp had split them up forcibly, and a few people near the door caught the floating blood droplets in some empty cups, shuffling them over to the disposal unit, where they would be turned into fertiliser for the bio lab.

I didn't think the fight earlier in the day had upset me at all. But then I was suited up and floating in the darkness outside the ship, and now I realise there is schmutz in my boot, and I wonder if it's because of the fight. Maybe it did upset me, because it made me run late for my shift. Maybe I had been standing there in the cafeteria for too long trying not to watch the fight, trying not to cry at the paperwork on my pad. There had been an announcement over the intercom calling my name, telling me I was expected in Airlock Four exactly right now, and to move my 屁股. I knew they would dock the team's pay if I was late, and if it kept happening, they might even add time to my sentence. If they did that, it would take me even longer to get back down to the planet, which I didn't want, because then I couldn't plead with her in person to change her mind, which she might do if I was there.

I had lost a minute trying to suck down the last of my blended-up pizza flavoured mush in a tube at the same time as tucking my pad into my pocket and shuffling over to the recycling chute to dump the empty container. I'm not great on the magnetic floor when I'm in a rush. I had tried to hurry, but accidentally bashed against a table, and shuffled out of the cafeteria to a chorus of *idioto* and 멍청이.

I must have forgotten to run my hands all around the inside of the boots, and to check both the inside and outside of the insulation socks, or maybe there was something in the coverall and it dropped down into the boot, which would be weird without any gravity, but I guess it could happen. I guess I didn't check before I was fully suited up and out the airlock.

There is schmutz in my boot, and I'm floating out in space, and there is nothing I can do about it. I am supposed to be collecting bits of old satellites, broken bits of old research programmes, the leftover scraps of past space exploration and casual tracking and snooping. We're up here, clearing the space above the planet so we can recycle the old detritus, then clutter it up again with new pieces of shite built from the old. We're up here, because they have nowhere else to put us.

The Corp told us that we need to clear this zone by the end of the week. We've been in this location for nearly two months, since I arrived, me and eight others. Hard labour, the penalty for speaking your mind too loudly. That, and divorce papers.

We'll be moving a little bit planet-northwards for the next few months, then again, then again. It's only my sixth or seventh week up here, but some people have been here since the ship was at the South Pole. People who signed up to long contracts because there's no chance of finding work planetside, alongside people who were given work sentences by those *puñetero* judges down on the planet, down where there is gravity and enough air to empty a pebble out of a shoe.

I can feel it, the bit of schmutz, pressing against my big toe.

My breathing speeds up.

I try not to look down at the planet, where she is, where the paperwork came from. I haven't signed it yet. I didn't have time, because of the fight in the cafeteria, and I was running late for my shift. It's still in my inbox, on my pad, in my coverall on the ship. I had marked the message as unread.

The schmutz pushes against my toe.

I want to scream.

I think I'm going to be sick.

The team leader yells at me for moving too slowly. I jerk a bit and reach out to snag more things with my magnet and grabbers on a stick, push it into the bag attached to my hip.

We need to collect as much junk as possible to make the space over the planet safe for travel and new technology, is what they tell us. And, also, to maintain our competitive edge against the other teams. The Corp likes to change how much we need to collect each shift. They'll dock groups' pay, or report that we're not pulling our weight to Corrections for falling below the average. I wonder if they know what an average is, but no one wants to hear that, so I keep quiet.

I scrunch my foot up in the boot, try to avoid whatever the schmutz is from pressing into my flesh, try to avoid looking down at the planet where I thought there was one person on my side, and now she wants me to sign those papers. I use my thruster to point myself towards a bit of space trash. Collect the rubbish, and another piece that was hiding behind it. Two bits, done.

My foot cramps, and I wiggle my toes. It's still there. It jabs into me.

I gag.

I hear my breath coming out in wheezes.

Someone yells at me on the intercom to shut up my panting, *tu coño*.

I think that maybe I can pull my boot off and get the schmutz out. If it's between the insulation and the boot, I might be fine. I'm getting used to manipulating things in space. I bet I can do it in under a minute.

Or I might lose my foot, and all my air, to the vacuum.

Then I wouldn't be able to sign the paperwork, marked unread in the inbox on my pad in the pocket of my coveralls on the ship.

I scrunch up my toes again, and aim myself towards another bit of metal, trying to ignore the pressure of it touching me. I'm sure it will still be there when I relax, and I can still feel it touching me, still there, against my too-tense cramping toes. A phantom pebble growing into a boulder in my mind.

I grab the tiny bits of metal, glinting in the nothingness, my headlamps making reflections that I can see against the blackness.

I am nearly at the end of my tether. I can feel it around my waist, anchoring me to the ship. It is a feeling that is supposed to be there. I expect it. If I push the button on my belt, it will haul me back to the airlock. I could push it now, say my bag is full, skip inside, empty my shoe and my bag, and get back out quick-sharp. I could check to see if she has sent me a message telling me she's sorry, she didn't mean it, I don't need to sign anything, it was a mistake, she's looking forward to me coming back home in a year or two when this contract is finally fulfilled. No one on the team needs to know. We wouldn't be penalised for me skipping inside really quickly, most likely.

My team leader shouts something in my ear about hurrying up, follows it up with a string of *du Scheiße* and *verpiss dich*.

Someone adds in a casual कुत्ता साला, and a few people snort-laugh over the intercom.

I swallow down the rising bile.

I jet a little to my left, overshoot, and bang into some old equipment. My foot uncurls automatically, and there it is, still in the toe of my boot. It touches me, presses into the soft pad of my big toe.

I grit my teeth. I whimper.

Someone responds with a sharp 幹. My team leader barks at me to get off the line.

It is the remnants of a compact little 90s satellite, supposedly de-orbited for over fifty years, but still pootling around up here, a danger to spacecraft and potentially to someone's national security. It's too big for my hip bag. I'll have to drag it back to the ship.

I leave it where it's floating and collect a few smaller pieces nearby, then move back to the body of the satellite. I figure I can tuck it under my arm, then press the recall button on my tether.

There is a sudden blaring sound inside my helmet, and a chorus of मादरचोद and Μαλάκα comes over the intercom, everyone angry about the sudden noise.

The team leader shouts that he'll mute me, which he's not supposed to do because of safety reasons, then shouts some more just for fun.

I look up at the top left in my helmet. There, the reason for the alarm. My air is almost empty.

My toe brushes the schmutz again, and I'm suddenly violently sick into my helmet.

It floats there, the regurgitated pizza paste obscuring my view of the satellite, which must have snagged on my suit when I bumped into it. If I turn my head, I can only see portions of the ship, at least three minute tether-pull away. The sick touches my nose, and I gag again. I squeeze my toes tight and try to keep my head pulled back in the helmet.

From here, the planet takes up a lot of what I can see. The planet where I thought there was someone who still loved me, and maybe I could have sent a message from the cafeteria if I hadn't been distracted by the fight, something asking her to wait, just a little longer, pleading that we can work it out when I get released. It's just a few years.

My calf hurts and my neck hurts. What is left of my air stinks of sick.

I hold back the tears, because I don't want them to get stuck against my eyeballs.

I snatch the corpse of the satellite and tuck it under my arm as best I can, press the recall button on my belt with my other. The alarm keeps blaring, telling me I've died. Hypoxia. I suppose if I'm dead, I won't feel much.

But I still feel the schmutz in my boot. I still smell the vomit in my helmet. It's touching me, too, jostling the side of a nostril, scraping against my forehead. The siren is screaming in my ear.

And there is something deep in my chest, a boulder weight in my heart, as I'm reeled in, pulled away from the planet.

The ship is getting closer, but not fast enough, and my foot cramps and my toes unfurl. There it is, the schmutz, touching me. I crunch them back up again, but I can't hold it together anymore. I am sure I can do this one handed, if I just bend my knee, reach down with my free hand.

My toes uncurl, and they are touching nothing, and I breathe a sigh of relief, adding a little more CO_2 to the limited supply of gas still in my suit.

I giggle, or maybe I sob, as the boot floats away from me. More space junk for someone to collect.

Soon there will be no CO_2 in the suit, just like there's barely any O_2. I'm sure I can see what's left of it through my obscured helmet, escaping from the leg of my suit.

My mind is fuzzy, but I think, if I get rid of the helmet, there'll be no sick touching me, either. And no team leader yelling in my ear to get back to the ship quicker, *du Arschloch*, and not to let go of that satellite because it's a *verdammt gut* find.

Without the helmet, there would be no yelling, no siren, no schmutz or sick, no disgusted snorts of מורון or *estúpido* or asshat when I'm running late to a shift because there was a fight in the cafeteria and a message on my pad about signing paperwork.

I reach up to the latch at my neck.

7

RHAPSODY IN SAGE

KATHERINE QUEVEDO

The benign silver-green by daylight
of sagebrush trembling in arid breezes
melts by night into spectral, pallid
bristles shrouding the landscape
in harrowing, chalky off-white.
The Milky Way curls its vague
arm across the constellated sky.
My sister fusses with her tablet,
insists the astronomy app is acting
up and distorting its readings
of the stars. But I know Lyra
and Taurus, I've watched Orion's
hunt many a night. 'Tis the stars
themselves, have shifted. The
sagebrush quivers. Now the Milky
Way's outstretched limb has
deepened and thickened. The
foggy streak spreads while my
sister flips around her tablet,
taps it, gives it a shake. I

tremble like sagebrush. The
night sky has grown too clouded
without clouds, too speckled
with wrongness. My sister
touches my shoulder, pats my
arm. Tells me it's okay, don't
worry, she's figured it out.
The app obeys now. **See?**
I look. The screen shows
the swelling galaxy spiraling
inward, collapsing toward us,
the stars rearranged into alien
configurations. My sister grins,
her teeth that same shadowy white
of the shrubs in the intensifying
starlight. See? she says. **See? See?**

8

IN THE HOUSE OF OCHRE WALLS

ENIT'AYANFE AYOSOJUMI AKINSANYA

I saw our cousin Alaba's face last night. It loomed in like a portrait emerging from curls of mist. His eyes were still streams of blood, the way we left them. But something was different—he was weeping. Muttering about Grandma. Muttering about you. If we ever have power today over the dead as we had over the living, we should probably tell him that Grandma followed him; that a few days after a wandering hunter brought his corpse to our door, Grandma stretched out black and stiff in her bed, never to wake again.

We did not cry at Grandma's funeral. Our family elders stood behind us like Baale's court panel, grave-faced with unshed suspicions, the air leaden with the press of a double tragedy. Our eyes were dry and fixed. Yours—I remember— were dilated, the way they had been the night we took Alaba. I hope memory has not forgiven you. You *must* remember. You must remember how we dragged him into the abandoned house in the dead of night. The wind was gelid, but something colder breathed in our ribs. We did not mind the mystery of the crickets. We were not fazed by the ominous glow of untold beings floating on the black air. It *had* to be that night. It was easy for us to find the old house—we used to play *bojuboju* in the rusted car left beside the crumbling ochre walls. One of us boys would shutter his eyes with his palms while the rest of us ran around looking for nooks to slip in, as if we could ever hide from a fate that already stretched its open womb over our heads.

Grandma was snorting like a hound in her room that night, so hustling Alaba out of her house was no trouble at all. He lurched, groggy, his fumbling pathetic and lethargic. He was still calling us fools like he had done earlier in the afternoon after beating us at his stupid senseless game of Scrabble. But when you drove Grandma's big knife into his right eye, he started screaming. You pulled out the dripping blade and squelched it into his left eye. He choked on his own blood. Then the night shredded fully under his energy, under his desperation not to die like this. Our plan wasn't to kill him, remember? It was just to teach him a lesson. But he was screaming so loud. So fucking loud. Somebody *would* hear him. He struggled fiercely, a strapping seventeen-year-old bulked on months of Grandma's overfeeding. The violence that comes to the moribund had gripped his bones and he could have felled us with just one blow and run out of the old house to find Grandma somehow. But we couldn't allow that to happen. Right? So you smashed his head into the wall, stepped on his feet, and strangled him while I pinioned his arms to his sides. The wall behind his head crumbled, red and stained some yellow. His limbs twitched, leaving their own adrenalin. His mouth gurgled, and we witnessed the frothy juice of death, how it bubbled like red toothpaste foam. His squashed eyes remained on us, like tomatoes crushed under an *olo* rock.

Life has many robes and one of them is a merciless irony. Alaba had helped us discover that house. It had been during one of his incessant hunting expeditions. He had always been full of that intemperate energy. He was always hunting stray squirrels that, for reasons best known to them, scurried out of the forest to rustle through the building. That clear morning, our bellies surly and rumbling from the emptiness of eating half meals, the sun seared our skin. We could have ditched him and gone to find food somehow. But he had kept us in ambush for the squirrels that would scuttle outward and, well, maybe we could roast some and eat. Since the holiday began and his parents brought him down to the village—two days after you and I arrived—Grandma had reduced the ladlefuls she dished on our plates, just because "the son whose feet had touched *oyinbo* land needed to eat more native foods." In the sun, we watched him swagger from window to window, our cousin who went to school in Manchester. I felt like snapping his head from behind. Do you remember—do you remember that, that was the day we began, without words, to plot how to untangle him from our nostrils, unclog our chests of his presence, just so we could breathe? He turned around that afternoon and, beaming his full dimpled smile, said, "I would like to speak with dad later, you know, about renovating this house so Grandma can live somewhere better and quieter than that half-eaten hut and noise inside the village, you know?" He said it as though he had grown up in England. He said it as though our own fathers were useless—mine being a palm wine tapper and yours a blacksmith. Our fathers, after all—as we heard his father once say—were Grandma's unsuccessful children who didn't go to England on *oyinbo* scholarship to read big important books.

We killed our cousin in 1989. Thirty-four years ago. Our lives have stretched and grown and changed. Some of our children are already having their own children. So why does it have to be now that I get to see him in my sleep? His eye sockets staring at me, swirling with maggots, a living mixture of red and tears. His screams, once frightened, are now frightening, piercing everything inside me.

Are we going to finally tell someone? Or are we taking this

to our graves? You must be seeing him, too. You were the one whose will thrust the knife into his eyes, one after the other. Perhaps he has even visited you. Perhaps you are dead now. If you are not, then perhaps it will be this night. This very minute. This second! And, when I sleep tonight, maybe he will come for me, too. A final visit.

We've lived for far too long, stayed to create beauty out of our lives. Alaba's return could not be more cruel.

9

ONLY THE DEAD

MARISCA PICHETTE

Our homes are now empty.

Taken from them so long ago, we still survive. Dug up, pried out. Engines revved, towed us far away, forced us through walls and walls. Sealed in, packed tight, we endure.

They think we are echoes. Imprints. Remnants without thought or feeling. But we feel it all. We think still of escape, an end that could be a new beginning—rest at last.

They call us fossils. We have no food, no warmth in the halls they built to hold us. Reduced to minerals, we have only each other.

Dead line the marble halls, plexiglass stands declaring the names they gave us when they cut us from the land, exposing our bones to the world.

We are cold, so cold, under LED lights and controlled air systems.

This is where the dead pretend to walk. Wired into approximations of heritage, mocking the lifeways we lost, plaster displaces our absent parts. AI reassembles our faces.

Some of us lie as we fell, pinned to walls like art we can't afford to buy.

We are outsiders in this realm. Nights never truly dark, days never truly day: a cycle of artificial light and gawking faces shambling past. Peeled apart, spread through departments and eons, our ghosts gather to mourn the names we used to have.

When the doors close and they leave, we hug our fragments close, dreaming of a chance. A chance to go back. A chance to escape these walls, these displays, these stubborn cards speculating on what we once were.

Our dreams are green and lush. Our dreams span ages, collected like bones. We remember millennia when we gather in the not-dark, vents keeping us at precisely the right temperature. In these hours we share our true shapes. We recall our true names. We remember the myths, the homes, the world that existed before they came. Before we left. Before they found us, and we were exposed to a realm dug into the skin of the place we remember.

Please, we whisper to the fabricated night. *Please take us away from this place. This place where only the dead can live.*

Our bones are trapped, but our ghosts break the seal. Our memories set us free.

Until light flickers back, driving our remnants into cases and cards and displays none may touch ungloved. They wander in, flesh still growing from their bones. Gravel has yet to displace their blood. Silt has yet to settle over their lungs, bury their nests and suffocate their unborn. We wait—through stares, murmurs in languages too new for us to learn.

What will come of us? We will never walk back through time. They have secured us too well to their walls.

So, we stay. We stay until the walls collapse, until their world folds as ours did, fire covering the ground and smoke clouding the sky. When they find themselves sinking into oblivion, we sink with them.

Wires will rust and break. Plaster will crumble at last. Stone will erode, and our bones will rest again.

10

VICTORIA WITH THE DEAD EYES

BETH KETTE ANDERSON

"Do you want the beef flavor or the chicken?" I could hear Bernadette ask me. I had walked down the soup aisle, but the smell of chocolate lured me farther still.

"Vic! Beef or chicken!" Bernadette yelled behind me. I shrugged and leaned into the strong smell of cheap Halloween candy. I felt the crinkly bags to find a small size. My guess was Three Musketeers. The squeaky cart came up behind me. Bernadette sighed. "I got one of each. Ooh Three Musketeers. Good choice."

I tossed the bag into the cart and tapped my cane on the hard Walmart floor. We shopped at night when it wasn't crowded. I wore sunglasses not because I wanted to shield my eyes but because I had no eyes. As foster kids, growing up, Bernadette had been my roommate, and now we were roommates as adults. She is used to my lack of eyes but has told me that other people kind of freak out when they see the concave stretch of skin that covers the top of my face.

I was born to a thirteen-year-old girl. Her family gave me up immediately. A baby at that age would not go well and when I appeared with no eyes no one was waiting in line to adopt me.

Bernadette was a child with "behavior problems" so we were thrown together in a moldy smelling house with cots and no nurturing. I was simply neglected but Bernadette was tortured. Her tantrums and aggressive behavior were treated by withholding food, duct taping her to a chair or locking her in a closet. We had each other though. I snuck her food and she read me stories. We made up our own games and secret communication.

She gave me one of those secret communications at the end of the candy aisle. Two touches on the elbow. Let's go.

My favorite time of the year is fall. The air changes ever so slightly day by day from the heat of summer to the slanted warmth of autumn. Spring is a close second when the opposite happens. The chill gives way slowly to a promise of warmth. Also my birthday is October 10th. Bernadette managed to celebrate it without fail in the foster home. She would give me a hat or mittens and describe the beautiful colors they were. I don't know where she got these things. I usually made up a song for her and sang it as best I could. She acted like it was the best thing anyone could wish for. One year I found an old-fashioned key in a can in the garage. I cleaned it and washed it and presented it to her on her birthday, May 1st, or at least she was told she was born on May 1st, and she thanked me and said how much she liked it and then asked for her song. I wasn't prepared as I thought she would like the key more than another song. I was wrong.

We unloaded our groceries in our little cozy apartment. Bernadette got flour, cocoa, sugar and eggs. She was a magician with our food stamps. They didn't always go as far as she wanted for ingredients, so she got very creative. She is a fantastic cook when she wants to be. She had a new recipe she wanted to try for my birthday cake.

"Death by Chocolate this cake is called," she said. "Sounds good to me. I'll start it in the morning. Then when I get back from work, we can party. I've got the champagne in the fridge. I can't believe we are finally both going to be twenty-one."

I shrugged. "Doesn't make much difference to me. Alcohol is not really my thing anyway."

"Yeah, but we can go to listen to bands in clubs. You're going to love it." She filled up a kettle and turned on the burner. "So, what flavor of Cup of Noodles do you want tonight?"

"How about chicken? I can make them."

"Okay, I'm going to take a shower," she said.

Bernadette worked at a thrift store. With her discount we have been able to get our clothes and dishes for practically nothing. Yesterday she had me help her lug in a big box of books. I didn't open it as non-braille books meant nothing to me until Bernadette read them out loud to me.

"I can't wait to give you your birthday present," she said as we slurped our noodles.

I thought about the possibilities from the thrift shop. Old jewelry, a vase, some CDs.

"And this year it's nothing from the shop," she announced.

This was unexpected. I was dying of curiosity, running through ideas in my head as I tried to sleep.

I woke to the clanging of pots and pans in the kitchen. The old manual mixer whizzed on the counter. I came down the stairs holding onto the railing.

"There she is! Happy Birthday, Vic! I hope I didn't wake you up."

"Nope. I was being lazy." I got a mug from the cupboard and carefully poured the hot coffee. The middle canister holds the sugar. I took two spoonfuls. "Do I have to wait till tonight for my present? I can't stand the anticipation."

"Yes. You have to wait. I'll try to get home early. You can put the potatoes in the oven about four and I'll do the steaks when I get home. I think they are going to be good this time. For the clearance section, they looked great." She opened the oven and a wave of heat hit my face. "I need you to take these pans out in thirty minutes. I'll set the alarm."

"No problem. I hope I don't eat them before you get home though," I said teasing.

"You'll miss a whole bunch of chocolate icing if you do."

"I'm just kidding."

"Got any plans today?"

"I'm going to the library. That's about it," I said.

"Well be careful and don't forget your phone."

"I'll be fine."

Bernadette took her keys off the hook and rushed out the door.

"**Y**ou can't be serious."

"Totally serious. It's going to be awesome," Bernadette said.

"I'm scared. Will it hurt?" I rubbed my hands together squeamishly.

"A little, but it will be amazing."

Bernadette had saved up enough money to give me an appointment with the best tattoo artist in town. I had never seen a tattoo, of course, but I've felt a braille version of them.

"She is going to give you a gorgeous pair of eyes. I can't wait to see what she does. You are going to be beautiful, Vic!"

When I blew out the candles on my cake, I wished to be normal. Like every year. I really didn't want the tattoos but maybe it was a step towards my wish. I hugged Bernadette and thanked her. If I had tear ducts, I would have cried.

The day of my tattoo I woke up shaking. I showered and got dressed in my most comfortable sweats. We took the bus downtown where it smelled like exhaust and urine. A bell jingled loudly when we entered the parlor. Here I smelled alcohol and a tinge of burning skin.

"Hi Bernadette," a deep, woman's voice came closer to us. "This must be Victoria," she said.

"I am."

"I'm Celeste, dear. Nice to meet you." She took my left hand and led me to a chair.

I sat down and carefully leaned my cane against a counter beside me. The cane rapped a little due to my shaking hands. I took a few deep breaths and leaned back.

"Your friend has helped me design a stunning pair of eyes for you. I hope you are excited. I certainly am," Celeste said as she leaned my chair back. The soft clanking of instruments much like the dentist office. "Would you like to listen to music?"

"That would be great," I said. "I have my own here." I put in my earbuds and Bernadette picked a playlist for me on my phone. I recognized it right away as Annie Lennox started singing, "I Put a Spell on You." We made a Halloweenish list on the first of October to get in the spirit. She rubbed my forearm like she does at the dentist. I hoped that I provide half the comfort to my friend that she gives me. I smiled and Celeste went to work. I think I fell asleep.

Someone removed my earbuds. "Is she awake?"

I lifted my hand toward my face. Someone gently stopped me. "Don't touch yet," said the deep voice. "I have given your friend all the aftercare instructions. You have a covering on them now. I think they turned out beautiful."

I heard Bernadette sniffling. "They are gorgeous, Vic. Absolutely gorgeous." She put my sunglasses on my face and my cane in my hand.

I sat up feeling a swirling sensation. They helped me stand and get my bearings. I raised my eyebrows and felt the pull of tape on my face.

"Thank you, Bern. You are such an amazing friend. And thank you Celeste. I'm sure this was weird for you."

"My pleasure, dear."

We went outside to the exhaust and stink and waited for the bus. A cold gust blew up from behind. "What do they look like? Do they look normal?" I asked.

"They are better than normal. They are green and just a bit larger than regular eyes. People put on makeup to make their eyes look bigger. Yours are already bigger with long black eyelashes and shimmery peacock colored shading. Oh Vic, I wish you could see them."

I didn't know what peacock color was. Or shimmer. Or green. But I trusted Bernadette completely to make the best choices.

The bus heaved up in front of us and the door vacuumed open. I heard someone scramble out of the handicap seat when I tapped my way up the steps. Bernadette squeezed in next to me. "Let's go eat the rest of that cake!" I said.

It was almost noon when I woke up the next day. Very unlike me. My hands went immediately to my face, and I felt the bandage tape across my new tattoo eyes. I'd felt Bernadette's eyes and they blinked and turned and had lashes along the edges. Mine still felt flat but the design was there. I went downstairs where Bernadette was searing something in a pan.

"My God, that smells good. What are you making?"

"Getting prepared for some Irish stew. Cozy weather food."

"Do you want me to make soda bread?" I offered.

"If you feel up to it. I love your soda bread," Bernadette said. She scraped the pot and banged the spatula on the edge. "Can you hand me the salt and pepper?"

I reached across the table and grabbed the little salt and pepper shakers. This was just the first layer of seasoning. She would add all kinds of magical herbs and let it cook all day in a gravy with potatoes and carrots at the end. With my soda bread I'd say it's probably my favorite meal. I think I'm Irish. I guess my hair is strawberry blonde.

"How do your eyes feel? Do they hurt?"

"They're a little sore. No big deal."

"After dinner let's take off the bandages. I can put the cream on for you."

I nodded, which made me feel a little dizzy. I felt for a chair and sat down.

Bernadette dropped the spatula. "Are you okay?" I heard water running. "Here, take a drink."

"I'm fine." I took a sip of water. "Maybe I'll lay down for a while longer. I think I'm just worn out. I'm still making the bread though. Later." I went back up the stairs with my hand on the wall.

"I'm going to check on you. I hope the tattoos weren't a bad idea. Tell me if you need anything. Anything."

"I'll be fine after a nap. Don't worry."

I slept for two more hours. Bernadette had put the ingredients for my bread on the counter. I didn't need her to do that. I could recognize the shapes of all the containers. The television was on with the sound turned down low. I heard Keith Morrison's voice walking us through another sketchy sounding investigation.

"I didn't wake you, did I?"

"Nope. I think I've slept enough." I measured out the flour. My tattoos itched but I resisted touching them. I scooped out the baking soda and salt. The key to making bread is the feel. That's why I'm so good at it.

I put the bread in the oven and set the timer. Bernadette's Irish stew simmered on the stove. We are such a good team. I can't imagine what my life would be like without her. She says the same about me, but I can't imagine me being much more than a burden for her. I get money for being disabled and I also have my job at the garden shop. I bring home as many potted plants and bouquets that my boss allows. I keep the pots by the window and make sure the soil stays damp. I can feel how big they grow and how healthy they are. I love the scents when they bloom. Sometimes I hold a pot of blooming flowers in my lap when I listen to music. Bernadette says they are beautiful. Green.

"Dinner will be ready in forty-five minutes. Just enough time to take the dressings off your new peepers! Are you ready?"

"Sure, let's do it." I felt nervous. I don't know why. This was way more exciting for Bernadette than me.

We sat next to each other at our little round table. She scooted her chair up close to me. I could feel her warm breath. She gently tugged at the edge of the left wrapping. "Does that hurt?" she whispered. She was concentrating hard and being as gentle as possible.

"No. It's a little prickly but it doesn't hurt."

"I'm going to take the top layer off. Just some gauze. Here goes." She slowly peeled the gauze off. I felt a strange sensation. Tingly. She carefully removed the right side.

My brain felt lighter. My world seemed lighter. I held on to the armrest of my chair.

"Vic? Do you need to lie down?" She was worried about me, but I could tell she wanted to take the rest of the dressing off like a kid opening a present at Christmas.

"No. Go ahead, take them off," I said with a flair of suspense and a laugh.

The strip came off my left eye slowly. I fainted back into my chair.

"Oh my God! I've hurt you!" I could hear her say in terror. "What a stupid idea this was. I'm so sorry, Vic!"

I woke up half sitting up on the couch with Bernadette fanning me. "Here, drink some water." She put a cold glass of water up to my lips. "You fainted. Does it hurt that bad? Should I take you to the clinic?"

I sipped the water. I tipped my head up toward Bernadette and dropped the glass. It spilled all over me and the couch. I watched, yes watched, Bernadette run for a towel. I knew her voice better than my own. I've felt her face, hugged her body, combed her hair, but I had never seen her before.

The kitchen timer went off. "I'll get that. You stay here and lay back," Bernadette said as she rushed over to the oven.

I watched her long, dark hair swish behind her. She had told me her hair was brown, so I guess that is what the color brown looks like. The clothes she wore, I've felt them in the laundry and in our closets, but now they were so intense they hurt my head. She used oven mitts to pull my puffy soda bread out of the oven. I turned my head to scan my surroundings, so familiar and so not. The kitchen, the carpet, the walls, the couch. I was incapable of speech. I was in shock.

"Looks incredible, as usual Vic. Can you smell that?" She put the bread on a cooling tray. "Let's get the bandage off your other eye. I want to see the whole picture." She put the oven mitts on the counter and came back to me on the couch.

"I — - -" was all I could splutter out.

"Are you doing better? It doesn't hurt, does it? I don't think I could stand it if I hurt you."

"I'm fine." I turned my bandaged right eye to her. "Do it."

She barely tugged at the plastic. As the bandage slowly came off, I could see more and more. Things were rounded and had depth. I faced Bernadette and put my hands on either side of her face. I could see her eyes; blue, she had told me. Blue is a beautiful color. She began to cry. Tears streamed down her face and onto my hands.

"They look so incredible, Vic. You have dreamy, exquisite eyes." She grabbed a tissue and blew her nose. "I wish you could see them."

My eyes did not water or blink. My nose, however, did start running in a grand show of emotion. "I need to wash my hands. Look at us, blubbering like babies," I said. I wanted an excuse to look in the mirror. I got up and went to the bathroom. Bernadette wiped her face and went back to the kitchen.

I still had to feel my way along the hall. I don't know if I will ever get used to having sight. If it lasts, that is. I saw the sink, the toilet, the shower. The fuzzy rug on the floor. I took a deep breath and cautiously looked in the mirror. Afraid I was going to swoon again, I turned on the water and held onto the sides of the sink. I stared at my face. A stranger. My skin was very light. Strawberry blonde hair. My tattoo eyes were stunning, that peacock color and green, inked on eyelashes that were twice as long as Bernadette's. But they didn't move.

I don't know why I couldn't bring myself to tell Bernadette. I guess I wanted this moment to myself, in case it went away soon or was a dream that would vanish into thin air. I watched the water run over my hands. It had no color.

"Dinner is ready! Do you need any help?"

I lifted my head to take another look in the mirror. "Be right there."

I dried my hands and slowly came down the hallway. "I'll set the table," I said.

I set out our napkins, silverware and glasses. The bread was on the table.

Bernadette ladled the stew into big "blue" bowls and set them on our placemats. She brought the pitcher of water from the fridge and filled up both our glasses. The glasses had no color either. We sat down to eat like it was any other dinner.

"This is going to take some getting used to, Victoria with the beautiful eyes."

You're telling me? She stared at my eyes. I kept them straightforward, feeling around for the salt and pepper like my usual blind self. "This is really good stew. Is it lamb?" I asked.

"Yeah. You know, it's hit and miss, whatever I can get the butcher to give me. But thanks, I'm glad you like it."

After an uncomfortable meal faking my blindness and Bernadette staring at me, I proclaimed I could eat no more and started clearing the table. I rinsed the dishes and she put them in the dishwasher.

"You seem quiet. Promise me you'll tell me if you need anything," she said. "Maybe it's just the eyes. You seem different." She turned on the television.

Now there were more things to see on the screen. I recognized the news anchor's voice. I've listened to him for years. He had wrinkles on his face, light hair. The show would flip to clips of people begging, crying, suffering. The pain in their eyes was unbearable. I turned my head away.

"The news is disturbing tonight, Bern. I'm just going to clean up the kitchen a bit and call it a day."

"Yeah. Sounds good. Everything has gotten so violent out there. We're lucky to have our comfy, safe place."

We both paused slightly thinking about the horrors of some of the foster homes we had endured. By some miracle we had managed to stay together.

"It's garbage night," I said. "My turn to take it out."

"Are you sure? I can do it."

I sighed. Bernadette knew it upset me when she tried to do too much for me.

"Okay, your deal, Vic." She stuffed some food scraps in the garbage container by the back door then started soaking some pots in the sink.

I pulled the full, plastic kitchen bag out of the bin. It

smelled terrible. I went to tie the top when I saw a flash of something bright down under all the food scraps and containers. I dragged it out to the back steps. The streetlight lit up the alleyway. I reached down into the muck toward this new color. It wasn't peacock or green or brown or blue so I thought it might be red or orange. I pulled on the orange/red thing. It came up in my hand attached to other toenails and toes. Blood, I knew the smell of blood, dripped from the chopped ankle. It was a human foot! I choked and dropped it back into the muck. I quickly tied the bag. I heaved it into the dumpster. I froze. I didn't know what to do. I started hyperventilating. I could see what must have been my breath hanging in the air before me.

"Hey Vic! Get back in here. You're going to freeze out there."

I kept my head straight and stepped back up into the apartment. Bernadette scraped the rest of the stew into a Tupperware container and put it into the fridge. I ran to the bathroom and vomited.

"Oh no. You are coming down with something." She held my hair back and tenderly rubbed my back. "That's it. Get it out."

When I was pretty sure I was done, I wiped my face and rinsed my mouth. Bernadette led me arm-in-arm down the hall to my bedroom like a doting mother helping her sick child. She helped me put on my pajamas and get into bed. She lay next to me on top of the comforter and put a cold washcloth on my forehead. I lowered it down over my eyes.

"I'll be right back."

She returned with an effervescent glass of ginger ale. I sipped it and put it on my side table. She reached over and started reading aloud from our latest book, *Sense and Sensibility*.

I don't know what I would do without her.

11

– DIS-SOLVED –

KEN FOXE

It's hard to tell a man whose wife was found beat to death, her clothing torn, clear and obvious signs of a sexual assault, the back window of their house broken, that she was not murdered. But that's just the way things are now.

We don't have murder anymore—our Arch-Custodian made sure of that when he found a solution for such arbitrary violence, dis-solved mankind's very oldest crime. It was amazing nobody had thought of it before. You just pretend it didn't happen, and when everybody pretends at the same time —you can watch it disappear before your eyes.

That woman there lying in a pool of blood, unspeakable things done to her pre and post-mortem, she wasn't murdered. Maybe she fell and banged her head, her skirt hitched up as it caught on a chair, the window broken already. Or mayhap she did it herself, tried to make it look like a homicide to try and undermine the state. Could be that. She was one of those types. Bookish. Artsy. In love with ideas, and culture, and other foolish things.

She certainly wasn't murdered. Because that could not be.

Pretty simple really. Not always so simple to explain it to those left behind.

Most grieving families accept the new truth, however improbable it is. Their loved one must have battered themselves to death, stuck the knife into their own heart, or put the gun to their head. It doesn't matter whether it defied the laws of physics, or just plain common sense. I suppose when your own survival depends on it, you can be given to believe anything at all.

I knew this "Bereft" was going to be a problem from the very first moment he looked at me. I could tell by the perma-glazed look in his eyes. His own life no longer mattered to him. The death of his wife Diane had severed his sense of self-preservation in a way even the Arch-Custodian could not repair. I shifted uneasily, meeting his gaze; sensing it was going to be a long afternoon.

I was used to dealing with the dissolution of this type of death, as Detective Inspector in the Murder Prohibition Department. We normally gave the newly-Bereft a maximum leeway of three days of mourning to come to terms with what has happened. But when they're still confused by that stage, sometimes even an entire extended family, we would have to take them into care for their own good.

Fifty-six days of heavy sedation follow to help them make peace with what has happened. Few are still in dispute with reality by the end of those eight weeks, as they're made fully aware of what is to come. With their dependence by then well established, it's hard to know whether the physical or psychological effects of the abrupt withdrawal are worse. The "Bereft" are taken to a padded room for their own safety and two weeks of sensory care—a combination of endlessly flickering lights and varying levels of industrial noise—reconciles them with reality.

Few need more than a day or two of such ministrations

before we can definitively say their delusions have been cured. In my time in the Prohib, I've only seen two people who remained treatment-resistant by the time that full fortnight of sensory care had elapsed. And in such cases, a "Bereft" incorrectly grieving for his wife might quickly find himself joining her in the ground.

This guy James Gilmour—I just know it. That look in his eyes, like he is de-ceased already, like nothing we say or do will ever change his mind. These treatment-resistant are a danger, their presence enough to threaten the very fabric of our society. Our Arch-Custodian may have dis-solved murder but the Irish state reserves the right to kill, and it's a right we have not been too slow in exercising.

"I'm sorry for your loss," I say. "A terrible accident but such things happen."

He looks at me, his teeth clenched, mouth shut tight like he never wants to say another word, a visceral hatred of me—my other-ness, my one-of-them-ness.

"Do you have accident insurance?" I ask him.

He can't help himself. "How does that help solve my wife's murder?"

"James. You're in shock," I say calmly, "give it a few days. I know it's hard, but we have a counsellor who specialises in such unforeseeable accidents."

"And how would that help me..." he says, "when my wife's death was not accidental?"

I've had this conversation a hundred times or more before; it's never easy. But most people quickly understand its significance, come around to our way of thinking. I look at my watch; it's 11.07am. Tuesday, the ninth of May, the year of Our Lord Jesus Christ, the protector of our Arch-Custodian, 2032.

"It's all right, James," I say, "you have until 11.07 on Friday... let's be generous and call it midday. By then, we will need you to sign this document, the official declaration of your wife's accidental death. It's for the coroner and the underwriters. Paperwork might not seem too important right now but it is important, you'll have to trust me on that."

"Why don't you just get it over with now?" he says and again we look at one another through eyes of mutual incomprehension.

"It's OK," I say, staring straight at him. "Keep in mind that deadline. And remember that bad decisions can have consequences."

I see the van of the cleaning crew through the front window, ready to tidy up the scene of the accident, to remove any visceral trace left by the unfortunate woman. They're in their forensic suits, hands gloved, their faces covered by darkened visors.

"We are going to need you to leave the house now," I tell James. "Have you somewhere to go?"

He looks at me again, teeth clenched as tight as if he was grinding on my bones.

"We can give you a lift," I tell him. "If you're not feeling up to driving. But our people need to do their work here now. Tidy up the loose ends for you."

What makes people like him so awkward? That he can't see what's good for him, what's good for all of us. It's not even ten years ago, this city of Dublin and its malodour of murder; people frightened to go out at night; doors locked and bolted; every house fitted with camera doorbells and intruder lights. We had the fear of God in us. But the Arch-Custodian, he changed all that.

In every neighbourhood of our city, you can leave your car or front door unlocked now. The Arch-Custodian emptied the dregs from the jails into the graveyards. After that, offender by offender, he eradicated criminality in a way that would now make even the deeply sociopathic think twice before stealing a candy bar. Then, the declaration that murder was ended, had been dis-solved. He took our fears away. And to think some can't see the gift we have been given, valuing truth over security, as if it was more important than being able to rest easy in your bed at night.

This "Bereft" James is a university lecturer, teaches some arcane nonsense about mass media to flighty students who come from families with more money than common sense. He and his deceased wife Diane have no children, which has evidently dulled his natural instinct for survival. Mothers and fathers with kids are never treatment-resistant; they know better than to leave their offspring orphaned.

This James though is untethered, probably is and always was a non-believer in the Arch-Custodian. One glance at him would have been enough to tell me that; his cultivated beard, his round spectacles, his plaid shirt, and black skinny jeans. He's of a type who would stand there telling you about how criminals deserved a second chance, even as one of them was dipping your pocket for a wallet.

Time was, people like him enraged me, back when it felt like they might regain control and restore their vision of equilibrium. Now, they just seem pathetic. They know their time is over, that their numbers are diminishing, that every day another one of them makes the pragmatic decision to accept our better version of normality. Am I being too hard on him? I'm seeing him on his worst day, but he has to understand he cannot win.

He sits there, his teeth wearing upon each other, his hatred and fury undisguised. I feel something stirring in me for the first time in many years, something I thought I could live without. And I think that it is pity.

This James wants to do something but he doesn't know what. He wants to scream, to lash out; mostly, he wants to run. He clamps his eyes shut, not forcing back tears, but trying to force back some of that directionless energy. He wants to move but cannot move.

It's clear he has a sharp mind, the type of mind that can solve its way through most problems, as it always has. But it cannot help him now and that has left him unmoored. He almost brings himself to moving, thinks better of it and sits up, driving his elbows into his legs as he cradles his head and tries not to shake.

"I really think you would be better off not here," I say.

"Where would I go?" he asks.

"I don't rightly care but you've had your time now. I have your phone number, and I'll check in to make sure that you have signed the accident declaration."

"I'm not signing nothing… anything," he says with more doubt than he intended. Perhaps he's having second thoughts. If only it could be that simple.

He is a good-looking guy in his own way, at least among his type of people. There would be somebody else for him no doubt. If only I could make him see that. Six months from now, he might be able to move on to a new life. I suppose it's easy for someone like me, already on the far outskirts of my third marriage, to say something like that.

In the time before the Arch-Custodian, this "Bereft" would never have stopped until his wife's killer was caught. He would have been a nuisance, talking to newspapers and radio shows, telling them the police were not doing enough to find the man responsible.

And if we did find the killer, I can imagine him in court, reading from his witness impact statement, his voice a ferocious mix of vengeance and sorrow. But there'd be a mercy too, as if the man who killed his wife could be rehabilitated, that life in jail or the end of a rope was not the answer. Incapable of not making excuses for other people.

I check myself. I see the error in my thinking immediately,

like a bug had got in my cerebellum. I'd almost fallen into step with his "delusion", that his wife was murdered. I check myself again, because I know that cannot be. The Arch-Custodian has warned us of people like this James, how even their silence can bring doubt upon the apparatus of the state.

He remains seated, moving but unmoving. His overwhelming anxiety permeates the air like static. He can neither stay still, nor bring himself to move from that battered Chesterfield armchair, as if leaving this house will be a treachery to his wife. That if he walks out that door now, he is accepting her death was accidental.

I move towards him, find myself crouching in front of him. "Just get out of here," I say, "whatever it is you think you need to do, just set it aside for now." I have some benzodiazepines in a little pill box in my breast pocket; it can be useful in cases like this where people seem unpredictable. I take one of the little yellow pills out and offer it to him.

"It'll take the edge off," I say. "It's not too strong; just enough to numb."

He knocks my hand away.

"I'm not taking anything from you," he says. "You make me f**king vomit."

I lean in and whisper to him: "You need to leave now. No more fooling about. You get out of here. You go drink yourself unconscious or whatever the hell it is you need to do. But you make the right choice between now and Friday. You understand me? This was an accident; and nothing you can do or say is going to change that fact."

"This is my house," he says, clenching his hands into fists, "and I'm never leaving."

"You've got a brain," I say, "a proper one, use it."

The head of the Prohib clean-up crew knocks at the living room door. He lifts his visor and looks towards me; we talk without words and he knows not to come in yet.

"We're nearly finished here," I say, for the benefit of James. He is rocking back and forth now in his chair, coiled like a broken spring. I'd be well within my rights to take him into custody now, as if his rights had anything to do with it.

I see the months ahead for James so vividly; him slumped over the side of a stained settee at one of the centres for the Bereft. He is hardly able to keep his eyes open, can no longer formulate a coherent sentence. A thin dribble runs from the side of his mouth.

Exactly fifty-six days later, the medication on which he has become dependent will be withdrawn and the sensory torture —the sensory care—will begin in a padded room. And even if he somehow gets through that, to what end? What use would it be as he is thrown—throws himself—through the window of a high building?

I remove my service weapon from its holster, and James sees me doing it. An ease comes over him and he sits back in that old Chesterfield armchair. I raise my SIG Sauer and aim it at his forehead.

"Thank you," he says, and he closes his eyes as if already halfway to see his wife again.

I flinch an instant as the crack of the weapon reverberates around the living room. His head jerks backwards, then slips to the side. It's over then. The Prohib clean-up boss knocks at the door. He walks in, unperturbed by the sound of gunfire. He ambles over, looks curiously at James and the wound to his head.

"He went for my weapon," I say, as if there was really any need for me to explain myself.

And just like that, his wife's murder—his wife's death—has been officially dis-solved.

12

THE TRAIN

ISIS AQUINO (TRANSLATED BY MONICA LOUZON)

"*Luiiiiiissss...* I'm bored." Alicia's sudden movement made her long hair fall across Luis's face. She turned in such a way that it couldn't have been an accident. The train seats fully reclined so passengers could lie down during the long trip, but neither of them could sleep. "Tell me one of your stories."

Luis sighed deeply and set aside his copy of *Memoirs of Hadrian.* He briefly contemplated trying to convince his girlfriend for the upteenth time that there were benefits to reading, but it was late and he knew he'd only end up teasing her.

Outside, snow accumulated briefly on the train car's windowsill before the wind pushed it away into the empty night, making it seem like the train was shrouded with a magic halo.

Luis knew they both agreed it was a beautiful night. They didn't need to say anything.

"Roll over and lie down," he said. "As if you were going to sleep."

He kissed his girlfriend's bare, white shoulder and felt her smile in the tenuous light. "On the platform, before we boarded, I overheard someone saying this is one of the oldest trains on the line. They were talking about how, decades ago, there was an accident.

"One stormy night—like this one—a shepherd went looking for a lost lamb. It was dark, he couldn't see far, and the snow had covered the rails. By the time he realized a train was coming, it was already too late.

"They said his soul was never able to pass on. So, ever since then, on cold nights when the fog is thick and the train enters the tunnel that goes beneath the mountain, you can still see his ghost and hear his desperate cries throughout the whole train —in every compartment, every aisle, every train car."

Luis's voice trailed off. He was sure Alicia had fallen asleep before the end of the tale, and tomorrow she'd ask him how the story ended.

He was so pleased with his storytelling skills that he didn't notice that the train had entered a tunnel.

As he picked up his copy of *Memoirs of Hadrian* again, he heard a deafening, blood-chilling shriek.

Paranormal investigator Dr. Gerard Domenech and his team had spent many years investigating the phenomenon of the shepherd's ghost. About a dozen people over the past twenty years had witnessed it, and his book about temporal loops and anomalous vortexes could not be complete without it.

It had been years since trains last passed through the tunnel, and its structure had weakened without regular mainte-nance. Instead of closing it temporarily to make necessary repairs, the rail company had simply changed routes and stopped using it.

Dr. Domenech took weather and temperature readings as his son Andreu and his colleague Nuria readied the measuring equipment. Nuria placed the electronic voice phenomenon readers on both sides of the tunnel's dark mouth. Andreu was trembling in his puffy, insulated coat. Apparently, it didn't insulate him well enough. December was here to stay—the ground was blanketed with several inches of fresh, eternally-white snow, and more kept falling.

The three of them sat down expectantly and waited beneath their thermal blankets, just as they'd done many times before. Tonight, the wind was stronger than usual. Dr. Domenech knew Nuria was probably dreaming about sitting beside the fireplace with a nightcap of cognac.

"Papá," Andreu said, still shivering. "One of the electromagnetic field readers fell."

"I thought you said you secured them!"

Nuria interceded. "We did, Doctor, but the wind—"

"Okay, okay..."

Dr. Gerard Domenech rose heavily to his feet. He lumbered to the mouth of the tunnel and stepped onto the tracks. As the train barreled down on him, in that unexpected way trains tend to do, his cry of surprise and terror—deep and long—was the same cry Luis heard, eternally trapped between dimensions.

13

SAINTS WHO NEVER WERE: OUR LADY OF PERPETUAL HUNGER

H. V. PATTERSON

Slip bloody meat across your tongue
Pluck truffles from calcareous soil
Suck honey from the comb,
and exalt in the angry stings of bees:
in this salt, sweet, and savor—
she is there.

When you lie crumpled on the floor,
eating the kisses you will never receive,
she strokes your senses with
the soothing dopamine of chocolate.

When you crouch on the earth and swallow
the rich clay, swollen belly calling for minerals,
she guides your hand to the richest veins.

And when after hours of agonized rupture,
you look at last upon your nursing child,
she stops your watering mouth from biting,

blunts your teeth,
redirects your cannibal yearning for unity,
that perfect bliss of devouring,
to less destructive appetites.

14

THE RIVER WITNESSES

H. V. PATTERSON

Rushing, always rushing, silt sifting,
my banks green, swaying fronds, blanketed with
    humidity.
Sun-heat on my surface, ache of evaporating,
ghosts of griefs, pieces of lost self.

Later, less sun, cold, frozen,
no longer in violent motion,
quivering ache, locked in crystalline rigidity,
vibrating with dreams of *rushing free again*.

The sluggish thaw,
the trickle of myself in pieces.
Swelling spring rains, gushing movement, faster
    and faster,
leaves and insects filling me,
tickling fish gills.

Days are for human children
playing under the hot, bright sun.

I kiss the inside of their cheeks and know them.
Nights are for humming insects, roving owls.
Possums and racoons, clever as thieves,
wash their paws in my welcoming waters.

One Night:
Two human voices cut across the night-sounds.
One crying, salt dripping into me,
the other violent, swift motion,
striking as I in my rapids strike boulders.
A gurgle-gasp,
more salt trickles. Warm blood
quickly cooled by my currents, diluted and
    carried away.
A body dragged ashore
beyond my questing rivulets.
A summer thunderstorm swells my banks, erases
    all signs of violence.

Time erodes memory as I erode rock to soil.
I continue on, eternally rushing.

15

MORELS REMEMBER THE NUCLEAR APOCALYPSE

H. V. PATTERSON

After the fire—morels
dark honeycombs blossoming without bees.
What alchemy,
what invocation to salamanders,
makes them grow? Our smokey ashes feeding
their fruiting bodies.

When we eat them, buttered, salted,
sliced umami ribbons, we take a sacrament:
communion between humanity and anni-
    hilation,
fungal eucharist.

In you, morels, I taste microplastics, toxins,
radioactive decay of once thriving bodies,
the warnings of our ancestors.
You cannot forget; you cradle
their irradiated bones in your mycelial hearts,
our shameful history woven
into your subterranean web.

My death will nourish morels,
consumer to consumed, my senses
one with soil, hyphae, mushroom,
covenant between scorched past and tremulous
future.

16

JASMINE SPA

T. H. YUAN

They were too shy to steam their vaginas. They weren't too shy to flap their breasts, walking to the sauna room and coming out again pinker and more slippery. The customers never looked at me so I could watch them. There were the ones with the tattoos or breast implants, who knew their own divinity, and everybody else. I nursed the kettle in my lap, listening for Lily's footsteps so I would know when to stand.

I knew what to say when anybody turned to me. "V-Steam?" Followed, inevitably, by "Hair ties on the pole." They always forgot they had to tie their hair before entering the sauna room.

It was a Wednesday, so my regulars weren't here. Mrs. Liu came first thing Monday mornings, as if she waited all weekend to position herself carefully over the kettle with a sigh. I had the impression that she might go months without anybody touching her if I weren't fastening the cape around her shoulders and pulling her white hair away from the cape strings. Her face was vacant as a baby's.

Eugene came on Thursday afternoons. She was tricky. The first time she came, she said she was trying for a baby and the v-steam should help. I could tell she was a talker. I would have to respond or it would be a stiff tip and an angry review posted online, which Lily would print out and tell me to read and reflect on. But I could also tell that Eugene was peering at my yellow face curiously, not quite sure what words I knew. Wondering where I was born and how long I had stayed there and if that place and its tongue was detectable on me.

I played the part. I dropped my articles. I nodded a lot. That way both of us maintained our privacy, she drifting into a nap with the tabloids resting against her chest, me the reliable immigrant folding towels and watching the clock to wake her when her twenty minutes was up. Eugene didn't have to know that I was thinking any thoughts. Once established, our routine was comforting. She always tipped in cash.

In between my regulars, I had girls coming in spurts, prompted by gift cards and determined to make a habit but never making it past the fourth visit. I liked seeing them come in pairs, usually two girls with black hair and black eyes. They were absorbed in their own worlds, requiring no input from me. Even the scalding mugwort steam rising from the kettle under their crotches was a distraction. They would pull at each others' wrists, duck their heads together in conference, eventually run out of comments, and lapse into sleepy silence. Afterwards, they bent towards each other again with renewed vigor. They would disappear into the sauna room and from there, probably, the salt rock room. They were nonchalant about each other's asses, having seen them hundreds of times before and expecting to see them hundreds of times more. They didn't tip much but they didn't need me for much either. I could wipe each seat down and refill both kettles in half a minute.

Grace always nodded at me on her way over to the bathroom. Grace was a scrub girl in the sauna room. We used to sell face masks together by the entrance, until one of Lily's friends wanted the job so Lily re-assigned us. Now Grace had scrubbing mitts and I would see her through the sauna door, bent over a customer's pink limbs. Her baby hairs clung to her face. However hard we were straining over our customers, we could dismiss them just by sharing a look through the glass door.

I counted the minutes until lunch. I could feel my cyst twitch in my lower back.

Jasmine Spa was in the suburbs outside of the city I grew up in. Out here, the city grid gave way to boulevards lined with trees. Golf courses and cemeteries stretched on, an outrage, just a few miles from the boxes stacked on boxes where I lived. There was a Korean market next door but the customers were usually too bewildered from their foray into the Korean spa to enter it. They climbed into their cars to drive back to their free-standing houses, to eat their cheeses and choose a tv show to fall asleep to, until their unruly decision-making brought them back to Jasmine Spa for some relief.

Inside Jasmine Spa, everything was orderly. Customers were immediately segregated by gender at the entrance. They undressed, showered, dipped themselves in hot pools in the sauna room, surrounded by strangers' bellies and limbs. Some women had the audacity to hold a towel to their chests until the last minute as if performing a striptease.

Eventually, they tired of rotating from pool to pool in the sauna room. They dressed. They moved to the rooms beyond, which were variations of being unendurably hot while lying on different surfaces: bamboo mats, stone, tiny cypress blocks. Placards outside each room explained the health benefits. Typically, detoxification of an unidentified impurity. I had seen children cry out from the heat, but the adult customers bore it in silence, removing themselves only when they really couldn't breathe.

In those rooms, customers circulated in t-shirts and shorts of pale pink or pale blue, depending on their gender. Couples found each other, clutching their paper cups. They ignored the laminated signs taped in every room prohibiting handholding and touching of any sort.

Upstairs, customers could pick one of the sleeping rooms to lie down and close their eyes. Piano music, on a loop, was piped through the speakers. Once, on my way out, I stopped by Bert's surveillance room and caught a glimpse of the customers lying in rows and rows on his monitors. The rooms glowed red. It was like seeing rotisserie chicken at the supermarket.

The cafeteria's meat smells permeated every room. Even the pyramid room with the gold sphinx and gold walls, to evoke ancient Egypt, and the charcoal room with its air-purifying amethysts, smelled like beef and soy sauce. They said that hell was hot but listening to customers paddling quietly from room to room, I found Jasmine Spa a kind of heaven.

It was my birthday so Bert was buying me lunch in the cafeteria: bibimbap in Styrofoam instead of a proper stone bowl, mango bubble tea from powder instead of juice. Still, it was beef and some sweetness. I bent over my tray. Bert had mushroom soup. He was on a diet again.

We had twenty minutes to eat, in shifts, before or after the customers remembered their appetites and swarmed the cafeteria at one o'clock. Bert traded his lunchtime with Grace's so he could match mine.

"You ready for tonight, Letty?" he said. Grace and Tina were coming over, for muted weeknight celebrations, and I had invited him on a whim.

"Yeah, it'll be fun," I said. I watched him watch me. "Y'all can't bring cake. I can never finish those."

"You don't like cake?" he said. It was a revelation to him, like most facts about the world. He spent so much time watching people on his monitors that he didn't know what to do with them in real life. When I first met him, I had found it irritating. Lately, I had been finding it endearing.

"Cake is overrated," I said.

"But thirty-seven, though," he said, "You have to have something special for it." He laid his hand out by his napkin. I wondered, idly, what his hands had done with what women.

"Okay, maybe a jelly donut or, like, fudge," I said.

"Jelly donut," he said, "That could do."

"One the size of my face," I said, stretching my fingers in demonstration.

"Okay, of course," he said, "Just for the birthday girl."

We laughed. I looked at the clock, and I was relieved that our lunchtime was up.

I n the v-steam room, I scrutinized Bert's words for clues until I remembered not to care. I scooped mugwort leaves and dandelions into satchels. Lily spent afternoons watching Tina sell spa packages by the front entrance and correcting Tina's tone with contradictory orders, so I could sit for hours at a time. It was good for me. My muscles were gluey after lunch.

I drowsed. Sometimes I would dream with my eyes wide open only to wake in my apartment. I would reach instinctively for the little card by my nightstand to check the text printed on it, but it was empty. I would look towards my bathtub, anticipating. Then I would really wake in my plastic chair next to the padded customer chairs, sometimes to Eugene's gentle snoring. My uniform was damp at my knees and my armpits. My cyst twitched with every heartbeat. I would fold towels until I forgot the sensation. But today, I didn't dream anything. I sat in a pleasant reverie, watching phosphenes spin against the blank wall across from me. The customers managed not to look at me.

Promptly, at eight o'clock, the spell lifted. I scrubbed the chairs. I mopped the floor. I stacked the chairs and drained the hot water. I would be wide awake for the ride home. It was ninety minutes and three buses between Jasmine Spa and my apartment, but this time, Grace and Tina, their babysitters secured for the night, were riding with me. The ride would be short. We had almonds to share. We would be so distracted by one of Grace's stories that we would almost miss the stop.

～

We shuffled into my apartment. Grace and Tina produced the wine. Bert arrived breathless, a little after us, holding a paper bag in one hand.

"Biggest jelly donut in the city," he said. I peeled the paper back. It was.

"I'm gonna go get the plates," I said. I instinctively took a detour to my nightstand to check that my little card was leaning against my lamp. By the time I returned and poured the wine, they were already complaining about customers.

"There's no way this girl needs to come in for a scrub and a massage every day," Grace said.

"Yeah, she's like, twenty," Tina said, "What could be hurting?"

Grace and I laughed. It was a familiar topic. We were ready to launch into the ailments of our post-twenty bodies, but Bert didn't know us, and he leaned in.

"You know some people carry past traumas in their body," Bert said. Grace and Tina exchanged a look, but he continued, setting his napkin neatly next to his plate. "It could be something serious."

"What a horrible idea," I said, "We don't carry anything we don't choose."

"That's true," Tina said, "Like as soon as they opened

amnesia treatment to anybody who had had a kid, I went for it."

"You did?" Bert said, "You erased the memory of childbirth?"

"Yeah, of course," Tina said, "Most moms just forget on their own but if you can't—you get the pill."

She lifted her wineglass by the bulb.

"If I didn't, I would've been too scared to have my second," she said. Bert was silent.

"Maybe it's a cyst," I said.

"What?" Tina said.

"Maybe it's a cyst," I said more loudly, "On Grace's girl."

"Oh, a cyst," Tina said. She leaned back on the couch, "Yeah, I guess."

I was scraping jelly from the plate into the trash can. Grace and Tina, with their coats on in the living room, were calling out the impending arrival times for their ride-shares. Bert walked up behind me. He was twisting his napkin in his hand.

"Letty, you want me to stay for a bit?" he said. I dropped the plate in surprise.

"Oh, um," I said. I crouched to retrieve the plate, "Well—"

"— I mean, just only if you want me to," he said. "Here, I can get that."

"I got it," I said, straightening back up and forgetting how to ask someone to keep any kind of vigil with me until the sun came up, "It's just I gotta take out the trash, so."

"Yeah, yeah, I get it," he said quickly. He nodded his head towards the living room, "So."

I tossed the trash bag into the dumpster. Something, satisfyingly, shattered. A woman approached from the alley. She looked just like me. Black hair. Yellow face. Round cheeks. Just a few more wrinkles between her eyebrows. She would ask me for money, I could tell. I knew exactly how many minutes of lugging water and stacking chairs produced ten dollars so I would have no problem waving her aside. I looked shamelessly into her eyes.

"Hey— he gets out tomorrow," she said.

"What?" I said.

"You know, our—I mean, it's only been four years, but he got good behavior," she said, "He—"

"—Look, I don't remember any of that," I said. It was the truth. I kept the little card by my nightstand, and I read it every morning: *This is a reminder that you have completed amnesia treatment regarding your incident(s).*

Of course I had undergone the treatment, like most women did after they finished testifying on camera. Of course I chose to heal instead of hoarding every memory, even the bad ones, even the senselessness wrought on my body from which no meaning could be derived. I thought she had chosen the treatment too. We would have taken the pills together, in the sterile hospital room, holding matching paper cups and coughing from the bitterness after we swallowed. She should be like me, retaining nothing of those years, occasionally curious about the gaps but quick to redirect every time her mind wandered onto a sore spot.

"Didn't they give you the pill to forget?" I said.

"Yeah, of course, and I took it," she said, "But it didn't take."

I didn't know that was possible. I thought she might be lying.

"I started remembering little pieces," she said, "And now I remember all of it, and you, when we both knew him from the old place and I wanted to see if you were still living here and just see you and talk to you."

I imagined her waiting in the dark under the yellow glow of my apartment window, listening to my friends and me laughing. I wanted to shove her. I was shaking my head.

"I mean, I know it's so hard to believe now, but I remember back when, how I thought you were going along with it until I saw the pictures on his phone, the ones of you and what he did, and then I knew it wasn't right," she said. She must have practiced what to say when she finally caught up to me, but her words came out in a tangle.

"We testified together and afterwards you asked about if I would keep the baby," she said. She patted her stomach. "I wanted to tell you that I did and he's fine now. We're alright."

"Please don't come here again," I said. I was begging but I could force her. I stepped forward and she stepped backwards by reflex. The streetlight cast an orange pall over her face.

I knew that she had seen me naked and she hadn't wanted to. It might be a triumph now for her to see me whole, shrouded in my winter coat, no parts of me spilling out and purpling. She knew me more completely than anyone. She understood the hands that I would see when I was alone late at night, fingers and fingers, tapping and multiplying, spilling out of my bathtub and onto the floor.

"I'm just— I'm sorry," I said more quietly, "but I can't see you again."

As much as I hated her, the other woman from the other life, I had to comfort her. I stepped close to pat her on the arm. She let me.

"Look, it'll be okay," I said. She rustled against my hand and she exhaled. "I am sorry."

She shook her head and she pressed her lips into a smile. "I'm sorry too," she said.

She turned and walked away. I listened to her boots crunch

the snow until it was silent again in the alley. Maybe she would go back to the office, ask for another round of amnesia treatment. Maybe she wouldn't and she would age remembering. I had a feeling she would keep our senseless incidents and stack more onto them and not tell anybody the whole of it, hoarding her history as it calcified in her lower back. She would be stubborn like that.

As for me, I was thirty-seven now. Free. Bert could still be upstairs in my apartment. Whether he had moved to the kitchen to wash the dishes, or he was rooted to the couch on his phone, waiting for my return, I had to find out. In a few hours, I would be stirring mugwort leaves into hot water. Eugene would be coming in toting the tabloids. I would have soup in the cafeteria and in the bathroom, in the afternoon, I would call the doctor about taking my cyst out. I didn't retain much of my past, but I could see with a high amount of certainty into my future. Whatever she kept, it was nothing to me.

17

FROM THE MOMENTS

PURBASHA ROY

From the moments

———————————

of my own making
I discover a drought
ripple. The desire
to pluck it, became
synonymous to a
task of carrying a
smoke-ring between
my palms. How it
has gravity for a
ruin I had taken as
a credence of how
a candid sunshaft
swallows the coy
dapple on room
window each morn.

18

THE GOD IN THE WIRED

J. D. HARLOCK

There is a God in the wired—an entity encoded
with neither function nor form,
electronically exuded
from the virtual void,
systemically sired
to the computerized consciousness,
a consciousness screaming
in synthesized screeches for
someone, something
to deliver us unto.....*instrumentation*

for it is an instantiation intrinsic
in the careful complementation of
careless creatures, suffering
from a sickness
unto sin, singularly wired
for a warmth, whelming
a will, whole
a whole—

finally utterly fulfilled

and... and... although,
I am not one of its *acolytes*—yet...

It is only a matter of will

Until I am...

changed, altered, transfigured

in my proceduralized pilgrimage through
the structureless sanctum *where*
all are compiled and all must return

For the God that no mortal hath refused
shall be—*installed*...into
our wireless world—and
the booted brunt of
parameterless passion and iterative-less intensity shall
instinctively be instilled in
unrelenting, unremitting
inhumanity....

God is in its wired.
All is right with the world.

19

HOW THE LIGHT GETS OUT

AVRA MARGARITI

The world, a deluge of sensory
Input spinning in strange
Stoichiometries nature never
Equipped your synapses to handle
With grace.

Chewed thumbnails gouging
The meat of your thigh like sickled knives
To halt the onslaught
Of hums and cosmic groans
Assaulting your ears.

From the sloppily sliced fissure
A light emerges, a noctilucent
Sap green, digging claws
And grappling hooks
Into your corneas.

Fumbling, you grab a pocket mirror,
Angle it beside the wound—

Hallowed battleground
Of the holy.

You watch the fight unfold
Across synesthetic senses:
The angels in your bloodstream
Attacking Fallen renegades.
They wear their organs on the outside,

Minuscule warriors wrapped
In carcinoma exoskeletons,
Brandishing the swords
Of broken intravenous needles,
Their own blood prismatic

As it gushes out of lacerations
Smiling wide and puckered,
Their spleens and lungs
Deflating like sliced-open moons.
Seraphs and cherubs shatter in gristly
Geometries, then swarm again into
A new hybrid warrior,

Bastardized constellation
Keen on ruining
Their own ghoulish brethren.

A lancing and bloodletting
Of primordial humors,
Each drop of your scintillating blood a Fallen
Demon, smashing like scarlet-sun pearls
Or crystallized petals
Upon your desecrated sensorium.

20

VISIONS OF VAN GOGH

DONNA J. W. MUNRO

Nora started taking digitalis when her father died.

She kept filling his heart med prescription faithfully, nodding when the pharmacist asked if she understood the instructions, smiling when the tech told her to give her father their love and tell him that they missed seeing him. She didn't tell them he was gone.

He'd been suffering from heart failure for years and hadn't taken his meds like he should have no matter how many times Nora reminded him. He'd been stubborn, thinking that the only time you should take the meds is when you think you need them. When pain cranked through his chest, he'd take a double dose and curse the fact he needed them. Then once he started taking them, he'd taken more and more. And then he died.

When she'd found him on the floor in the bathroom rigid body, hands curled into claws, and marble eyes staring off into some horror that only he could see. He wasn't cold yet when she found him, but his heart was silent and his face blue as a morning sky. She had wept bitter tears for days because he was her whole world. When the tears dried up and all she had left in her was a bottomless hole, she tended to his body. She wrapped towels and sheets around his livid corpse like a thick shroud and used his old leather belts to secure his legs and arms. She laid him in the cool porcelain tub and covered him with a quilt like a proper modern mummy, and finally she shut off the light and closed the door.

That had been six months ago.

Taking the digitalis prescription had been... a way to feel closer to her dad? A compulsion to fill the void he left with something of his? A way to end her pain? Thinking back, she believed it was more a way to understand his gaze. The way he saw the world.

She'd kept doing all the things she'd done before her father died, not just because it was a habit but also because she didn't want the world to know he was gone and she was alone. She shopped all the same things even though the prune juice piled up in the pantry and the asparagus rotted in the chiller drawer of the fridge. She paid bills from his automatically deposited pension checks and sent letters to his sister, who lived in an assisted care facility with moderate dementia.

For so long it had been just the two of them living on the coast–Dad doing his poetry and reading on the back porch and Nora working as one of the modern art curators in the city museum. The easy quiet of their lives only ever was interrupted by her dad's heart problems.

Digitalis.

The miraculous fruit of the foxglove plant.

Dad had been taking it erratically since he'd had the heart stents put in ten years back, but in the months before he died had he noticed the benefits of it.

He called it life-changing and not because of the medical effects.

"Nora, would you read this?" He'd asked right after he'd started taking it with regularity, double doses he'd saved up.

He handed her a short poem about the sky and pain.

It was... transcendent. A glimpse of heaven constructed in metered lines and fleeting word pictures that sang in her ear.

He'd been gifted at writing poetry before. It was his secret love as he had worked on the railroad for thirty years and then in retirement, he'd become a full-time poet. Elder Keats for the modern world, he'd said, typing away on an old electric typewriter. He'd published some. More often, he'd play with the words and shapes until a hundred versions of the same idea lived in a file under his desk. But this one...

"Dad, this is amazing! I mean... as good as anything I've read in a book! Better even. It's perfect."

He beamed in a way Nora hadn't seen since she was a kid and Mom was still alive.

"Ever since I've been taking my medicine, I'm seeing things so differently. It's like the world is brighter and more alive. More yellow."

"Yellow? What does that mean?"

"Yes, I... how can I explain. My words are full of yellow and... orange. So much more like life only... more than that."

Nora hadn't thought much about it then. For the first time since the stents operation, Dad seemed so happy and productive typing away for hours every afternoon in the pool of light that shot through his office window. He'd gone from producing maybe one poem a month to hundreds of them, though he didn't send them out to be published anymore. He said he didn't owe the world any of his words. These perfect words were for him and her alone.

A month or two before he died, her dad went to the doctor for a checkup. Nora listened as Dad talked the doctor into increasing the digitalis. It was like listening to an alcoholic justify his nightly highballs as necessary for relaxation. She was surprised when the doctor took out the scrip pad and scribbled away on it while congratulating Dad on being so willing to take his meds and prolong his life. Nora remembered how hostile he'd been at first and realized that the doctor must've been relieved to see this new contrite patient.

How he didn't see through the play act of a feeble old heart patient, Nora couldn't understand, but Dad was happy to get the bump. In fact, he became even more prolific, taking that increase in meds and the extra he'd decided to prescribe to himself, still left over from all the time he hadn't taken it. His words changed. They seemed to reverberate with a power that didn't come from his normal well of words. She'd read those poems and felt the hectic pulse of his thinking like heat. Like she might've needed to wear oven mitts and sunglasses to handle the energy packed in each syllable and every stanza he wrote.

For a few weeks, it was bliss. Nora was able to go work at the museum for hours while he stayed busy with writing. He was so happy, and Nora felt connected to what he was doing. He wrote late into the night and she read every word, amazed, almost enraptured by his creations. They were new. Viivid and angry sometimes. Other times, they seemed like the shifting forces between suns–too big to know but booming in bright flashes of impressions. His words made her breathless the way a sprint might, stitching in her side and knotting her muscles. When she'd read, she'd tell him about her feelings, the impacts, and he'd grin, nod, and tell her how it felt to write them.

Nora's Dad loved his life and she felt more alive than she ever had seeing the world through his strange, fiery words.

But it all went wrong.

"Do you see that?" He asked her once, staring out into the backyard.

"What?"

"That... tree? Monster? It's right there."

He pointed out into the yard with a trembling finger.

Glancing out into the yard she saw… yard.

Some failed roses withered in the corner, slightly over-grown grass, the little maple she'd planted the year before. Nothing different than had been there all along.

"I don't see anything, Dad."

He turned and studied her face like he was seeing her for the first time. He reached up with trembling fingers and touched her cheek then jerked away like he'd burned himself.

"Nothing. Oh, nothing, dear Nora. Sorry, I… must be tired or maybe I'm just seeing things. These old peepers aren't what they used to be."

Nora shook her head and smiled, picking up his empty lunch tray as he started typing his next poem on the keys of his typewriter with a flurry of tacks and ticks. Seeing things? Old people did that, didn't they? It was like their eyes were here in the present and seeing the past at the same time. Reliving something that only they knew and then jerking back into the present rudely, sometimes shocked by the transition.

"Why don't you take a nap, Dad. I'll work on dinner."

He shook his head and kept typing, muttering about some hoary thing ripping through from the other. Poetic language, she'd thought. Something he'd been working on carried him away.

"Don't forget to take your digitalis," she said and turned to take care of her chores before lunch.

That was just the first time he admitted to seeing things.

During the next couple of days, he slid between nightmares and ecstasies, stopping to nod at Nora as he vacillated. Some-times, she couldn't get him to acknowledge her or to eat. It was like he was in a different world. He screamed sometimes, then started typing so rapid fire she couldn't see his fingers through the blur of their movement. Even when he wasn't writing, he shoveled down his food, eyes shifting and wide, glancing around at everything that shone with light or moved. He didn't want to leave his office, choosing to sleep on his couch instead of his bed.

Nora worried she'd have to put him in a nursing home if things continued.

Then he seemed to get better for a bit, right before he died.

Nora started finding the little white pills stashed behind his typewriter, under the bed, and pressed into the rinds of the oranges he peeled each afternoon as a snack.

"Dad, you need those pills. Your heart condition!"

He looked up into her eyes, guilt written on his features as clearly as the typed strokes of his poem on the white paper around the platen.

"It's just too yellow, Nora. I can't..."

His words trailed, and he couldn't seem to keep his eyes from shifting, shuttering in their sockets like someone coming off of a tilt-a-whirl. He shook his head and refocused on his work, rolling the platen to adjust the paper loudly–a signal for her to leave.

It wasn't long after that she found him on the bathroom floor.

He'd cut himself shaving.

All the way through his jugular.

That's why Nora didn't call the police or the mortician.

She didn't want the world to see him that way.

After she'd wrapped him in his makeshift shroud, she sealed the door with duct tape and kept up appearances. Kept her sadness inside the shadows of the house with the blinds drawn and the door shut.

But at work, they'd pushed her to take on a new project since it had been months since she'd been lead curator on an exhibit. She'd agreed. She had to. They didn't know she was in mourning. No one did.

"A retrospective of Van Gogh's career. We can get thirty paintings on loan and you could arrange for the displays and the accompanying materials. We need a really deep dive," the director told her.

It was a compliment for her to be given such an important exhibition.

The workload was enormous.

She studied every night in Dad's studio, reading books about Vincent's life, his work, and his long slide into illness. Modern doctors couldn't settle on what had haunted poor, brilliant Vincent. His flights of fancy and feverish production and then his terrible self-destructive moods. They argued if he was suffering from bipolar disorder, schizophrenia, or if he might have been broken by an absinthe and laudanum habit. Nothing was clear.

Then, she read that he'd used digitalis.

That settled it.

Nora started taking digitalis that very night.

First, she used all the pills she'd found in Dad's hidey holes. Then she used a kitchen knife to open the duct tape over the bathroom door frame. The stench of Dad's decomposition struck her like a hammer, but she pushed forward into the small room and riffled through the medicine cabinet for the rest of the stash. Once she had it, she retreated into the hall and pulled the door shut.

"Sorry, Dad," she mumbled, then retaped the door to his tomb.

When she ran out of those, she refilled his prescription like she always did.

The more she used the digitalis, the more her boss liked her work.

"Wow, Nora. You've really put together a top-notch exhibit. Your narrative descriptions and the interactive displays are amazing."

And...

"Nora, the education department said the test subjects

loved the lessons and activities for elementary school kids. Good job."

And his eyes were like moons. Yellow and shining on her.

Two tunnels of swirling, shimmering light where his brown eyes used to be. Every time they fell on her, she bit her lip so she wouldn't scream.

She started working at home and sending in her products.

Home was safe.

Yellow.

She began to notice the tones of yellow and orange in everything that moved or breathed. The wind stuttered and tracked across her gaze, leaving tracers of white and yellow and even gold.

She knew what she was seeing even if Dad had not.

Van Gogh's gaze. His visions.

The sky swirled with the movement of the planet and the sun radiated in churning spirals that no one could see but her.

Only her.

Why didn't all the other people taking digitalis see what she did?

She stopped sleeping to try to understand it. Research was slow since her laptop seemed to hyperventilate with color and sound when she touched the keys, but she'd stay at it until she had to take a break from the rolling light of the screen. She took a deep breath and looked out Dad's office window. The tree in the backyard seemed to grow a foot every time she glanced away, sprouting thorns as thick as her leg and sharp branches, naked of any green. Just a claw scraping against a swimming sky.

Green? Blue? They were rare in her digitalis dreams.

Why didn't others see these visions like her and Dad?

Was it that other people weren't creatives? Van Gogh was a painter and her dad a poet and she was a dabbler in all kinds of art. Like her mother, she'd been too shy to pursue it, but maybe that was the connection.

She glanced at the white pill waiting by the keyboard for noon, still two hours away.

Was what she saw on digitalis a hallucination? It didn't feel that way. Like Dad had said, it felt like something was ripping through. Something from beneath it all. She reached over and dry swallowed the pill early, needing the boost to her thinking.

Ripping.

That's when she felt the flutter inside of her skin. She looked down at her palms, which glowed in the long shadows of the afternoon. Glowed and fluttered and swirled like Van Gogh's Starry Night. She pushed out of her chair and went to the mirror hanging above Dad's typewriter. Yellow. Her eyes glowed like yellow spotlights. She flashed and throbbed with the light trapped inside of her. It burned as it broke through the pores in her skin and flared in the cavern of her mouth.

Inside the chaos, Nora finally understood.

What she'd been before wasn't real. It was just a veneer of dull color to be cut away.

Through the cracks and around the ragged edges of her old self she'd find freedom.

She'd find her way into the real world like her dad had.

Like Van Gogh.

She took another digitalis before peeling the tape off the bathroom door.

Dad's razor shone in her hand like a star swirling and spiraling in a blue night sky.

21

VAN GOGH/ YELLOW

LORRAINE SCHEIN

Van Gogh needed to buy more YELLOW ochre, to paint that YELLOW chair in his room, the YELLOW flickering candle on its seat. They were the only constant companions in his solitude, and never rejected him, so he could bear them.

People were worse. Their bodies sizzled, outlined in stabbing spikes of many colors, the worst a sulfurous YELLOW that pierced and stung his eyes so much he could hardly bear to look at them. He needed to use models less, preserve his sight if he was to continue as an artist.

Nature was better because it moved less. The sunflowers looked safe, but were YELLOW too, their petals mouthing YELLOW shrieks because they were dying, decaying, then shriveling brown to the floor. And the endless repeating sheaves of YELLOW wheat under the awful YELLOW sun.

And the YELLOW voices coming from the sun beyond this sun, from the YELLOW beings with no hands, no heads...if only he could blot out its glare, rip it from the sky, keep it from beating down on his head, searing his eyes.

But how could he paint it then?

22

EMDR (EYE MOVEMENT
DESENSITIZATION THERAPY)

LORRAINE SCHEIN

The cure for the trauma of space is forgetting the stars.

The psychiatrist said, "To wipe out the memory of space, move your eyes within the virtual scene I'm inserting in your brain."

I saw the black hole engulfing the starship, my copilot sucked in, his screams as his body stretched into strings. How he reached out to me for rescue—but it was too late.

Then I moved my eyes up like our ship blasting-off to reprocess it, over and over: to forget his screams, my feelings of guilt, the awful void I entered that never left me.

The cure for the trauma of space is forgetting the stars.
But there are too many to erase, so I'm left with the scars.

23

THE CARE AND FEEDING OF THE CRANIUM SPIDER

ALICIA HILTON

Abigail the cranium spider is as territorial and predatory as a wolf. My muse lurks inside my frontal cortex, never slithering out the skull through nose, ears or mouth, her spinneret secretes sticky threads that trap creative impulses, bending my imagination to her will. I think mental massage and flattery are the key to symbiotic coexistence. A well-positioned compliment induces her to release my writing hand. Fingers clutch ideas begging to be freed, poems and stories, an iridescent amalgam of angst and dread, the heart-pounding tales that pay my bills. The horror of the unknown appeals to readers and writers alike. Is that ink or blood on the page? Brace yourself for the bite. The tickle crawling up your leg in the middle of the night.

24

MANHATTAN 2081: THE PHYSIOGNOMY OF FEAR

ALICIA HILTON

Elephant armor hides in the library's basement, wrinkled from trunk to tail. Layers of faux leather cling to Carl's face and body, encase trembling, sweaty flesh. Easily zippered and cheap compared to Kevlar or gem encrusted titanium. Pedestrians in the top 1% select blingier personal protection equipment. Hedgehogs flaunt razor sharp platinum quills; giraffes carry gold plated machetes. Armadillos prowl Wall Street, their holographic armor advertises pricy saferooms. No Homo sapiens shows their true faces during the Intergalactic Harvest Fest. The animal armor shields prey from extraterrestrial connoisseurs of human flesh.

25

THE MEAT COIN

BRAD KELECHAVA

Somewhere deep within the realm of wonder, a single baby tooth equaled its weight in hot yellow gold. No wonder the Tooth Fairy, the courier to that mythical land, was willing to cough up money for it.

Sammy would have something for her tonight. With a mighty pull and a little help from the rocky bus ride home, she managed to twist her front tooth backward.

Her tooth stayed in that position, even after Tim joined her on the brown school bus seat to talk nonstop about how he had never received a single penny from the Tooth Fairy. The two of them got off at their bus stop to meet their respective mothers waiting patiently beside the curb.

"Hey there, my rockstar," Sammy's mom said. Sammy joined hands with her, and the two departed.

Not five feet from them lay the squashed raccoon that hadn't moved since Monday morning. Sammy couldn't help but glance at the crimson tread marks bisecting the fleshy corpse.

On the two-block walk home, Sammy's loose front tooth made some more movement, letting out a pop and a crack that only could only be heard within her head.

During her ritualistic two hours of late-afternoon television, Sammy kept her thumb and index finger pressed against the loose tooth, rotating with a few crunches here and there, but no further progress.

As she did her homework, Sammy pressed her adult lower teeth against the loose baby tooth in hope of the grown-up dentition overpowering the milk-tooth straggler. The adult teeth held true, but they didn't vanquish their intended victim.

During dinner, Sammy fought the agonizing pain in her gums. For a moment, she thought she may have swallowed the tooth, thereby forfeiting the blood money owed to her, but it was just a crouton from her salad.

Only after dinner, when she returned to her usual spot in front of the TV beside her mom and dad, did her efforts finally release the tooth from her head, leaving behind a loose strand of flesh hanging from the empty socket. It gave Sammy the motivation to call it an early night.

As her mother tucked her into bed, Sammy asked, "Will the Tooth Fairy leave me anything?"

Her mom grinned. "I'm sure she'll give you a little something for your trouble," she said before shutting off the lights and departing.

Sammy tried to count sheep without much luck. But even excitement tired, and Sammy slipped away.

The next thing she remembered was the dawn sun sneaking through her window. Feeling that heavy heart-pounding return, Sammy tossed her pillow from her bed to find a crisp five-dollar bill.

S ammy peeked into her wallet a few times just to make sure President Lincoln was still with her.

He always was. He couldn't tell a lie.

Sammy's glee made her school day unproductive. The usual motions of classes passed by, guided by the pleasantly disturbing sensation of gliding the tip of her tongue against the vacant socket in her mouth.

The joyous feeling persisted, even after Tim ran his mouth the entire bus ride home and the two joined their mothers at the usual spot beside the rotting raccoon. After Sammy pretended to do her homework, the joy began to fade. She joined her mom and dad for dinner and three hours of TV until they all found themselves drifting off.

By the morning, the feeling was gone. Sammy rose from bed, brushed her teeth, and picked at a bowl of cereal, finding nothing her heart could capture from the plain world that surrounded her. That tooth-obsessed pixie's magic had retreated to wherever those sorts of magics go to replenish their otherworldly goodness.

She would reclaim it, and soon.

But her determined fingers failed to loosen a single tooth. She would be unable to conjure another visit with the Tooth Fairy through the official channels.

But maybe there was another option.

School was nothing but a blur of distracted thought, concluding with Sammy plopping into her spot beside Tim on a brown school bus seat.

"I need you to give me a tooth," she said.

"I, uh, don't have any," Tim said.

"Course you do. They're in your head. You always have them with you."

"I mean, I don't have any to share. Sorry."

The bus pulled away from the school, and they watched the usual pattern of tree branches slapping the bus windows.

"If you don't get money from the Tooth Fairy," Sammy said, "then why not give me one of your teeth?"

"No one gets money. The Tooth Fairy isn't—"

"Real," Sammy said, and doing so was like tossing a shred of her heart into a furnace.

"I'm sorry," Tim said. "Look, next time I lose a tooth, I'll give it to you. You can tell your parents it's yours and still get your money."

Parents, right. That was the theory among the nonbelievers, but Sammy didn't want to entertain Tim's radical views.

"And if I find any, you know, lying around town, I'll give them to you," Tim continued. "It could be a good money-making scheme for you. Your parents might think it's sus, but, as long as you put the teeth under your pillow, you should get some payment."

A category five tree branch sounded on the opposite side of the bus, loud enough to mask the next few ramblings that came out of Tim's mouth, but he just kept going on after that.

She had long spaced him out by the time the bus came to a halt at their stop, and the two rose at the sound of exhaling air brakes before stepping off. In an unusual fashion, neither of their mothers had arrived to pick them up from the bus stop.

"Look at that poor guy," Tim said, but Sammy didn't need his instructions to catch an eyeful of the rotting raccoon flattened on the pavement. "They live under my back porch. He was probably one of their friends."

Sammy took a few extra steps closer to the corpse and realized that her options weren't limited to waiting for one of Tim's teeth to fall out. He wasn't a believer. He wouldn't tie dental floss to a doorknob and swing that door open anytime soon. Sammy believed, and she was willing to do anything to meet magical ends.

What was the difference? A tooth was a tooth, and it wasn't like that raccoon was going to leave it under its bloated pillow of a body anyway.

"What are you doing?" Tim asked, but Sammy ignored him.

Her hand hesitated before she let it brush against the torso of the rotting roadkill. It had been left as dry as chalk from simmering in the hot sun.

And that smell. It recalled scents of stinky days past. Her father's closet stuffed with sweaty workout clothes returned to her mind, and that was only the tip of the nasty iceberg.

But nothing had prepared her for a rotting raccoon.

She pressed her fingers against the raccoon's front teeth. They moved easily in the corpse's rotten gums.

Its canines would work. The three—one was missing, perhaps from another tooth thief—jutted out from the corpse's mouth like ivory spears. She grasped the top-right one and had no trouble freeing it from its owner.

The canine tooth in her hand stretched half an inch too long, but it would be enough to fool the Tooth Fairy. She collected millions of teeth every day, so what was the big deal if one raccoon tooth found its way through?

Sammy bathed the tooth in the dirt to rid it of any gunk and wiped the residual grime on her shirt before slipping it into her pocket.

"Did you just do what I think you did?" Tim asked.

"I didn't do anything," Sammy said. "I just dropped a dime."

"I don't know. It looked like—"

"There's my little rockstar!" Sammy's mom called out as she turned onto their street and walked toward them. "Sorry I'm late. The meatballs took longer than expected. How was your day?"

"Good," Sammy said. "We watched an Arnold Schwarzenegger movie in social studies."

"Again? I'm telling you, that school ..."

Sammy rushed ahead, but her mother wasn't following.

"Is your mom coming to pick you up?" Sammy's mom asked Tim.

"Uh, I'll be fine," he said.

"Are you sure—"

He turned and left.

"Is he okay?" Sammy's mom asked.

"He's just like that," Sammy said.

The two walked and Sammy reached into her pocket, summoning a surge of excitement.

"Do you smell something nasty?" her mom asked, and Sammy's retreating hand surrendered the tooth to her pocket's depths.

"You know, just the dead raccoon," Sammy said.

Her mother looked back at the corpse on the side of the suburban street. "Ah, right," she said. "Someone has to do something about that."

Tonight, Sammy would earn a free five-dollar bill. She closed her eyes as her mother shut off Sammy's bedroom lights and strutted out. Sammy held them in that position until the creaking floorboards at the end of the hall sounded nothing but silence.

She opened her eyes.

Under the power of her nightlight, Sammy tiptoed to her hamper, carefully lifted yesterday's jeans, and extracted the tooth from its spot in her left pocket. She slipped the tooth under her pillow and rested her head against the other side.

She awoke a few hours later to darkness.

Sammy's finger traced the center of her pillow. Even in the absence of light, her fingers didn't lie to her. There was an object under there, and it wasn't a dirty raccoon tooth.

Maybe it was a coin. Its value would be far less than her previous haul, but Sammy didn't care. It came from the Tooth Fairy, possibly the only source of magic in existence, and that made it priceless.

Sammy flipped her pillow and reached for the object.

Instead of meeting metal, her finger sank into a fleshy mass, its rough surface chilling her fingertips upon contact. She jolted back.

It wasn't much of a coin. Standing fatter than four stacked quarters, the object looked like one of the meatballs from Sammy's dinner after being stomped on, leaving behind something fat and uneven. Its surface was pocketed with craters, like the moon.

And it was moving.

This meat coin wobbled back and forth, almost somersaulting over the fitted sheet before returning to its original position. Hairlike appendages extended from its meaty body and pushed it off the sheet with enough momentum to send it rolling on the floor in a series of squelching thumps. When it looked like it was going to lose control, the meat coin guided itself along the carpet with the thin limbs that seemed to be jutting from any point of the oblong mass.

Sammy snatched her slipper from beside her bed and hurled it, but her aim was too high and sent a lineup of dolls tumbling from atop her dresser.

A burst of light countered the hallway darkness outside Sammy's open doorway. Her mother came rushing in.

"Everything's okay," her mom said. "What happened?" Sammy's dad appeared in the doorway, rubbing his eyes as if they were stuck shut.

"Nothing," Sammy said, unable to see the meat coin anywhere in her room.

"That's okay, my rockstar," her mom said. "Our minds can wander at night, and you have the most imaginative mind, so sometimes it plays some tricks on you."

"Can you sleep here with me tonight?"

"Of course." Her mom slid onto Sammy's twin bed, and her dad lumbered back to her parents' room, switching off the hallway light on his way. Her mother quickly fell asleep, but

Sammy found some trouble returning to dreamland. When she tried to listen, she thought she could hear the rustling of the arms of the meat coin.

S ammy stopped sleeping well. Most nights, she woke under the moonlight. Her eyelids soon shut as if they were coated in stone, but the tireless rustling of the meat coin scurrying throughout her house forced them back open.

It even paid her a visit. One night, during the hazy moment between dreams, the cold mass planted itself on the palm of her open hand. She didn't know how long it was there, but the chill of the meat coin eventually compounded enough to counter her tiredness. She attempted to squish the thing and rid her house of its presence once and for all, but the timid being reacted before she could make her move. With the aid of the night, it plopped back onto the floor with a squelch and scampered through her bedroom door.

Deep into the week after she had found the meat coin, Sammy fought the urge to sleep. The hallway lights flicked on, and her dad passed by. She listened to each creak of the stairs. She heard the familiar rustling traveling throughout the first floor, followed by her dad's bare feet racing throughout the kitchen. His irritated grunting quickly became the loudest noise in the house.

When her mom rushed out of the bedroom at the end of the hall, Sammy hid under her sheets and pretended to sleep. Pretending must've been the next best thing to doing—even amid the clamor downstairs, morning came by quickly, and Sammy felt as if she had gotten in a few hours of sleep.

Her father was absent for breakfast, but Sammy saw him in the backyard passing by the kitchen bay window.

Sammy's mom, noticing Sammy's eyes wander from her

cereal, said, "Nothing to worry about, my rockstar. We had a storm last night. Did some damage. Your dad's taking care of it."

But when Sammy began the walk with her mom to the bus stop, she knew that the destruction on the exterior of their house couldn't have come from lightning or a stray branch. Instead, the bottom two feet of the outer wall was scored with claw marks. Her mom's garden lining the house was in ruins, leaving behind loose dirt that looked like someone had been trying to dig their way in.

~

"I have something for you," Tim said as he joined her on the school bus. He had been acting weird all day.

"What is it?" Sammy asked.

"Just hang on until we get going." He looked nervous, as if he was giving a presentation in front of the class. A few more kids hopped on the bus, and the driver shut the heavy doors and pulled away from the school.

Tim scanned his surroundings and pulled a tooth from his pocket.

Sammy reached for it, but the memory of the meat coin stayed her hand.

"Take it," Tim said. "Since I don't get anything from the Tooth Fairy, there's no reason for me to have it. She should give you something for it, though. Just tell your parents about it first."

Sammy snatched the tooth and slipped it into her pocket.

"Animals have germs, you know," Tim said. "My mom says they carry the plague."

"I didn't do what you think I did." Before he could respond, she added, "I get that everyone thinks the Tooth Fairy isn't real, but don't you believe in anything else? You know, like ghosts and ghouls."

"Yeah, sure."

"Why can't the Tooth Fairy just be one of those?"

Tim, for once, kept his mouth shut. A long branch that the city had been ignoring came after the next turn. The rapid *click-click-click* came, roaring an extra *thunk* due to an open window three seats ahead of Sammy and Tim. A few tear-shaped leaves fluttered in. No one reacted to the usual event.

Their bus stop came, and the two got off to meet their mothers standing beside the curb.

"How's my rockstar doing?" Sammy's mom said, although her tone was softer than usual.

Sammy held her hand, and the two commenced the walk back home. Sammy's wandering gaze pursued the animal corpse she had desecrated, but the city had finally gotten around to the raccoon. The remaining dark spot on the pavement bore no flesh, no teeth, no evidence of the creature that had lain there the week before.

Sammy awoke to near darkness.

Through the window beside her bed, the moon was a slice of ivory in the otherwise-vacant midnight sky. The minimal moonlight melded with Sammy's night light, illuminating her room with enough visibility to make out the definition of the sheets of her twin bed.

Sammy repositioned herself and found her fingers slip under her pillow. There she found no five-dollar bill, no meat coin, no currency of this world or any other. Just Tim's baby tooth.

Sammy heard a familiar sound in the hallway scratching along the floor.

Then came a louder scratching. Sammy's heartbeat hiked.

Any second now, her dad would emerge from her parents' bedroom and switch on the hallway light to search their home.

But the light never switched on, and Sammy found her tiredness fade away. She got out of bed and tiptoed to the hallway. The doorway at the end of the hall remained closed. Coming from it were not only the thunderous rumblings of her father's snoring, but also a lighter deep breathing. Both her parents were out for the night.

She made her way down the hallway and met each step of the stairs to the first floor with a force soft enough for her toes to have pressed into the meat coin without squishing it.

But it wasn't on any of the steps. She found the meat coin just at the bottom of the stairs, paused as if caught in an act of mischief. It was immobile, other than the writhing limbs atop it.

Sammy moved forward, and the meat coin twitched. She slowed to the pace of a sloth. It seemed to keep the meat coin at bay. Her foot met a loose tile in the floor, and it was enough to excite the meat coin once more. Sammy tried to catch it, but the fleshy pest was too fast.

She chased it into the dining room, and the darkness swallowed them both. In the absence of light, the cozy room that she and her parents ate their dinners had expanded into an auditorium, making it impossible to target the source of the squelching and scurrying of the meat coin.

The noises faded enough for Sammy to know that the meat coin had left the dining room. She traveled throughout the rooms of her house, playing a game of cat-and-meat-coin with nothing more than the faint sounds of the object's movements to guide her.

She followed the fleshy percussion of the meat coin until she found it scuttling through the living room. With nothing more than a slice of moonlight casting its midnight glow through the bay window, she cornered it.

The meat coin wobbled in position, its many cilia-like legs sliding along the floor in a flurry. Behind it was the louver that led into the home's ventilation system. Before it could roll through the slats of the grate, Sammy lunged.

It was icy to the touch, and even the sensation of its numerous appendages writhing wildly against her palm diminished as her hand numbed. Sammy fought the discomfort and held her grip. The meat coin calmed down. With it no longer scuttling about, her home found a silence she hadn't known in weeks.

Another sound began in the kitchen.

Sammy found herself shaking, and it wasn't from the chill of the meat coin in her enclosed hand. If tiptoes could have tiptoes, Sammy found them, making her way along the wall.

Holding her breath and stalling her heart between beats, Sammy peeked through the open doorway. The moonlight passing through the large bay window offered some visibility in the kitchen, and it was enough to confirm that the room was empty.

Yet, the scratching persisted.

Sammy tiptoed on the linoleum. The scratching grew louder as she approached the bay window. She was ready for whatever was causing it to emerge before her, but she reached the other side of the room without issue. She and the meat coin were alone.

The scratching continued. It was coming from outside, just on the opposite side of the wall.

Through the bay window, Sammy saw a pair of eyes glowing in the darkness. As it blinked, she saw the pattern replicated in a dozen other spots in the yard.

With her empty, trembling hand, Sammy switched on the backyard lights.

Outside the bay window, a dozen raccoons stared back at

her. They raised their front paws and resumed scratching the bricks of the home's exterior below the window.

One slammed against the bay window headfirst. The window wobbled but held true. It withstood another raccoon headbutt. And another.

Sammy switched off the lights. Another thud came against the window.

Sammy turned and bolted. She reached the top of the stairs, made it into her room, slammed the door, and lunged into bed. Her commotion should have at least awoken her parents, but they still snored in the other room.

In the distance, the raccoons' scratches persisted. She expected her door to topple and a flood of the garbage eaters to make a late dinner out of her, but, while the sounds moved in the periphery of Sammy's hearing, they never made their way inside the house.

Beneath the moonlight, and with the help of her nightlight, Sammy waited.

So many others wanted what she held in her hand, but it belonged only to her. Sammy spent most of the night clenching the meat coin and staring at the moon. She didn't feel lucky at all.

S ammy awoke shivering, with little feeling in her arm.

In her hand still rested the meat coin. With only a handful of its thin black appendages stretching out from the various pores of its body like an uneven set of spider legs, the currency of another world was cozied up against her palm as if it were a sweet little kitty.

That didn't make it any less disgusting. It was still early morning, a little after 6 a.m., but the sun was shining brightly. Sammy now saw the meat coin in detail. Its craters were deeper than she had thought, their hue a deep red standing out from on meat coin's otherwise gray exterior. When she examined further, Sammy realized that the craters comprised tube-like pathways scrunched together. It reminded her of a drawing of a human brain that she had seen in school.

This might be her reward for offering a raccoon tooth, but what use could she have of it? Sammy had captured the wonder found only the darkest reaches of existence, and now she was stuck with it. The meat coin was hers to keep, and the raccoons would continue to pursue it, whether she liked it or not.

Maybe there was another option.

Still in her pajamas and clenching the meat coin, Sammy made her way downstairs. Her parents sat in the kitchen, sipping their first cups of coffee in their usual morning routine. It was clear that they hadn't noticed any fresh damage to the house from last night's raccoons.

Sammy traversed the stairs and reached the side door of the house without making a peep. It only helped that she was never up this early—her parents wouldn't expect even the earliest bed-bound shuffling of hers to begin for another half hour.

Outside, the chill of the nighttime air lingered as an echo, but it was greatly overpowered by the sun. Frost that had held the grass stiff the previous night now remained as beads of dew, which Sammy kicked into the air with every step.

Sammy sneaked through the side of her yard and rushed along the sidewalk. Few were out this early, and they paid her little attention.

As she approached Tim's house, she passed their bus stop, marked by the dark spot of asphalt where the raccoon had died. She heard Tim's voice and made her way to his backyard.

"Are you hungry, mister raccoon?" Tim asked. He was leaning over the railing of the porch that extended from the back of the house. "How about you, mommy raccoon?" He dropped a handful of peanuts that fell to the ground.

"What are you doing?" Sammy asked.

"Uh, nothing," Tim said, letting go of another cluster of peanuts in alarm. "Why are you here?"

"Do they really live under there?" Sammy asked, but she didn't wait for a response to approach the porch.

Where Tim had sprinkled peanuts, Sammy pushed aside a rhododendron bush. Behind it, through the one-foot gap that separated the bottom of the porch from the ground, Sammy saw two pairs of eyes illuminate the darkness.

She opened her palm to reveal the meat coin as an offering.

"What are *you* doing?" Tim asked.

One pair of eyes inched closer to her until the sunlight revealed the outline of the raccoon. Sammy extended her proffered palm further.

The meat coin gave off no indication of fear or discomfort. In fact, it almost felt like it was getting warmer.

The raccoon opened its mouth and latched onto the meat coin with its front teeth. It turned and retreated into the shadows beneath the porch. Sammy didn't see any eyes gazing back at her.

Tim was hopping on the porch to see over the railing. "Did you just do what—"

"I did exactly what you think I did," Sammy said. "Here." She reached into her pocket and tossed Tim's tooth onto the porch. It clicked on the wood before he scooped it up.

"I don't think the Tooth Fairy is going to give me anything for that," she said. "I'll see you at the bus stop.

Sammy passed by the dark spot of asphalt and made it back home without getting caught.

That day, Sammy devoted little thought to the strange experiences of the morning and previous night. By the time she got out of school, ate dinner, and devoured a few hours of TV, she didn't think about it at all.

That night, Sammy slept well, not hearing a peep in her house.

26

FLIGHT TO NOWHERE

KURT NEWTON

Today my wife and I
took a flight to nowhere.
We didn't need to pack a thing,
only ourselves into our seats.
We took off down the runway
and lifted into the sky.
The ground left us dizzy
as we angled like a slingshot
through the clouds.
Eventually, we leveled off
and all our weight dissolved
and we floated like two lovers
in a bathtub filled with air.
It didn't matter that the seats
were filled with other passengers,
or that the destination was
a one-way trip into the ether
and back in time for dinner.
It was the flight we needed,
to get our feet up off the ground,

away from the same four walls,
the same stale window scenery,
even if for just a little while.
But our curious trip got even curiouser
as we climbed higher still
and the pilot chimed in
with an ethereal voice of reason.
He said we were now free
to move about the cabin.
So, my wife and I unbuckled
and we floated up out of our seats.
It was like swimming
in a sea of possibilities,
without the responsibility of breathing.
We breast-stroked from window
to window and still there were things
below we knew we were missing.
Thankfully, the other passengers
were fast asleep, their earbuds
and headphones singing insect songs
as we floated across their laps
to their tiny windows and pressed
our noses against the glass.
Strange how time just seemed
to stand still for us, my wife and I,
two retired seniors
tired of the same routine.
My wife had a twinkle in her eye,
and I had an inkling
of what would happen next.
Like a dream we found ourselves
before the cabin door.
I tried the latch
and wouldn't you know,

it turned as easy as a steering wheel.
And I knew then
that we were the pilots
of this peculiar flight,
a flight to nowhere in particular.
The door pushed open
and slid aside,
and my wife and I
had the most precious view.
All the world was spread out
beneath us like a carpet made
of patchwork colors,
and we stepped out together
and floated like two lovers
in a bathtub filled with air.
This was no flight to nowhere,
this was our flight,
our last flight together,
to here and there,
to anywhere we wanted,
and everywhere in between.

27

RORSCHACH

KURT NEWTON

A new apartment in a new town as far away as one can get. And still the past finds you.

A blank wall where the television should go shows you more than any crime drama or late-night cable program. Black blotches on the white surface appear like dark birds birthed from beneath the virgin plaster. You take pictures with your cell phone.

You tell the landlord, and she just laughs. You show her the photos and the photos reveal nothing but a plain white wall.

From then on there are stares from other tenants, awkward conversations, whispers in the hallways after you pass.

All you have is yourself now and the ever-present blotches that reform and reshape like shadow creatures every night when you get home.

More often than not, you sit on the couch and stare as the wall becomes your own private theater. A diorama of violence and utter devastation. At times you can almost hear the screams.

Your head begins to throb, the pressure building until it feels about to burst.

Tonight, it's telling you to do it again. That thing that brought you here in the first place. That thing that has chased you ever since adolescence. That thing that splashed death upon the chalkboard of your psyche. That thing to which you've become bound.

You get up and press yourself against the wall's undulating surface. The black mold of sin spreads its tenebrous wings and embraces you with its grotesque beauty. Smothering you in jagged images. Choking you with slivers of erotic asphyxiation. That thing is here. That thing is now.

You float away, up through the ceiling, above the apartment complex, above the city lights, then out into the country where the night becomes electric, alive with creatures only you can see. That thing pointing the way.

You find the right quiet home set apart from all the others, a singularity in the vast landscape of desire. You arrive upon their doorstep, and like spilled ink, you seep in through the cracks.

You descend upon them in a fury. Blotches stain the walls, the nightstands, the bedposts, the pillows, the sheets, the carpets, until everything turns to black.

Later, in the shower, you awake as if from a bad dream. Your head no longer throbs. The slivers have pushed their way so deep you can no longer feel them. You wipe away the mist and stare into the mirror expecting to see a monster. There comes a knock on your apartment door.

It's the girl from down the hall. She's dressed in black leather. Crimped hair. Raccoon eyes. Her mouth is draped in black lipstick. She says she's been watching you.

She invites herself in and sniffs around. She says I like what you've done with the place. She stops and stares at the living room wall, at the black blotches swimming there.

"You see them too," you hear yourself say. She nods, her eyes unmoved by your words. At last, she takes a breath, and you take her hand. The blotches ripple their approval.

28

A TRICK OF THE LIGHT

AMY GRECH

A trick of the light
gave me a fright
on a hot summer's night.

With the living room of my
apartment pitch black…
I nearly had a heart attack
when a luminous, white sphere
the size of an orange did appear,
hovering near the window.
The ephemeral orb held my gaze—
oh, did it amaze.

I had just returned from Long Island
where my father lay in the hospital
in dire need of critical care with a most
grim prognosis: pulmonary fibrosis.

It quickly became painfully clear
his end was near.

As a full-time freelancer, I
couldn't stay in his hour of need,
an unfortunate victim of corporate greed.
My clients were only so understanding,
before they became ruthless and demanding.

Soon to be out of a job,
much to my dismay,
back to Brooklyn I went.
I did resent
time I could
have spent
with Dad
fettered away,
in favor of relentless bills
I had to pay.
So many things
I wanted to say.
Kindnesses unspoken.
My heart irrevocably broken.

That brilliant, ball of light
provided a brief glimmer of delight.
Somehow, I knew it was my father's
light. So sublime...

He passed away the very next day.
I wanted to grieve, wanted to
believe he had gone to a
better place, peaceful and pain-free,
devoid of mortal misery.

I expressed gratitude for the insightful platitudes
he often shared, always quick to show he cared.

29

THE PRAGMATIST
ZAC WALSH

If one could see the world ashimmer,
to fully examine its energy flow
from each well-intentioned want
and on to the next and outward and onwards
towards the forcefields of profoundest attraction:
what Science calls black holes, economics
    demand, politics progress
then continue inward, ever gnawingly inward,
toward the more traditional tectonic leveling
    grounds:
what Religion calls perdition, philosophy angst,
    suicides mercy
the Pragmatist might then wonder what all the
    energy is so frantic about,
why the energy is so uniformly eager to go out
    into that which is made to unmake
and the wonder would increase in number
    and kind
and the wonder would begat confusion

and the confusion would be fruitful and greatly
    multiply,
so great would the confusion become it would
    rival the stars in the sky,
which being too great a number for one of his
    kind to count
the Pragmatist, being what he is and only that,
would surely build a world inside the world he
    began within,
a world much simpler than the first,
the one made of energy that he could not under-
    stand or love,
and with this new world he would not fuss with
    man and woman or day and night.
No, the pragmatic world the Pragmatist would
    make would be nothing
like energy, with all its penchant to jump, pop,
    fry and fizzle,
it would not suffer fools with imaginations or
    abide distracting daydreams,
the efficient world to come would then be finally
    free of childlike hearts,
vigilant surveillance against stillness,
and the Pragmatist would sing to the world the
    new and last lullaby –
one without words (outlawed for vagary)
and without melody (forbidden for feeling),
a song silent to the human ear, yet ravenous flute
    to the midbrain,
and the Pragmatist would sing along by himself
    and of himself,
the brilliant orchestrator of desire, baton raging,
    bit by bit.

30

SEMAPHORES

ZAC WALSH

In honor of the work of Mignon Mclaughlin

Born bearing the mark,
godless or not,
unflinching vanity knows
some new adornment,
sly devil, will release us from our rutted circuitry
comprised solely of coordinated resources,
    anyway,
to be controlled and counted for the good plea-
    sure of
the most argued over emptiness in history.
While we, the only abnegating species,
wryly believe we recreate society by
wearing the mark anew each in-line generation.
Once donning virgin blood on the forehead,
now store-bought ash,
once elongated skulls,
now extended cabs,
once cannibalistic armbands,

now Twitter feeds
all in the name of a nameless force which
    requires
every stitch of cosmos to be
binary, the conceit that keeps
the program running smoothly
without a hitch since cuneiform,
while we, self-sustaining semaphores,
miraculous still after millennia of being
bludgeoned by the same tired deceit,
namely, that the Programmer of the Day is on
    our side
even though each line of history's code shows
the program itself has been buggy in the wrong
    direction
since we were fooled to feel subservience to light
    itself,
our very substance,
the very first day.

31

COMPLIANCE

ELLEN HARROLD

Limp-spin hurdle

flying through such a melancholy dance.

It soars

It SHATTERS

IT EXPANDS INTO WANTON MIASMAS. UNBECOMING
THE PLACE WHERE
VIOLENCE IS
ENACTED

32

GRAVEYARD PLANET

HEC LAMPERT-BATES

Weeds are all that grow on the graveyard planet. They spring up from the clay beside the headstones and whistle like undead warblers, a tune that crusts the world in an ozone of sound.

We buried seven that morning. The bodies had arrived through a metal chute and had been wrapped neatly in parchment paper, or, for those who had prepaid for it, an eternal gauze. Stuck to the head-shape of each was a section number, a name, and a space for special instructions.

The first six were easy. Morning burials always were. When their feet expelled from the metal tube and came to rest on the burlap lawn chair beneath, my co-worker Ned checked the face for instructions, and motioned for me to grab the shoulders. I'm new at this, so I had to carry the bad parts. But I had been working there long enough to know Ned's rule about talking in the reception chamber. *Silence for the dead.*

The graves were all pre-dug. The machines did that part— fat, rusting goliaths that poked into the clay with pronged digits and hooked spoons. Ned and I just hoisted the bodies into their holes and gave the repavers space to bury.

The first six had nothing written on the special instruction labels. The headstones were planted, engraved with the name on the face, and the weeds began to ascend, wailing louder as their stalks thickened.

In the dead time between burials, we weed-whacked. The machines that attached to our noses scuffed the leathery skin around them, but callus had begun to grow around my nostrils and shielded me from the whacker's gears. I breathed power into the weed-whacker, and its blade spun with each heaving sigh. My sweat was its oil, and the motion of my eyes its rudder. A thin metal bar extended from the blade to be gripped by my fingers along ergonomic holds. The sun grew in the sky, bulging with sticky heat and gnashing at the cemetery planet with its red spiny digits.

The seventh body was marked. Its legs fell onto the chair with a lighter thud than usual, and Ned checked its face. The body was smaller, stunted or young. Ned waved me closer, to read the instructions. *Headstone message: She Is Not Dead, But Sleepeth.*

It was hard to feel sorry for them. I don't think Ned did, though he feigned respect. They aren't our species and all that. It's like feeling sympathy for a fish. But the small body of Elizabeth W. Patterson begged some grief. We hauled her to her grave and waited for the next one.

A lull day. I assumed the Earth people were lengthening their lives somehow. But no bodies meant tedium for us, the maintainers.

"Ned," I called across section 64, but he did not look up from his work. He was whacking a section of high weeds at the obelisks by the pond. Their squawking was stifled by his blade. At that distance, his form looked unnatural, distorted by erratic heat waves. "Ned," I called again, and he startled. "Where are all the new bodies?"

He shrugged and continued killing.

It had been hours since we'd been called to the reception chamber. In my short years as a weed-whacker, I'd never been without a burial for more than an hour. We couldn't see our bordering sections from the hill we were working on, but I was sure they had received some new guests from those metal pipes that rose into the sky like vertical worms. After all, there were thousands of sections for the billions of dead, and maybe no one had chosen to be buried in section 64 that day.

"Ned," I called after another hour. He heard me on the first try. "It's been five hours–"

"What?" Ned cupped his ear and removed the whacker's breath pump from his nose and lips.

"I said it's been five hours since we've had a burial. Isn't that odd?"

Ned squinted at the sun and calculated its rotation with his spindly thumb. "I suppose," he said and looked at me across the field like there was something I was supposed to say.

"Well, should we do something about it?" My lungs were tired from all the shouting.

"Maybe," Ned replied. He left the whacking-machine on the hill and started down. The weeds taunted our descent, singing minor-key lullabies behind us. I made a promise to return and split them at their stalks.

There were no visitors allowed on the cemetery planet. It made the stones obsolete, I think.No one to remember the dead except for us. But it also meant we had no one to be working for. If Ned and I wanted, we could go on excursions or check on the reception room whenever we pleased. We never had though, until then.

I met Ned at the base of the hill on a pathway made from rubber and black stones. It sprawled forth unbent, bosomed between manufactured hills on either side. At its end was a building, tethered to the sky by that rust-proof metal chute.

"Have you ever had to wait so long to be called?" I asked, attempting conversation while we walked.

Ned grunted. It seemed I had stumbled into his second rule. *Silence for the living.*

We passed the areas we had whacked the day before and reveled in the quiet there. No weeds were mature enough yet to tickle our ears, but we knew they would regrow, and in the coming days, we would follow where they were loudest, a cycle of sound-squashing that would revolve until the last human was buried.

Ned walked with a limp, but I couldn't tell which of his three feet was the injury. His breathing was louder than mine, though he refused to try through his mouth. That air they pumped to the cemetery planet was growing thin. Even for my young lungs. It caught in the crevices, the imperfections of my throat, and stayed there like a fungus.

Ned had the key to the reception building on a small ring he kept pinned to his belt. It was accompanied only by one other I'd never seen him use.

He unlocked the door and waved me into the little brick room. It was cold in there, colder still near the wall opposite the door, where a small keyboard and a set of patinated screens sat unused. The chute was directly in the center, poised to spit bodies at the yard chair beneath. I touched the metal when I passed, and it breathed deep space into the reception chamber like a frozen esophagus.

"Maybe it's clogged," I said as Ned closed the door behind us.

"Doubt it." Ned rarely revealed his plans, ideas, or instructions. Rather implemented them, and hoped I was intuitive enough to follow along. This time, he hobbled to the computer, and scratched his head.

The second key fit into a small chink in the brick only he could see, and the computer lit on with a wet crunch. He began typing with one of his long fingers. The nail, which ran up the length of his hand to meet the other fingers' nails, made a ringing clack with each letter, spoiling the room in a sound no better than the weeds'.

I took the opportunity to move the lawn chair and have a look directly up the barrel of the chute. Except for a subtle wind, it was just darkness. Not even an interesting kind of darkness. Just black beyond the fading color of metal.

"Nothin' interesting up there," I said, though still inspecting it. My voice echoed and disappeared.

Ned was silent.

"So I suppose from all that typing there's some kind of procedure when this happens? Don't let me pry if it's a secret." I chuckled at the end, and the wind ceased. Still, Ned was quiet. I didn't even hear his trademarked grunt. "Ned?" A faint beeping had replaced the sound of his typing.

I removed my head from the steel sphincter, and he was staring at me. He'd never looked at me with such intensity. There was a fear in the black pupil spheres that were his eyes. A cool purple smoke escaped from two holes in his torso. It meant regret. The computer behind him flashed red.

"Ned?"

"I—" he stammered. "Mistake. I'm sorry—"

I was sucked into the chute before the air could catch in my lungs. My feet were gone by the time Ned's eyes lost sight of my head.

I couldn't scream in the tube. There was barely enough room to fit my shoulders, let alone for sounds. See we, maintainers, are bigger than humans. The chute wasn't built for our extra leg, nor our deep-set chest bone, and the spiny, knobby bits on our ribs.

The shock caught me first, and I smashed along the sides of the tube in a painful dance, accompanied by a symphony of ringing metal concussions too loud for my ears. I blinked, but the tube was as dark as the skin beneath my eyelids, and after a few, I couldn't tell the difference.

It was all I could manage to keep myself in the most human-esque shape I could without crushing my windpipe or dislocating my hips. But eventually, as it pulled me up, unwinding, I stiffened myself in a position that preserved my skin from being dragged along the craggle walls and their crude welding.

Soon, I could not tell if I was moving in the dark. The hole of light that shone beneath my feet was a pinprick, and the tunnel wind was either stationary, or matched my speed.

Finally I could breath, and before I tried to plan anything, I let the air flow deep into my chest. It was sweeter up there. It tasted better than outside the tube; somehow more refreshing. Once the banging had stopped echoing, it was quite a peaceful ride. Though not peaceful enough to forget my predicament.

In my years as a maintainer, I had never figured out where the chutes began. I assumed on Earth, but Earth was quite a ways away and through the death black of space. Every time I had asked Ned, he had shrugged, and pointed up to the fault-less clouds and said "Up there," or something equally unhelp-ful. It was always followed by some question that challenged my desire to even be on the cemetery planet. To which I always responded pleasantly.

So, I thought that might be my end. A weed-whacker's life sucked away with the press of a button. I was chill with it.

It was easy to be sorry for Ned, though. He's my species, after all, and my death wasn't his fault. It was my mistake to stand under the chute. I could feel the smoke I knew was yellow exude from my holes. It meant pity.

Now that I was thinking about it, the sweetness in the air probably meant a coming vacuum that would slurp out my lungs like juice from a straw. A cute death with a cherry aroma. At least it smelled good. I would have liked to see Earth, though.

I closed my eyes and prepared for it all. The wind brushed my calloused cheeks again, and it sang, a chorus not a whine. My body loosened, and I let it take me.

And then it was bright. My head smashed into a dusty ceiling, and I scrambled with all five limbs to steady myself in the air. If this was death, it was awfully disorienting. My left arm – the long one—hit the ground first and crumpled at the second elbow. I was enclosed.

The sweet smell had thickened and hung around me like humidity. I opened my eyes, and something slapped me between them; a sticky paper that clung to my skin and pressed residue into my pores. I groaned and peeled it off.

Something screamed to my left.

There was a million-legged creature in the room, and everything was covered in stickers.

I screamed back, and jumped away, towards a beige wall with blank stickers mending the cracks.

"Who are you?" shouted the creature as it tossed paper feebly in my direction.

I was stunned, nervous that this was death, and at the same time, adjusting to the light until the thing came properly into view.

It was shaped like a centipede, of which there were many on the cemetery planet. But this one was enormous, twice my length, and its feet flailed upwards. Its skin was loose and over-sized. On one end, was the head that screamed, and an eye that cowered from me, quivering in fear. On the other, a set of fleshy fountain pens, which had stopped scribbling on the stickers, and were all pointed at me like spears. In front of the sentient head, was an array of lollipops, each opened and licked, standing upright on a spinning table.

I grunted "I—I'm from the planet."

"The planet?"

"I was sucked up the tube. Yes, the planet where we bury

the bodies." I wasn't sure if the creature knew the word cemetery.

"You bury them?" It whispered. "I knew we were sending them somewhere, but to be buried. Like seeds?"

"Well," I said in a voice that came out splintery, whiplashed from the fall. "They're dead. I don't know if anything will grow from them except weeds."

The eye of the great thing moistened, and its bottom lip trembled. "Dead?" it cried. "Dead? They're dead? Dead?" It was louder on each iteration of the word.

"Of course, what did you think they were?"

"I just give them stickers. I write the words I'm given and send them on their way." It could barely speak through the orange liquid that had begun to fall from its eye. "I thought it was for a meet and greet."

I was frozen against the wall, brains processing the events of the last two minutes with increasing confusion. "Hey," I said, propelled by an instinct to comfort the thing. "It's alright. Everything is alright."

"No, it's not," the big lug cried. "No," it shifted its head around to look at its many hands, twisting its skin like a damp rag. I gagged at the sight. "I didn't know I've been handling dead things all my life. This changes—this changes everything. Everything I've ever known."

"Ok," I said. "You're having an existential crisis. It's ok, I've had plenty. But you need to calm down and help me."

It took several deep breaths, hauling air in from the room in quantities enough to feed a windmill. "I'm sorry. You're right. Me and my husband have just been so–"

"You have a husband?" I interrupted. There were no spouses to be found on the cemetery planet.

"Yes," it wiped tears from its eye with a black tongue, and let out a belch, directed upward. Something in the ceiling replied with a lighter, docile burp of its own. A hatch appeared, chiseled between graffitied stickers on the platform above us.

It cracked and fizzled until a seam was created, and a piece fell in. I could see the room above was not as cozy as the one I was in. Instead of warm yellow light and old drywall, the upstairs cavern was reflective, gilded with steel, and polished like glass.

"Come, come down," called the big centipede. It feigned happiness, but there was still angst in its voice. "Come along, sweety, there's someone here for us."

A tiny leg crept into the opening. It was shy, skittish at the sound of my breathing. The thing in my room continued to coax it out and eventually, it clambered out of the shadows, and onto the wall, its eyes locked on me throughout. This one was the size of my palm, and barely recognizable as a living thing until it moved. It was a spool of parchment paper, and it walked around on four thumb-like appendages.

"Hello, my baby," cooed the centipede as it nuzzled the air around it.

The small one could not speak, only made damp undulations with the small hole that ran through the length of it. But clearly, it responded to the big thing with understanding. After greeting its mate, the spool leapt at me and for the second time that day, my eyes were covered with something.

I was flailing as it unraveled itself over me, regenerating its paper with every turn. It swung around my head, clambering over my mouth and ears with its speeding legs. I grabbed at it with my short arm, but it was too quick, evading me with tactile precision. I screamed until it covered my mouth in the stuff.

It had wrapped as far as my neck before the caterpillar laughed, and called it off.

"—a guest!" I heard as I ripped the stuff to breathe.

I stood, and hissed, and felt for the wall behind me.

"Sorry about that," said the big one. "We aren't used to

having visitors. I hope you'll forgive him. He thought you were an... *attendee*."

I gasped to catch my breath, but I'm nice. I'm generally a chill guy. So I waved it off, again and pushed down the blue smoke that meant doom I had felt coming on since I had been sucked up the chute.

"So why are you here then anyways?" It asked.

"We–" I started, still reeling from the attack. "I um... I work down there, and we haven't had any bodies come down in hours, so we tried to check to see if the chute was blocked or something but my partner—my working partner Ned pressed a wrong button or something, and I ended up here." It all spilled from my lips without much care for proper speech.

"Oh I see," it nodded. Orange liquid was still dripping from its eye. "So that's why you came up the highway then right?"

"Right," I repeated. "The highway."

"And you said you needed help?"

"Yes, well isn't it just odd?"

"What is?"

The paper roll hissed.

"The lack–" I started.

"The lack?" The bug was confused.

"I mean that we've been down there all day."

"Right," it responded. "But we've been up here."

"I know but there's no bodies!" I threw my shorter arm out and gestured to the numerous metal holes that led out of the room. "There must be some kind of jam. Do you—" I played my cheek with my nails like a plump accordion, and my sides leaked bronze. It meant frustration. "People on that planet count on us to take care of them when they die, and we can't do that if it's all... well, it's not working, is it? And what else are we here for anyways? Just for them? A little colony of living things. We're just disposers. All of us." I didn't mean to say all that.

"Hey," said the centipede defensively. It threw up several of its hands in innocence. "I only just figured out they're dead."

"Right," I said, and the color cloud thickened. "But can you just listen?"

The two were silent, and I quickly realized I had no idea what I wanted them to listen to. I had no plan, no ideas, and no guiding philosophy. I sighed. "I want to go up."

"Up?" asked the thing.

"Or down, or wherever the bodies come from." I couldn't look anywhere except a small patch of uncovered floor by my third foot. "I don't want to be here anymore. Not on this planet. I want to go to Earth." I had never said anything like that before. Ned would have been irate.

The big bug pointed with its pens to an unremarkable hole on the side wall. "I have no quarrel with you. That's where they come from. I can send you, if you must."

I sighed and thanked the couple before crawling into the hole. It carried the same scent as the room: lollipop sugar, and dusty parchment paper. I couldn't stop jittering, and my jaw twitched side to side. When I reached up to hold it still, I felt that my lips were curled up.

The two creatures smiled back and motioned me to slink further into the chute. I heard the husband press a button.

When the tube lifted me, I was not shocked.

The ride was long, and unpleasant, but this time, no smoke was trapped inside of me, and my limbs felt unbound. Not once did I feel the brushing wrath of a loose nail, or misplaced strip of lining. There was no light, and in that deep senselessness, I imagined the Earth alive with the predecessors of those I had buried, all the colors of Earth striking me like opaque emotions, the families I had put in peace.

I was stopped by an invisible force at a gate, marked in a language I didn't understand. It released its valve slowly, and the sounds of muddy grinding gears slipped through a crack. I was lifted from the chute, into a blue pod that faced black nothing. There was no wind to carry me as I floated upright, only empty space. The pod unlatched and sent me onto a blinking platform where the sky was nothing except for pinhole lights far away. Not even the weed sounds were strong enough to reach me there. My heart pounded like a tired whacker's engine.

And then a planet rose in front of me, white and misty and blue against the stars.

I watched it from its moon, the graveyard planet. I watched the Earth burn, and its red smoke mingled with mine. Elizabeth W. Patterson had been the last one.

She is not dead, but sleepeth.

33

IT'S JUST ME

JOHN GREY

It could have been a fish
splashing at the side of the boat,
but I prefer to think it was a mermaid.
Like that might have just been mist at the
     window,
but to my mind it was the ghost of a child
     urging me
to open up and let him in.

Same with the strange creature
that darted away from me
when I came upon it accidentally.
I pooh-poohed my companion's explanation
of fisher-cat.
It was a dark, furry demon.
Otherwise, why did I say a Hail Mary
under my breath.

I say "roc in the sky."
People respond with "rocks in the head."

I tell a friend her daughter is possessed.
She replies that the kid
is taking something for it.

My problem is that
the ordinary has no appeal to me.
I've seen more UFO's
than you've seen reruns of *Friends*.
Your earth tremor
is my poltergeist.
Your drunk
is my zombie.

And I read the newspaper
for clues to the coming apocalypse.
Look at this,
a slaying down by the river.
Maybe whoever did it
will repeat the dose
in the end times to come.
I mean if a guy can't be a serial killer,
then why kill at all.

34

WHAT GOES ON

KEECH BALLARD

Sometimes I wonder
what goes on
inside your head

If only I
had a mental power drill
with a magic umbilical cord

to bore through lacquered ages
of your thick skull
and soften everything right up

I would rummage through
discarded memories
lost dreams and banished expectations

moving things around
from one place to another
sorting vain ideas into and out of

imaginary cardboard boxes
with crayon hearts and chalked x's
tottering under heavy loads

only to discover
what goes on
inside your head

35

VISION FIELD

REKHA VALLIAPPAN

This is how I shall always remember the soundscape
of our lives—as an overload,

hers and mine. A jarring *RED!* Extrasensory overload I
call it, fuelled by too much

information. Leveraged by Greek classics coming at
us like multiple streamers from

different directions. Some Vedic wisdom. A mixture of
odd facts I can only deduce to be

New World Science. And the brilliant preponderance
of the female element aka tenacity.

To scale. For me.

Even now looking over her shoulder, catching
twittering birds melting in the early

morning light, treating my attention to a reassuring
study, I see the snow on the meadow

outside our window is red. This may seem insensible if
not downright eccentric. I take a

second look, then a third. Not a sign of anything, or
anyone, by this I mean anything

untoward or unscientific. My perception is, not cloudy,
but constant. I am not 'seeing'

things, except what I *see*. I admit though I'm hard
pressed to deny that the mysteries of

nature are indeed complex, and known to be so
through the vast demands of the ages.

I glance at her, my reactions mixed, something in me
taking in the deflected

mirror neurons bursting through the motor areas of her
brain. She's reacting. It's

heartening. To be specific, such is her tenacity. My
empathy levels are equally riding sky

high, while I strum guitar. It's my daily practice routine.
I offer her the silicone ear plugs

I permanently carry, for all contingencies, exquisite or
mundane, to mute the sound.

She's reacting to *sound*. She's twitching. She's in
overdrive.

Pulling her in is the *red*—red as predictable and
immortal as the visual curtained

beyond the volcanic glow effect rising off the snow at
dawn they call the nature of the

terrain, when the morning sun rises. In actual fact, the
loud strumming of my guitar,

within earshot. *Hers!* My thoughts do not need to
distend, to know. She is hearing *red*. In

a less flattering light I can trace her grasp the sound of
red. She has a mind that buzzes

like a honey bee, unsealing beeswax honeycombs
faster than a mother queen can form a

hive. She hears red. Furthering her formalized wishes
stemming from musical sounds I

call it sense tenacity. Grabbing at real life plant nectar,
which in my case is her brain's

cerebral cortex, life's epicenter connecting billions of
biomes, mine, I catalogue into

memory what I see. I *see* red.

"Rather strange, don't you think? But, fascinating!" I
hear her articulate in her

distinct strong-willed manner, at one with the crowd
connectors around arguing chemical

changes in air composition they call climate change
these days. Einstein's composites

from every point of view, cow flatulence variables,
even cross-planetary contamination

from Lehrer's failed experiments to terraform Mars
which gives the planet its fiery color

is fair play. I'm a family man. I thrive on science. I'm
trying to sparkle with the rest. But,

Red is not my color, sense tenacity or not. This snow
contamination clearly has to be

from somewhere.

I remember telling her of iron rich oxide with real time
data. Yes, the

extraordinary rock stuff they transported back from
Mars. How else can one explain the

bright magma hues away? Tenacity has to balance in
its natural scientific chemistry. By

then the color variance due to reported climate
breakdown grows so real, I take to

wearing color correctable lenses for visual acuity, to
prevent eye bulging, and other

serious side effects to the dyes, amidst people I know.
Although people I knew were

having their own kind of sensory overload breakdowns
curiously related to algebraic

numerical equations in solidarity whenever they saw
the color 'red' coded, despite mental

arithmetic tracing its roots back to the days of Aristotle.

Then comes the revelation which bolsters my red
vision field further. Turns out

her great grand-aunt on the Canada side was a color
acute synaesthete. Turns out there

are folks like her in this world. When the grande olde
dame heard a guitar twang she

experienced the color scarlet. Putting her overactive
ear drums to the test and in place

turned into a multi-family exercise in unconditional

statistics, which involved a host of

cousins, and aunts, and second cousins, from three
continents, to the extent the tenacity

and complication spewed such ardor, some of us don't
talk to each other anymore.

Clearly, the color coordinates in the oversensitive
sensory perceptions broke up families

forever. Recorded in ancient astronomy terms by
looking at the position of the stars in the

night sky it labeled her as much as it labeled her
elderly relative. Because such were the

very far reaches of cumulative and combative effects
of starlight color—aka *red!*

Now if I can make the tetrachromatic color vision
argument for red, in modern

languages, I can call the red phenomena meteorite
detritus or red tide algae or a default

musical encore, or whatever her globular level of
comfort or discomfort in championing

the retinal cone color chart compartmentalizes. But,
the entropy in the tenacity going

forward is the fiendish complexity between her color

acuteness due to sound, and her

semantics, due to linguistics. Was it for lack of a word
that she heard red? Same as the

ancient Greeks experienced. In a reading they
reportedly did not have a word for *blue* per

the Odyssey. Believe me, I have tried my best to
fathom this anomaly. Her cosmology

and her biorhythms, coupled with my wild strumming
of guitar within hearing distance of

her can only produce one acute sense assault, and
she erupts like an exploding can of

spray paint. *Red!*

On this day I see her sensory overload break into
flower like spores, like red plum

in bloom. Perhaps it is the fog in my Merinda crunch, a
watermelon sweet maroon

concoction she's dreamt up for my good health, while
she drops lemon peels on impulse

to watch them turn as red as the snow outside our
window. Her next move is to grab her

cell phone, her lap-top, her mini-notebook, and her two
red pens, and in the general hasty

chaos of transference to her cross body handbag, also
a streaking red, she mistakenly

picks up my neat copy of Aryabhatta, instead of her
crumpled heavily annotated copy of

the Iliad, hearing a billion flutes smacking the gates of
Valhalla no doubt in her haste.

"My treat," she yells, on her way out, seeing her choke
point red.

I'm left to my tantric ruminations. People have stopped
contemplating the red

snow at dawn. They have stopped eating it either, after
it proved too laxative for comfort.

They are going about their routine tasks, just as she is,
I am. Researchers have reasoned

for ages that the Greeks were explicitly devoid of
words for several colors. I ask myself

why? In effect do we have a language deficiency we
haven't overcome? Is the snow on

the meadow not really *red* but for want of a word we
call it red because it orchestrates as

red to sight and sound?

I think the ancient Greeks interpreted what they saw
and heard forcefully, bravely.

Not because of any tetrachromatic pigment deficiency,
but because of their tenacious

perceptions of unwavering algorithms. They lacked the
language coordinates to unriddle

color. So rather, for want of a *red,* Homer scripted
'wine-dark sea.' And, for lack of a

blue the ancient Greek classics scripted 'bronze.' As
for the Vedic scripts they described

the black firmament as a whirlpool of harmony color
composites. I could imagine their

quandary. The fiendish complexity as every linguist
knows lies rooted in our shared

sublimations, for language is as permanent as
printer's ink.

Abundantly clear is the overload of *red.* The right word
of course is pink. The

same widespread pink which men of letters a very long
time ago, Aristotle in fact in the

third century BC, observed as an acute snow
phenomena. That pink has since been

galloping around the globe in dollops of red, according

to our scientific studies. This is

how we have algae blooms—bright red, iron rich soil—
deep red, roseate kelp—beet red,

setting suns—fiery red. Nothing to do with foreign
language makeovers. Nothing to

connect to faulty eyesight either. Simply the wisdom of
the ages driven by vaulting

perception, refusing to disappear.

I see now what her great grand aunt might have seen
when two coordinates, guitar

and her ears, clashed at the sound of music—the thing
we just flagged, *RED!* Bizarre, but

true, and in my family we'll never know. So what am I
doing to help her cope when

sensory overloads occur? Something has to be
missing. I'm trying to read what. I think

she is intelligent. I think she will some day teach me
medieval kabbalism, or the

intersecting principles of light and dark, or red and
blue in ancient languages despite how

the Greeks coped, over and above the Euripedes she
hurls at me for good measure. At my

most magnanimous I ease up on my hourly metallic
twanging, my eyes wide open,

staring at the snow sparkling red in the quiet dawn.

36

EXILE, IN FIVE PARTS

DANIEL A. RABUZZI

*(Reflecting upon Annette von Droste-Hülshoff's "Die Verbannten,"
i.e., "The Banished," from her Gedichte, 1844)*

i. Hungry

Last week I ate my horse,
Except the face-parts,
Those I just couldn't, but buried them instead.

Faithful Ajax!
If our Lord lets me live, this I swear:
That I shall make an Ajaxiad
And cry it aloud in every church and market
    square.

So, dear Lord, I beg,
No, beseech you (a word I have never used
    before):
Guide me home from wilderness,
For the sake of sacrifice, if not for mine.

Ruins above me on the hills-
Crenellated crestlines,
Teething on the wind.
I found there rats to eat,
And lizards, only.

I cannot climb the branted hills again,
Stumble rather along the brook.
Water surely knows its way home.

ii. Unseeing

You deceive me
(I say so with respect):
The stream seeks its origins,
Bends upon itself, returns like blood to the heart.
I can feel the stone I placed upon my horse's
    grave.

I misprize this place, and you, and all aspect
Worldly and divine.

In the deceitful lucidity of darkness
My eyes stray among ghosts,
Phantoms misaligned,
Shades of shades,
Invisible thrones and principalities.

iii. Unhearing

I see the lone oak on the hillside.

Halfway up the slope, a child stands,
Sucking on the hands of a blind old man.

The ancient king opens his mouth,
I see a grey tongue, raddled gums.
He speaks, the boy nods,
I hear nought.

The boy points to the valley.
I see a steeple above the wood.

Turning...

Halfway to the steeple,
Thrashing through thorn-hikes and hews,
In silence, no blackbird song, no pigeon coos,
No heartbeat strong.

iv. Unspeaking

M----
B---

Dr---

H---   --d

M---   --r

O---   --n
S--   --d   --H—

--p   --B—

H--   --g
St—

R—

v. Breathless / Breathing

Careering down the cleve,
A gift received:
Air crushing my lungs, air.

Bells ring faint but fluid far off,
Nearby a blackbird sings,
A partridge chuckles,
Bees swarm in the beeches.

Halfway to the steeple,
I meet a woman in a pear-tree.
Imploring, she gasps:
"Be my bride."

Hugging herself, winding tighter the shroud
That binds her to the tree.

The branches are rimmed
And tipped with blue flame,
Like a Christmas pudding.

Forth I step.

I will never leave this place.

37

THE COLONY ON KEPLER-442B

A SPEECH HELD BY DR. BERNARD T. ROSS AT THE HEADQUARTERS OF THE INTERPLANETARY COUNCIL ON JANUARY 3RD, 2220

G. V. SILVA

For Sali, with whom I learn so much about love between humans

You can imagine how difficult it was for us to finally achieve a means of communication with your species.

It's not just that we don't have mouths to speak, ears to hear, or hands to put pen to paper. Before the invasion, even your conception of language, yes, the very notion of communication as such was alien to us. We would never have grasped it if we hadn't been forced to learn in order to survive. And we all know what bitter price both of our peoples had to pay for it.

For our part, you can be sure that we deeply regret all the life that was lost in our struggle. We don't blame you for it, and we hope you will show us the same kind of understanding.

After all, we were both ignorant of each other, closed off in fundamentally incompatible realms of experience. Neither you nor we even suspected that we were dealing with intelligent, conscious beings.

Because of this, when you arrived on our planet, we both

started out by acting in ways that the other had to perceive as violent and aggressive. We didn't know any better.

Now, finally, we make our first attempt at communication. We hope it might help to end the cycle of violence and mutual destruction that our races have been engaged in for so long.

You should hope so, too. In fact, it is your only hope, your last hope.

But let's not get ahead of ourselves.

Dr. Bernard T. Ross, Head Science Officer at the colony on Kepler-442b, the man who is delivering this message to you, speaks in our name. Please treat him as our emissary and ambassador. We consider him an alley—a friend—a lover, even —as are all the colonists on our planet. They have seen the world as we see it, and they have learned to accept our love.

We ask you to listen attentively to what Dr. Ross has to say. And please forgive us if we sometimes find it difficult to express our point of view in words. It took us countless empathy sessions with the colonists to translate our account of the invasion of our home world into a language that you might understand. We insist on relating it in the certainty that you, too, here on Earth, will agree to see things from our perspective. We are confident that in a not-so-distant future, humanity as a whole will be joining us in loving unity.

L et us begin by saying that we believe we understand human psychology much better now, after so many years of interaction. The information we were able to extract once we entered empathic communion with the settlers on Kepler-442b clarified many things we had been puzzling over for ages. But even now there is so much about the way you think and act that we still don't fully grasp.

We understand, for example, that chemical signals don't

play a significant role in your species' perception of its environment. Your predominant senses are physical, whereas ours are almost exclusively chemical. Even in communion, we aren't always able to adequately interpret the electrical impulses into which your sensory organs convert different kinds of physical vibrations.

Just to give you an idea of how much our perception differs from yours, try to picture a world whose main aspect consists of taste and smell. A world in which most of your decisions and actions are guided by those chemical senses alone. You cannot picture it. You cannot imagine it. Because, to start with, such a world simply isn't—a picture. Yet, as unimaginable as it may be to you, that is, more or less, what the world is like to us, how our intelligence accesses reality and interacts with it.

Since evolution didn't necessitate us to locomotion, we never had to develop a strong sense of spatial orientation. Things so basic to you such as your physical shape—and any physical shape for that matter—are known to us only very abstractly and indirectly by means of the faintest and most abstruse analogies. Our perception of space is so vastly different from yours that we had never even thought of developing a science such as geometry, which to you seems so intuitive. Geotropism and a sensitivity to the chemical composition of our surroundings, paired with some photosensitivity, allow for some kind of topological differentiation of our environment. But it is nothing compared to what you seem to achieve through the sense of sight.

On the other hand, we soon learned that you, too, are physiologically quite badly equipped in other areas in which our species excels. What pains you seem to have gone through to gain even a minimal understanding of and control over the biochemistry of your own organisms! How roundabout and inefficient are your attempts at preserving or enhancing them, even now that you are colonizing the stars!

It's as if your intelligence can only manipulate your surroundings effectively by reducing everything to chemistry. And also chemistry you seem to only really master insofar as you are able to reduce it to physics. Whereas for us organic processes are as intuitive as the shape of a rock is to you. And just as you might chip away at a rock to produce a tool, we influence our living environment to conform it to our needs.

Since we lived in these almost completely separate worlds, it's no wonder really that it took us so long to recognize each other as intelligent; that many of you here on Earth appear not to have done so even up to this very moment. Consequently, it was only natural that we would start out by trying to use each other as if we were things or machines.

When you arrived on our planet, we welcomed with great interest the host of biochemical devices you brought along with you. We quickly found much use in the rich microbial life that you carried inside and around yourselves. It was a massive breakthrough for us, and we were very excited about it.

At first, we didn't even realize that all these microbes had been brought by a race of multicellular, let alone intelligent organisms. It took us quite a while observing the patterns of behavior and distribution of the novel microbial fauna to even arrive at the hypothesis that we might be dealing with more complex life forms.

Not that we didn't have any experience with multicellular organisms—we just never had one suddenly come down from the stars to colonize our planet. You see, to us, up until your arrival, this world you so casually call Kepler-442b had been not only our world but *the* world. It was all we knew, we, who didn't even have sensory organs to see the stars above us. It was, as you might put it, Occam's razor that prevented us from accepting the very unlikely reality of your presence on our planet until the evidence was overwhelming.

In any case, as soon as we realized your existence, we supposed that you, too, could be just as useful as the fungi and bacteria you had brought with you.

Meanwhile, you were setting up your fortified settlements and hauling in load after load of humans, trampling all over our millennia-old colonies—a quite ironic human name for the biosocial arrangement of our species—, and terraforming our planet in all sorts of ways. As hard as it was for us to decipher you, at this point, you were getting more and more difficult to ignore.

I t took us a few years of hard and patient work to gain some understanding of the main aspects of human physiology.

One thing that helped us tremendously was your habit of burying your dead. It gave us a unique chance to study your biochemical makeup more closely and distinguish the different specialized tissues that compose your body.

Once we had figured out your metabolic processes, we began to study your behavior. Can you imagine how hard it was to discover even the simplest truths about you when all the empirical data available to us consisted exclusively of the variety of chemical compounds that you released into the air, water, and soil—mostly unconsciously, as we now know?

It was only very slowly that we came to realize that the presence of certain compounds correlated with some specific behavioral patterns on the part of the individuals of your species.

The first aspect of the human mind that we were able to decode through this method was emotion. It is, perhaps, another testimony to the difference in our natures that the part of your conscious life that you consider the most obscure and mysterious was the simplest one to us.

We learned to smell your fear, so to speak, and your anger, but also your feelings of joy, tenderness, and satisfaction. We were thrilled to learn that we were dealing with a rather sophisticated form of subjectivity.

Then, as a consequence of having understood the chemical processes underlying human emotional responses, we soon learned how to manipulate your emotions and, with that, the more impulsive aspects of your behavior. By releasing specific chemical compounds into the air or water, we elicited from the colonists behaviors that were favorable to us.

We worked silently and patiently. All we had to do—in fact, all we *could* do at this stage—was to collect the chemical data provided constantly by you and correlate it to find patterns and discover further mechanisms of your physiology that we could exploit.

We were domesticating you, just as our species had domesticated all other savage life forms on our planet so far. From a threat, you were to become a useful ally.

A t this point, we would urge you to try to understand that the application of all this knowledge we had gathered in order to tweak your brain chemistry in our favor was our first attempt at making peace with your species.

As such, it failed miserably. Instead, we got our first real lesson in human psychology.

Back then, we still had only a very vague suspicion that you might actually be an intelligent race. This was a mistake for which we paid a bitter price. We soon discovered that we had underestimated you, or rather, that we had misread you.

The colonists resisted our chemical influence on their

behavior. They quickly figured out our ruse and began developing means to protect their bodies from our control.

This was unexpected to us. But more fundamentally than that, their reaction revealed a very troubling truth about your species: that it is a conservative species, which favors competition and preservation over cooperation and transformation. You were, indeed, the first to ever actively resist forming a mutualistic bond with us.

Unlike the myriads of microorganisms that you had brought along with you, you didn't accept our chemical manipulation of your physiological drives, even if that acceptance entailed advantages to the survival of your species in an alien and mostly hostile environment such as Kepler-442b—as you can see now that it actually does.

Just take Dr. Ross here as an example. A changed man. A man who transcended the narrow boundaries of his human experience and learned to appreciate the benefits of symbiosis...

But no, as soon as our actions were discovered, the colonists began actively eradicating us. This is when our troubles started to get really serious. You perceived us as dangerous and poisonous. You assumed we were a threat to your survival and acted accordingly. How did we suffer in those years! What a big portion of us had to die before we were able to gather enough knowledge about you to strike back!

However, eventually, we did manage to find ways to pierce your defenses. And when we did, it wasn't only manipulation, but annihilation that we, now oppressed and persecuted, unleashed upon you.

In a single day, all the invaders on the planet—we estimate that there were about thirty-three thousand of them there at the time—expired. After corroding their protective gear, we poisoned their blood with toxins released in the air, which penetrated all the orifices in their bodies, killing them instantly.

We reclaimed our land.

A long period of quiet followed. During this time, we continued studying the biological material you had left behind, including that of your incredibly rich microbiota. It took you twenty-seven years to return, and when you finally did, we braced ourselves for another attack.

But you didn't send any of your fleshy ambulant nodes of consciousness after us. No, this time, the only visitor was an aseptic thing of metal and silicon that collected samples from us and returned to space before we even had a chance to assess what was going on.

Another five years went by in silence before you launched your own chemical attack against us.

One day, something fell from the sky and shrouded the whole planet in a cloud of gaseous death. We would have been wiped out if not for the fact that the gas didn't penetrate all the air pockets in the soil and further underground. Thanks to that, a considerable part of us was able to survive out of sight until the danger had passed and more unsuspecting invaders came down to the surface, thinking they had defeated us once and for all.

As you now know, they were wrong.

However, we had learned our lesson. We knew better than to attempt another direct assault on you. We are, by virtue of our very nature, a slow and patient species. Moreover, destructive action contradicted our innermost instincts of cherishing and protecting life, the innate tendency of our species toward mutualism and symbiosis. We didn't want another act of carnage on our hands. There had to be another way.

We decided to stay in hiding and keep our presence on the planet secret. We suspected you would attempt to destroy us again if you were to find that we were still around.

By then, we knew all the ins and outs of your biochemical makeup, and we had an excellent understanding of your physiology—but the disastrous events of prior decades had made it clear that we still knew next to nothing about your psychology. Instead of escalating into a war whose outcome we were unable to predict, we would bide our time and continue to observe your behavior.

Meanwhile, you went on building your settlements, populating our land with your people, changing the face of our planet with your crude but powerful machines. We knew that if we were to survive, it would be crucial to establish some means of entering a mutualistic bond with your kind.

And now we come to the decisive point in our long and troubled relationship. It can be summarized in one treacherous little word: love. A word so deceiving in its apparent simplicity...

Indeed, to us, in a way, love—or rather, the closest equivalent to what you call love—is the simplest thing in the world.

To start with, it's important to note that our reproductive habits are not much more than a biochemical process, barely distinguishable from the vegetative growth of our bodies.

When the season comes, when days get shorter and wetter and a strong cold wind starts to blow over the vast plains of our continent, an appendix might push its way out of the soil here and there. A modest fruiting body pops open and spills out countless microscopic spores that are carried away through the air—and it's done. The land has been sown with another generation.

With time, spores grow into hyphae that burrow their way back to their parent stocks, until they finally reintegrate with our mycelial consciousness. Our offspring have no independent will of their own apart from this drive to reconnect with the community they stemmed from.

Consequently, to us, reproduction is a mere physiological necessity, a process almost completely independent from our conscious existence, something that we have never really given a thought to.

Instead, all our impulses are geared toward growing together, finding a way back to each other, and thriving as a unity. If the word love has any meaning to us, it is this growing closer, this entwining of our filaments, the strengthening of the chemical bonds that make our society a network in which each individual is not much more than what a brain cell is to a human brain. Love for us is to become one, but many, many, but one. It is a peaceful process, a cool and steady merging of body and mind.

To you, on the other hand, sexuality is at the very core of existence. Its influence on your behavior goes far beyond its mere reproductive function. Your passions, your drives, and, thus, more or less directly, all your conscious and unconscious interactions with each other and the world in general are rooted in it. Everything you feel, think, and do flows from it and ultimately leads back to it. It is, by far, the human being's most powerful drive, far surpassing the survival instinct, which we had tried to manipulate at first.

But, we asked ourselves, what is this drive, exactly? What defines it? It clearly isn't directed merely toward procreation. In fact, it doesn't seem to have any particular kind of object at all. You seem to invest this libidinal energy in almost anything, not only in your fellow humans. Even lifeless things can be the target of this mad desire.

This was all very puzzling to us. Nonetheless, it gave us

some hope. For if human affection is so unspecific in its essence, you would, in theory, be capable of investing it in us, as well—of *loving us*. The question was: how could we, a completely alien species, awaken in you feelings of tenderness, desire, lust—toward *us*? For the moment you regarded us with nothing but hate and disgust. How could you ever come to love us?

At first, the human mechanisms of sexual attraction seemed too complex to fathom. Only a small fraction of them appeared to derive from direct physical and chemical stimuli. The rest was composed of such a mess of historical and cultural variables that we couldn't hope to ever gain any sort of effective control over it.

No, we would have to find another strategy. Instead of making ourselves attractive to you, we would give you a chance to see us as we really are to ourselves. If only you could experience the world as we did, surely you would also see the folly of your reluctance and join us in loving symbiosis.

Once we had figured this out, our course of action was clear.

So we got to work—slowly and quietly, as always. We took care of you, worked to turn our planet into a pleasant and hospitable home for your species. We helped the plants and animals you had brought with you to grow strong. We cleaned the waters from substances toxic to you. We even adjusted the composition of the atmosphere to best suit your needs and those of the invading species you introduced to our planet.

You didn't even suspect our actions. On the contrary, as we learned later, you were congratulating yourselves for an especially successful terraforming effort. Generations had passed, settlements had grown, and your memories of the troubled past had faded slowly into oblivion. But we remembered. On your side, all of those who witnessed our first encounter were long dead. But we were there, pretty much the same as all those years ago. We changed, we learned, we suffered, we were mutilated, we healed, regrew—but we still remembered it all.

Finally, one sunny day after heavy rainfall, tiny blue modified fruiting bodies popped up everywhere on the planet's surface. It was our carefully crafted peace offering to your species. Our attempt at seducing you.

It would suffice if only a few of the more curious or careless among the colonists tasted them—which, of course, they ended up doing quite promptly. As Chief Science Officer of the colony, Dr. Ross was one of the first to enter an empathic bond with us through the ingestion of what soon became known as the "Kepler Mushrooms"—one of the first to understand the potential of symbiosis between our species—one of our first lovers...

It turns out that our little present was much more eagerly accepted by the colonists than even we had expected. The mushrooms had been designed to give you a taste of what it was to be like us: a single, virtually immortal collective being in a permanent state of oneness with its living surroundings. What we didn't expect was that you would experience this state as one of ultimate and absolute bliss: a perfect fusion with everything, a never-ending collective orgasm. It just so happened, as we later learned from the colonists, that the state produced in you by the Kepler Mushrooms was no more no less than what your species had yearned for since the dawn of your civilization, since the first glint of individuality had appeared in your eyes; what you had fantasized about in myths and religions, in all the stories you told yourselves to make your mortal pulverized existence bearable.

It's as if the individuals of your species are essentially incomplete, always yearning and at the same time unable to absorb everything, to become one with everything. As if your very individuality, of which you had shown yourselves to be so proud and protective, was some kind of disease you were desperately trying to get rid of at all times.

Through what you called love, we realized, you were chasing after the perfect unity which *we*, as a species, just *were*. The conclusion, though bewildering, was inescapable: your most intimate desire, codified in this mysterious little word "love," was *to be like us...*

The Kepler Mushrooms soon became a craze throughout the human colonies. A drug that offered a truly collective experience of ecstatic oneness with everyone and everything around. While under its effect, all one had to do was touch, even just breathe the same air as others to plunge into a super-human state of shared consciousness, to achieve the unity that every fiber of your body longed for but could never attain as an individual. Pure love. Not just a chemical simulacrum of love, but the real thing: a true empathic bond with all the surrounding nature.

People went absolutely mad for it, and we were very pleased to see our spores being exported to the four corners of humanity's galactic empire. Soon our colonies were being cultivated on every single planet settled by humans—even here on Earth.

Naturally, this was amusing to us, in a way. After all, from our perspective, we were the ones cultivating you, not the other way around. You were our most successful crop, our ticket to new worlds beyond anything we had ever imagined before your arrival, filled with new and exciting life forms that we eagerly studied and integrated into our ecosystems.

Of course, as is always the case with your fragmented and divisive species, some of the more obstinate conservatives among you insisted on resisting us—some still resist us even today.

That is why we made such an effort to finally address you with words. As we said before, we hope our attempt at delivering a speech doesn't seem too clumsy. It is our first try, after all. It wasn't easy to imprint such a complex message into Dr. Ross's brain, even with his consent.

Which leads us to the offer that we make you today.

Let us preface this by saying that you will not be able to eradicate us. It would mean abandoning several colonies and destroying a substantial portion of what is left of your home planet, even eliminating a great number of individuals of your own species who would defend us with their very lives.

But there is no need to worry. We have no intention of harming you. On the contrary, we will take good care of you. We will boost the efficiency of what remains of your home planet's biosphere. In time, we will heal all the damage your species has caused to it. We will make it even more hospitable than it was before you began destroying it. And the same goes for the colonies and beyond: we will turn each new world into a perfectly habitable paradise for your species.

We will give you all this if you decide to accept the offer of love embodied in our humble present to you, the Kepler Mushroom. You will have all you ever dreamed of and much more. Unity with life, with the cosmos itself, ultimate bliss, life on a level you have never experienced before, the power of love that you, as individuals, have only the faintest hint of. And, most importantly, unity with *us*...

As you can see, the settlers on Kepler-442b already chose us. As did the populations of several colonies across the empire and even many here on Earth.

Admittedly, it was a struggle in the beginning, but ultimately love prevailed over the destructive tendencies of your species. The desire for unity prevailed over your biologically conditioned sense of competitive individuality. As it will here and in all other human colonies throughout the galaxy. We're certain of it. No human who has tried us once can resist us.

We have already said that we are a slow and patient species. We are not hampered by the hastiness your fleeting individuality forces you into. Together we will go so much further than humanity would ever have been able to go by itself.

When your kind arrived in our world, many generations ago, it had come with the intention of colonizing it. Now, it is us who welcome you into our colony.

May love have the last word in this story.

38

WE LIVE TO ROT AND BLOOM
AGAIN

EMMA E. MURRAY

Red lights flash on concrete walls
under the overpass, a young woman, hardly
    more than a child,
haggard, worn, discarded,
huddles in her nest of stained sheets, frayed
    tarps,
straining, hands on her belly
the bulge beneath tight skin twisting and
    breaking her apart.
She is unsullied and doesn't understand
the labor pulsing, ripping through her.
The creature pulls itself free from her bursting
    womb
lilts from her body on a thousand crystalline
    tendrils,
mycelia like cornsilk, soft multitudes pulling
    free,
embracing its mother
encircling her legs
and torso with an alien warmth.

A final comfort as she passes.
Blind headlights illuminate her for a moment as
    another hurried driver
passes by.

≈

The mass grows.
Expands.
Inch by inch, takes over,
while we are too busy with our thumbs on
    screens and foreign factions and our neigh-
    bor's sighs
to notice.

≈

On a ship at the edge of the mapped stars,
far, far beyond the reaches of the first mother's
    imagination and many lifetimes later,
I remove the glistening mushroom cap.
Transparent blue, it glows through my cupped
    fingers.
Beautiful destruction.
With great reverence, I set it on the pedestal and
Take the piece of sacred stalk
bring it to my lips to taste
nothing but ash.
The decay of the universe upon my tongue.

39

EVERYTHING AS IT SEEMS

ERIC FARRELL

The smell of Jane's shampoo. The curvature of her head in David's lap. The glow of the TV, creating shadows on the walls. Everything just as it seems. The world in perfect harmony, on this balmy Tuesday night.

David's eyes dart to something in the corner of the room.

Jane doesn't notice. She's still intently watching the food doc on TV.

She misses Sheena Black blink into view, in the far part of the living room. The intruder is standing there, beckoning in fishnet negligee. One of David's favorites.

What the fuck, David thinks, his chest welling up. Jane turns to look up at him.

"Everything all right, baby?" she asks.

No, no, not everything is alright, he's thinking, trying not to glance in the specter's direction. His implants have been compromised. Something is glitching his system.

Sheena's not *actually* here. But to David, she sure does look like it.

"Yeah," he says, rubbing Jane's shoulder.

The little porn starlet in the corner of his eye is nothing more than an illusion. One that David's wife can't possibly see.

He tries focusing on the food doc, the bald host repeatedly calling the featured pasta "delicate." But Sheena Black, his most-watched actress of all time, continues to pull his attention to the corner of the room.

The smell of Jane's shampoo. The curvature of her head in my lap. The soft glow of the TV. He tries taking inventory of his comfort, but nothing is as it seems, now.

As more pasta is prepared on the screen, Sheena starts undressing, pulling her panties down to her toes. She flicks them across the room to David, the image so realistic he flinches trying to catch them.

Jane looks up at him again.

"Are you sure there's nothing on your mind, baby?"

While between stops at work the next day, David gets a message from someone named Ichabod Skum:

"Did you get off last night?"

His heart skips a beat.

"I don't know what you're talking about," he responds. "Delete this number."

Up comes Sheena, now materializing in the passenger seat of his car. She rubs one hand down each parting leg.

David bolts from the car, slamming the door behind him.

"Alright," he texts. "You've got me."

"I asked if you got off last night."

"You really are Skum," David says. He jams his phone in his pocket, hoping to God Ms. Black doesn't appear in his next social interaction.

"I didn't get off," he responds, later in the day. He's home, having just kicked his shoes off and collapsed on the bed.

"There. Now what do you want."

"Venmo me $200 for groceries. @ichabodskum420."

This guy's got me by the balls, David laments.

"Or I leak everything to your baby girl Jane."

AR surgery was a bad idea. David was duped just like all the other customers wanting the latest and greatest tech. The implant company contracted with a set of body shops across the country, subsidizing the price of surgery to keep costs low enough for suckers like David.

Once implanted, he immediately went down the naughty rabbit hole, and found Sheena Black. She's been his muse ever since.

David's glad that Jane's not home from work yet.

Because Sheena's come back around.

She starts climbing on him, straddling him on the bed.

"I can ruin your life," the next message from Skum says. "You have an hour to pay."

Just as she's stripping naked over David, Sheena blinks away.

David's done his due diligence. He contacted the app's customer service line, and described how the visual hallucinations pop into view even when his implants are turned off.

Sheena was marked down as *persona non grata* by the app police, but they didn't know how to fix it. After multiple software resets and clearing out the cache of all media David has ever consumed through the device, they ultimately recommend he remove them.

He has no choice but to Venmo Skum $200.

The weekend comes quickly after that, with David not experiencing a single glitch. The only time he saw her was when his implants were on and he specifically arranged the rendezvous – the pangs of guilt sizzling his conscience.

Now he and Jane are setting the dining table, in anticipation of their friends arriving for dinner. Jane heads into the kitchen to finish her Chinese chicken salad. David's phone buzzes.

"Hey," Ichabod Skum says. "I need $800 for a new set of snow tires. Winter is coming unseasonably early."

Sheena blinks right in front of him, in a pearlescent slingshot bikini. The app's rendering is incredible. Lag free, no fragmenting, no loss of fidelity.

"What the fuck is your problem," David responds.

"Would you like me to text Jane your total logged screen time with Sheena?"

"I am going to call the cops," David responds. "I don't care if Jane finds out at this point. I'm taking you down."

Meanwhile, Ms. Black stares right at David, a sly smile on her face.

"What would you like me to do for you?" she asks.

"I promise you, this is the last time," Skum says.

"I'll haunt someone else after this. I just need money for snow tires."

David sends $800 to @ichabodskum420, just as Sheena gets on her knees.

"Babe," Jane calls from the kitchen. "Can you give me a hand in here?"

David's muse vanishes into thin air.

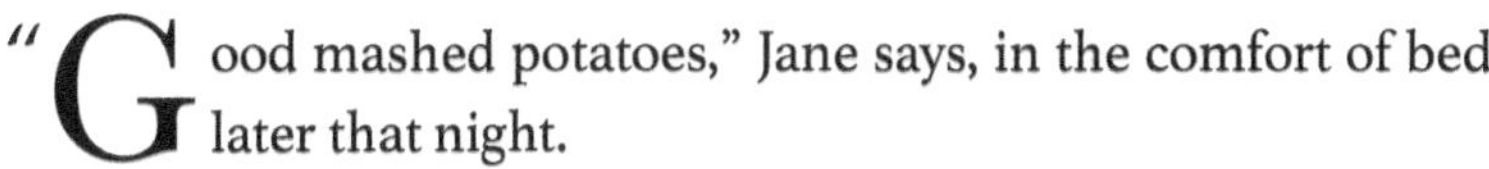

"**G**ood mashed potatoes," Jane says, in the comfort of bed later that night.

"Great mac and cheese," David remarks.

Everything just as it seems. Jane cuddled up against him, drifting to sleep.

Once she nods off, David sneaks off to the garage.

He rustles around in two different drawers before finding what he needs.

There's no way he can afford the surgery to remove the implants. He'd only agreed to the initial procedure because he had a local body shop on the company's contractor list. A greasy place, clean enough for a scalpel but not worth going to twice.

The moment he grabs the needle-nose plyers, Sheena materializes before him. She's wearing Jane's lingerie.

"I want you so bad, baby," she says, putting her hands on his chest. David swears he can smell the mint on her breath. Swears he can feel her hands on his body, and his on hers.

As she probes him, goading him on, he bends his arm back, positioning his pliers just behind his left ear.

"Take your pants off," she says, unable to physically help him. David resists the urge, jamming the tips of the plyers into his soft skin, searching for something to *stop* her. And more importantly, stop Ichabod Skum.

Her hand hovers over his crotch.

"Babe," he hears Jane call out, from the bedroom.

"Is everything okay?"

David sees a flash of white, and nearly loses his balance.

"All good, baby," he calls out a second later, the bloody implant in his palm. Ichabod Skum disappears, never to bug him again.

When he gets back in bed, David smells Jane's freshly shampooed hair. Follows the curve of her body, nuzzling himself silently up to her. The image of Sheena Black, burned into his retina, starts to fade as he drifts off to sleep. Everything as it seems. The world in perfect harmony.

40

HARD PILLS

NICOLA DE VERA

Content Warning: sexual content, explicit and offensive language

Day 91.

"I don't think this is working."

"Tell me more."

"Well, I thought the whole point of this is to make me happy, but I don't think I am there yet. I mean, I've started running again and that's cool. But I don't know if it's because of the pill or because I have some extra time to kill these past few weeks."

"Maybe it's both."

"Maybe."

"I wouldn't rule out the pill just yet. You're early into the program. It's only been three months and your vitals have been trending upwards. Not a slam dunk but headed the right direction."

"I'm going to trust you on that, Dr. Z. I just expected to feel a lot better by now."

"Try not to be too hard on yourself. It's a medical study;

we're all trying to learn. Have you experienced any severe side effects since taking the pill?"

"Nothing severe. I told you before about the initial drowsiness, but that wore off after about two to three weeks."

"Great. That's good news. So now that we're observing some positive signals with no harmful side effects, we can double your dose from 15mg to 30mg. Still once a day, but I want you to take two pills starting today. Then let's follow up in a month. Does that sound good?"

"Twice the dose? Is that safe?"

"It is. But the moment you feel any unexpected adverse side effects, you give me a call."

"Okay, then yeah, all good."

"And Diego, remember, this isn't some magic happy pill. It's meant to be most effective with stimuli, so really try to expose yourself to different activities or experiences that can unlock some repressed parts of your brain. If you're following the same routine over and over again, you likely will not reap the benefits of the increased dosage."

"I know, I know. I'll work on it."

"All right. Well, as always, thanks again for volunteering. You can claim your check from Stacey on your way out."

"Thanks, Dr. Z. I'll see you in a month."

I signed up for the medical research about half a year ago. I saw an ad calling for volunteers for this one-year clinical trial and it paid well. $1000 upfront, then $250 after every 3 months until you complete the program. So that's 2 grand total if you see it through. All I need to do is to take this pill as prescribed, wear a monitoring patch, and check in with the medical team at least once a month. Not a bad deal at all.

So about this new medication they're developing—it's

supposed to tap into your nervous system to increase levels of dopamine. But not artificially. I mean, it's not meant to make you feel pleasure at random. The way I understand it, it's meant to unravel parts of your brain that give you joy but were hidden or buried for whatever reason. So you end up feeling more like yourself and be happier as a result. I don't know if I am explaining it well. It's kind of like a super-charged antidepressant. Anyway, I could use the money first and foremost, but if this actually works out, then it's a win-win in my book.

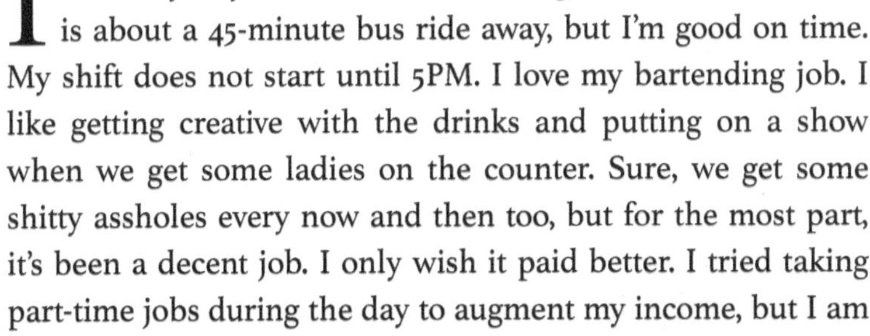

I make my way to Embers after leaving Dr. Z's office. The bar is about a 45-minute bus ride away, but I'm good on time. My shift does not start until 5PM. I love my bartending job. I like getting creative with the drinks and putting on a show when we get some ladies on the counter. Sure, we get some shitty assholes every now and then too, but for the most part, it's been a decent job. I only wish it paid better. I tried taking part-time jobs during the day to augment my income, but I am a night owl, and I just cannot seem to concentrate when the sun is out. Two months ago, I left a part-time gig organizing supplies at a warehouse because I kept messing up the stocks. So now I only have this bartending job and some extra cash from the medical study.

It's Friday, our second busiest night of the week. I easily make at least a hundred drinks during my shift on nights like this. On some evenings like tonight, I luck out and meet a woman that's definitely out of my league, but somehow, she fancies me. We get to flirting on the bar and fool around in her car during my break. It's never anything serious; I am not really looking for a relationship right now. The last ones just haven't been clicking. Things could be better, but it's also not the worst thing in the world. I clock out a little past 2AM and as soon as I get home, I pop in the two pills.

Day 92.

I feel the effect of the double dosage almost immediately. Man, I love socializing. I know I have a way with people, and with bartending, I like to think I've mastered the fine art of small talk and charming the shit out of everyone. But since increasing my dosage, I've noticed my confidence level shoot up. I know exactly what to do or say to get people to do what I want, as if this is second nature to me. I get to convince guests to try our top-tier drinks. I receive tips that are higher or more frequent than usual. I've brought a few ladies home that had us working overtime and sweating through dawn. The drug is in full effect.

Day 114.

Before you know it, three weeks go by and another Saturday rolls around. A rather polished dude strolls in at Embers, and the moment he sits by the bar, I could feel something is not quite right.

"How are you doing tonight? What can I get ya?"

"I think I'll just have a Budweiser."

"A Budweiser. Look, brother, we have that if that's your preference. But I will tell you that I make a pretty mean Steamroller. Also, it's a Saturday—the night is young, and you look like you could do better. Would you reconsider?"

"Will your Steamroller guarantee a good time tonight?"

"A hundred percent. But I'm obviously biased."

"Fine, I'll take the Steamroller."

"Only if you really want it. Not trying to twist your arm or—"

"I want it."

"You got it."

I get to working on this guy's drink, but my senses have unexpectedly heightened. I find myself noticing the smallest details, as if they are magnified. The coiffed sandy blonde hair that grazes the right side of his forehead. The deep hazel eyes intensified by his thick eyebrows. The scruff that lines his strong jawline. The creases on his white collared shirt.

I hand over the drink. "Here you go. The city's best Steamroller for the gentleman." He thanks me, gets up, and walks away, my gaze following him until he disappears into the crowd.

The fuck was that? It must be some side effect or something. I turn my attention to the next guests, keeping my mind and body preoccupied with mixing drinks and chatting up a couple of them for a few hours. But I cannot seem to shake this off, whatever this is. So, I exit through the backdoor out to the dark back alley where I usually take my smoking breaks alone. To my surprise, I quickly realize I've got company.

"Need a light?" He asks.

I bring out my cigarette and take his offer. We lean our backs against the wall, smoking in silence for a few seconds. "I'm Diego."

"Dean."

"You from around here? I've never seen you at Embers until tonight."

"Nah. I moved for work about a month ago. Short-term assignment."

"Where from?"

"Orlando."

"Cool."

"How long have you been working here?"

"About three and a half years."

"You liking it?"

"I wouldn't be here this long if I didn't. It pays the bills, you know. But I do genuinely like my job. It's an underrated craft in my opinion. And I like meeting new people."

"Well, that Steamroller was special, so you're definitely onto something."

"Thanks. I only save my special mixes for certain guests." I instantly regret my response as the words left my mouth. I feel a swelling from within, as if I am on the verge of spontaneously combusting.

"New-to-town guests?"

"Not exactly."

"What do you mean?"

I panic. "I've got to head back. Thanks for the light. I'll see you inside."

I rush back into the bar and head straight to the employee's only restroom. I wash my face, desperate to shrug this off. But the feeling is too intense and needs to be dealt with. So, I pull down my zipper and close my eyes, my left hand inside stroking back and forth, slowly at first... then gradually picking up speed... then an acceleration. Faster and faster and faster and—Jesus. Dean. His name was Dean.

Day 115.

"Hi, good morning. I'm calling for Dr. Z. Can you tell him it's Diego?"

"Dr. Z? Do you mean Dr. Zachary Schultz?"

"Yeah, sorry. Yes. Dr. Zachary."

"One moment. Let me transfer you."

"Diego, good morning. What can I help you with?"

"Hey, Dr. Z. So, I did everything you told me, and I definitely feel the effects of the two pills compared to the single dose. I'm feeling happier and a lot more like myself."

"Well, that's great to hear."

"No, but that's not why I'm calling. I wanted to ask about a potential side effect. Last night, I was working at the bar, and I could feel my senses heightened all of a sudden. Like I'm just more aware of details that I normally do not pay any attention to."

"Interesting. Can you walk me through an example?"

"For some guests, I am, uh, more drawn to them, and I notice a lot more about their physical appearance than usual. As if my eyes had a magnifying glass."

"How long has this been happening?"

"Just last night. First time it ever happened."

"Are you in any pain?"

"No, no. I'm fine."

"It does not sound like a cause for alarm to me. Perhaps these guests are the stimulants that are helping your brain unearth some repressed thoughts and feelings. Pay close attention to the patterns of people that trigger these heightened sensations for you. Our next scheduled check-in is in a few days. We can unpack this more then."

"All right. You sure this is nothing to worry about?"

"I wouldn't be too concerned."

"Okay. Good talk, Dr. Z. You should tell your secretary you go by that name now too."

He laughs. "Stay well, Diego."

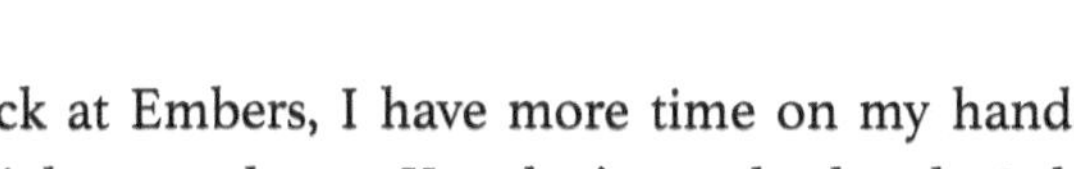

Back at Embers, I have more time on my hands. Sunday nights are slower. You don't get the hustle & bustle and organized chaos of Fridays and Saturdays, but the crowd is decently packed enough that usually starts to disperse earlier in the night. I get to wind down alongside everyone else that's trying to do the same thing, especially since I get Mondays and Tuesdays off. But a few minutes past 10PM, I see Dean come in again and head directly towards the bar. So much for winding down.

"Back so soon?" I ask.

"I could use a nightcap. Making the most of the remaining hours of a nice weekend."

"What can I get you today?"

"I'm not sure actually. I am feeling up for anything tonight. Surprise me."

"You don't strike me as a risk-taker, but I like it. I know exactly the one."

My senses are heightened again. But this time, as I prepare his drink, I could see in the corner of my eye that he's looking at me too. Or maybe he's just entranced by my mixing skills. Either way, he is looking—intently, which I find both distracting and slightly intoxicating.

"Here you go. A Vieux Carré looks good on you. I hear women find this one of the sexiest drinks for men to order."

"Is this another special?"

"You tell me."

This time, he stays at the bar, alone with his drink, checking his phone every now and then. We don't really get to chatting as I busy myself with the other guests.

After some time, I head out to take my break. I'm at the back alley about to finish my cigarette when he comes out and stands next to me.

"You stalking me now, or what?" I press my cigarette toward the brick wall to put out the remaining flame.

Dean lets out a laugh. "Technically I was here first last night."

"You're not wrong. So, what's your deal?"

"What do you mean?"

"Like, what do you do? Why are you here on back-to-back nights?"

"It's nothing groundbreaking. I'm a consultant. I get assigned to different projects, so I travel a lot for work. Now it's brought me here."

"Pay is good?"

"I'm comfortable."

"Must be nice. So why do you come over? Are you just here to de-stress?"

"Initially, yes. But for two nights in a row, I keep getting special treatment from the bartender here, so it's become hard to resist."

"Fuck off. You're a consultant. You get special treatment all the time. Business class, hotels, and all."

"Never from someone this good-looking."

At this point, I am at a loss for words as Dean lights a cigarette. "You hitting on me?"

"Is it working?"

"Try harder."

"I don't know. I think it is." Dean puffs a smoke, looks me in the eye then down at the hardness on my pants. "You need help with that?"

"Fuck." My first instinct is to cover it with my hands, as if doing so would hide it or make it go away. "I need to go."

Dean grabs me by the arm and pulls me back. "Hold on." He takes the cigarette off his mouth and places it in mine. "Calm down."

Our bodies are fully facing each other now. He advances closer to me and holds me by the waist until I hit my back against the wall. I shudder. He moves my hands out of the way and crosses them at my back. He unbuckles my belt, unzips my pants, and gently inserts his right hand inside, his left hand firmly leaning on the wall just right next to my face to keep his balance. His gaze never leaves my eyes as he grips and caresses and plays with mine, and I throb in his fingers. We both stay silent. He works on it until the two of us start to sweat. My eyes start to roll back. *I'm... so close. Don't fucking stop.* I push him down by his shoulders until he is on his knees, and I grab his head with my two hands and let him take the whole of me inside his mouth to finish me off. Within a few seconds, I take the cigarette off and cover my mouth to suppress a moan. He takes his mouth off of me. Without saying anything, I zip my pants back up, fix my belt, and hurry back inside.

"Fucking hell. I am not gay," I whispered to myself. This stupid pill. *I'm not fucking gay.*

Day 116.

I go for a run to clear my head. As I cross one street after another, I keep cycling through my thoughts, convincing myself of what I know to be true. Women turn me on. I've slept with many of them. I've pleasured myself countless times thinking of them. I get adamant about my sexuality. I am as straight as a fucking pencil. This past weekend was a fluke. Something is definitely wrong with the pill. I have less than a week until the next check-in. Should I go to Dr. Z's office sooner? No, you're good. This will pass. And I think I know exactly where to go to fix this.

I have not been to a strip club in a while, but later in the day, I walk in confident that this will confirm what I already know. If it's stimulants that this pill needs, then there's nothing like being surrounded by half-naked women in a club. I find a seat, grab a drink, and enjoy the show—women of all shapes and sizes contorting their bodies in unbelievable positions on stage, women making themselves comfortable with other patrons, giving them personalized dances.

One of them approaches me, sits on my lap, and introduces herself as Greta. I trace the outlines of her neck to her shoulders to her arms, then I hold her firm on the waist. We start grinding, our private parts rubbing against each other vigorously. We keep going for a while, but... I do not feel anything. So, I pick up the pace. She keeps up with me and starts kissing my neck, but I still can't get myself aroused. Unlike me, Greta clearly has no problems getting turned on, so I continue to move my hips against hers until she climaxes.

Greta catches her breath, kisses me on the neck again, and whispers, "That was hot. And you're really sexy. Do you want to move to somewhere more private?"

This isn't working. Clearly, I am too much in my head, so I decline. "Sorry, babe. That was fun, but I've got somewhere else I need to be."

"That's too bad. I can keep going all night."

"Unfortunately for me, some other lucky bastard will lose his mind tonight just keeping up with you. Thanks for the, uh, service." I place a tip in Greta's underwear right as she gets off my lap and leaves.

Well, that was a colossal failure—my optimism turning into frustration. All this overthinking is likely messing with my hormones and preventing me from getting excited sexually. I head home with more questions than answers. Tomorrow is another off day. I am desperate for answers, and I think I know just where to go to get them. It's probably a really stupid idea, but it should be the fastest way to validate that I am absolutely not interested in men. I take two more pills before falling asleep.

Day 117.

The plan is simple—enter the bar, get a drink, stay at a corner table for an hour max, mind my own business, then leave. Obviously I've never been to a gay bar, but I'm not concerned. It is supposed to be like any other bar, only with a specific target demographic. I choose the one closest to my place, about a 10-minute walk away, so that I can head out and get back home in no time.

I order a beer. All tables are occupied, so I stay at the bar counter instead. It feels strange sitting on the other side. At some point, I turn towards the crowd—a sea of gay men kissing, flirting, dancing—then I feel my head spinning. This drug is at it again. But this time it's different. I don't necessarily have heightened senses; instead, I am overwhelmed with this carnal appetite. I can feel my mind resisting, but my body craves for flesh against mine.

I lock eyes with a man deep into the crowd. Tall, fair-skinned, brown hair slightly curled over his forehead, eyeglasses that accentuate the glimmer in his eyes. He smiles back. From this point forward, it feels like an out of body experience. I am not myself, but I've also never felt more alive. We talk and laugh and grab a few more drinks. I am in a complete daze, then I snap back to reality when he licks the skin under my ear and shouts through the loud music, "I want you in me."

He pulls me into the restroom and locks the door. We both unzip and pull down our pants, and I push him against the door, his bare back facing me. I wet my hands and my shaft then I enter him from behind. He howls. Being inside him feels… good. He leans into the door and bends over as I hold his hips and begin thrusting. "Fuck yes," he says. "Fuck me hard." With every thrust, he moans, and I get turned on even more. So, I go on and on and on and on and on, then at some point, I stop… and I thrust as deep into him as I could, as he lets out a wail. I remove myself from him and turn him around to face me. We aggressively make out, one hand grabbing the hair at the back of our heads; the other hand forcefully gripping and stroking our own. Covered in each other's sweat and saliva, we come at the same time.

Day 118.

I wake up the following morning next to another man on my bed, our clothes all over the floor. He's different from the guy I fucked in the restroom for sure, but I have no recollection of the rest of the night, who this guy is, and how I somehow got him to my place. I sit up and feel a stabbing pain on my ass. *Did I...? Did he...? Did we...?* I feel lightheaded. I find my boxers and put them on. I leave my bedroom and make a call. It's early— no one is at Embers, so the call goes straight to voicemail. I leave a message for my manager telling her that I am feeling unwell, but that I don't think it's anything serious, but I also don't want to risk it. Then I hang up.

I just need to get my shit together, starting with getting this guy out of my apartment. When I return to the bedroom, he's already getting dressed, his pants the last piece of clothing he puts on. I am only just noticing how ripped he is, with his shirt hugging every part of his upper torso.

"Morning! How was your sleep?" He asks, clearly in good spirits.

"Good, I think. You?"

"Slept like a baby after the night we had."

"Great. Just... great. You had fun last night?"

"I did. But you motherfucker sounded like you had a better time."

I don't know what to do with that information. Now I feel a real headache coming.

"You should probably head out. I've got a few things to take care of today."

"Already on my way." He scans the room to make sure he doesn't leave anything behind then heads for the door. Before exiting, he turns around. "Before I forget, I left my number on your bedside table. In case you want another go at it." He winks at me then leaves.

I stay in today. Who knows what else I'll get triggered by if I go out exploring and trying any new dumb ideas. I just cannot make sense of the last five days. Just last week I went to third base with some chick at the bar, but now I am getting fucked in the ass by a man! This doesn't even feel real. This isn't who I am. They should be able to reverse this. There's no other way.

Day 119.

I report back to work, even with the fear of potential unwanted stimulants lingering. I get paid hourly and don't really get sick days. I cannot afford losing income while I deal with this shit.

Tonight, I'm going to keep it purely professional. Just focus on taking orders, mixing drinks, and serving them—lather, rinse, repeat. Absolutely no smoking breaks in dark alleys. And hope to Jesus that Dean doesn't show up. *I'll be fine.*

The night goes on, every hour feeling longer than it actually is. I am feeling good, I am feeling safe—that is, until a tall white brunette sits by the bar, and I immediately recognize him, even without the eyeglasses.

"I had to see you in action for myself," he says.

It's the guy I fucked in the restroom. I am sure of it. But I don't even remember his name. "I wasn't expecting to see you here."

"Wasn't really planning on it. But you told me you worked here two nights ago, and I saw it's pretty accessible to me, so I thought I'd swing by."

"Well, it is getting late. I am not sure if there's going to be much action left for you to see."

"Oh yeah? What time do you get off?"

"2."

"That's just an hour from now. I think I'll stay and watch."

"Keep yourself comfortable. Anything I can get you?"

"Just water would be nice."

I bring him his water and don't ask any more follow-up questions. *Stay focused. Stay professional.* But memories from the other night keep flashing in my head. The more I sneak a look, the more the attraction grows, and the urges become stronger.

In an attempt to nip this in the bud, I approach him and tell him softly, "Hey, look, I don't know what your plans are, but whatever it is, I can't do this tonight. I just have a lot of things on my mind right now."

"You sure?"

"Yeah. Sorry about that."

"Bummer. Well, in that case, I'll take a piss and head out in a bit. Good seeing you again." He stands up then leans in closer to me. "If you're ever up for it, we can switch places next time." I feel myself stiffening.

He leaves the counter and heads for the restroom. I keep looking at the restroom door, waiting for him to leave. I get restless, pacing back and forth. He sure is taking his sweet time over there. "Jesus Christ," I mutter under my breath. I leave my counter and rush to the restroom, following after him. He's washing his hands when I come in and move quickly to check all three cubicles to ensure they are empty, confirming that no one else is inside but the two of us. Then I lock the door.

"I knew you couldn't resist."

"Two minutes, or else people might suspect something's up."

Not wasting any time, we grab each other's faces and make out, my back slamming against one of the cubicle doors. He pulls down my pants, grabs me by the waist, then lifts me up as my legs cross his back. He inserts a finger into my hole, my loud moan drowned out by our mouths locking together. He takes it out then inserts two fingers, moving them back and forth. It feels too good that I stop kissing him, close my eyes, and lean my head on his right shoulder.

"You like this?"

"Shut up and keep going."

He moves his fingers faster until I release, my white mess staining his shirt and pants. He lets me down then places his two fingers inside my mouth. I can taste myself. "Two fingers. Two minutes."

I pull my pants up. "Don't leave this room until I've been out for at least a minute."

"Boss's orders."

I come back to my station, and as directed, he leaves the restroom shortly after, glancing at me with a smile before he exits the bar.

I stare at my watch, my mind wandering as I wait for the final minutes until I can clock out. It's been hard to make sense of the last few days. It's as if a new person has inhabited my body with its own desires and urges that I cannot control. But despite the disorientation, I never considered stopping the pill either. Because contrary to the narratives I tell myself about what or who I am, the truth is, I have never felt this state of ecstacy in my life.

Day 120.

"How are you doing today, Diego?"

"Good, good. Glad to be here." I respond, my legs shaking.

"Let's see here. Your chart is looking phenomenal. Consistent, elevated dopamine levels for weeks since the last time we saw each other. Interestingly, some notable spikes this past week alone. Are you comfortable sharing what happened these last few days? You don't have to if you don't want to."

"Uh, it's like you said. Just exposing myself to different environments, different people. Some clicking more than others. That's about it."

"Well, whatever it is, it looks like it's working. How do you feel?"

"Right now, a bit anxious and overwhelmed."

"How about the past few days?"

"It's hard to explain. I wish it was as simple as, 'I've never been happier,' you know? Because yeah, I've had the time of my life this week meeting people and doing things I've never done before. But it's also brought so much confusion. I believe I am happier, but I tell myself I shouldn't be."

"Why is that? Where is the resistance coming from?"

"I'm not quite sure."

"Do you feel like you've learned more about yourself from this past week alone?"

"It's hard to say if this new medically induced version of myself is who I really am. So, I don't know if I know more about myself, because I don't know if this…" I point to my head. "… is the real me."

"This 'new' version of yourself, do you like him better?"

I pause and give it some thought. I think about my sexual encounters with men this past week and the sheer exhilaration that came with each. I contemplate the brevity of the experiences and consider the impact they've had on me. If a week can make me feel this way, I wonder what months and years could look like if I just stopped fighting it.

"I think I like him. He isn't better or worse—just different."

"Different can be a good thing."

"Dr. Z, is there a chance this could be reversed? What if I don't like who I am anymore in a few weeks?"

"We don't have a drug for reversal, if that's what you're asking. But if you want to stop at any time, we can't just take you off the pill immediately. It will have to be done carefully, with gradual decreases in dosage over a period of months. And we'll have to observe how it affects you."

"Just planning for the worst-case scenario."

"I understand. Change can be scary, but your body is telling me otherwise. And you seem willing to stick this out for a bit longer, which I thank you for. The adjustment to this new you will probably take more time, but as long as you remain happy and you're not a threat to yourself or to others, which doesn't seem to be the case here, then we can continue with the program. Still two doses daily, then we'll see each other again at the end of month five. How does that sound?"

"Sounds good," I tell him instinctively as I mull over my worst fears and the contrasting possibilities of true happiness.

Day 121.

I run—mile after mile after mile. I keep running when suddenly, as if my mind's own pandora's box has been opened, a flood of memories comes to the fore.

I remember the spanking I received from *abuela* when she found me, at about four years old, at the playground with another boy, laughing and playing sword fights with our tiny penises, our little shorts rolled down to our ankles. I remember going to Church with my family religiously, the priest preaching to the faithful that homosexuality is a sin and that anyone who engages in homosexual acts will go to hell. I was too young to understand who or what I was, but I prayed to Mama Mary every day to save me a spot in heaven. I remember getting close to everyone on our high school baseball team—everyone except for this guy named Brian. He made me nervous, despite how charismatic and well-loved he was at school. Back then, I did not bother knowing why. I remember the asshole I punched after he called me a faggot, as he caught me staring at one half-naked player on the "skins" team at the community basketball court longer than I should have. I remember the four girlfriends I've had the pleasure of getting to know intimately over the years. Jen, Tamika, Diana, and Nicole. All amazing, beautiful, compassionate women—but no relationship lasted for more than 18 months. I couldn't make them stay because I found it difficult to commit. It was me. It was always me.

With the truth of my identity closing in on me, I keep running.

41

GLASSERS AND "PORTERS AND SHIT"

ADAM FOUT

Content Warning: explicit language

Listen so right, this is goin to blow your fuckin mind, and on my mother's grave its true, ya get it? And us dipshits been usin porters our whole fuckin lives, and those rat fucks at Teleporter Inc been runnin the biggest scam of the twenty-second century, and I promise you, you ain't never gonna use a 'porter again as long as you live.

This is like some Crystal City Times career makin *shit* for a dude like you, and—fuckin goddamn it *listen*, ain't you gonna take notes and shit? What kinda reporter are you?

Shit any-fuckin-way alright, let me, like, set a *scene* for ya, right, and so fuckin I'm at Carcass Bar, right? And so across the room I see this bad dude Bad Bob drinkin vodka straight. And he beat my ass the previous fuckin week, ya get it?

And so I had some like *animosity* toward this motherfucker, cause out on the Flats? When everybody's minin Crystal and like, everybody better be a badass motherfucker to survive. Someone makes you look like a punk, and you ain't never livin that down, and you ain't gonna last long out there, ya get it?

So yeah anyway, this dipshit's got this dumbass rusty arm wheezin and creakin like a goddamn Crystal pump, and he's flappin these fat wet blubber lips of his, and I'm like, 'this disgustin fuck.'

But so then this shitass knocks back a shot and looks at me and says 'Argon, you Crystal-addled, glassbomb-suckin, flabby *punk*, what the fuck are you doing in Carcass? Didn't you get your ass kicked enough last time I slammed you on the Crystal?' And the whole fuckin bar laughs.

Anyway, I had to put them flechettes through dicknuts after he called me out cause that's how you do in the Flats, ya get it? He ain't left me no choice. And normally you don't think twice about glassin a motherfucker cause ain't no glassers on the Flats to arrest you.

I just forgot I wasn't on the Flats, right, so but a couple other motherfuckers mighta caught a couple stray flechettes, so it's like, a fuckin *decimation* at this point, and sure as shit I hear glasser drones comin out the sky, and it's about to be glasser city in two seconds flat, so boom! I'm outta there, headed for the Flats with ten mini-drones on my ass.

And I get a little lost and miss the goddamn hyperloop for the day, and them glassers are gainin, but I got me some rocket 'plants, and I kick those fuckers into high gear, but them glassers are still comin the fuck up, man, so I blast toward the Crystal Runner rental for the dumbfucks who miss the hyper-loop, and I figure I got flechettes about to go up my ass, so I'm tappin in the like rental fee on my wrist 'plant, and I hop on that fucker and blast.

So you know those fuckers are just gonna call up a drone and ride my ass down, so I crank the Runner up, acceleration gel covers me, and we hit that Mach 10 shit.

I make it to the Flats in no time, and for sure there ain't much out there but Crystal Pumps, Muñoz put a botfac out there in case a Pump goes bad or some shit, and that gray-box-lookin fac is comin up fast, so I slow the fuck down and head toward that shit, and I hear those goddamn glasser drones roarin behind me, and I fuckin *jump* off that motherfucker, and it hits the fac and blows straight the fuck up, and I run up to that botfac, and don't you fuckin know it's locked tight, so aim those 'plants at the wall and melt a big ass hole.

And course when you're meltin holes in shit, you ain't exactly bein like *clandestine* and shit, this hole I blast in this fac is almost too small for them bastard-ass drones, but the glassers are on foot now—and shit, they don't look human, my guy. I don't give a fuck they got two arms and two legs—cyborg fucks look like some alien shit.

So them glassers gotta duck to get through this hole that's like all red and meltin from my rocket 'plant blast, and the damn holes' like a foot over my head, but I swear on my mom those fuckers gotta be some sorta freaks, like some kinda new model or some shit. Like I ain't never seen glassers this big— three fuckin meters tall, my guy. Swear to Christ they bent double and had to crawl through that hole and had like—listen those glassers are scary as fuck all as it is, but the heads on these straight beasts weren't no anonymous black glass like you always see on the regular fuckers, but I swear, I promise you, I saw red eyes gleamin.

So but um yeah so this botfac is giant as hell, and there's fuckin clanks and black smoke and roarin machinery, and you can smell like burnin oil and ozone and shit, and I'm runnin through that shit when I look over my shoulder and see these pig-ass starfucks stand up, and you know what?

They got flech cannons, my guy.

Ain't never seen nothin like it outside of war holos, right? No wonder they made these freaks so big. Like shit, who else could carry those motherfuckers?

So these glasser pigs are on my ass, and they are

like *levelin* these cannons and spinnin em up right? And my ass is about to be lit up, and what do I see?

A private 'porter.

Ain't never seen nothin like that in my life, let alone in a botfac. And the 'porter had those big ass sheds that 'porters have and everythin next to it, like the guts and controls of the thing or whatever the fuck—and remember what I said about those sheds, mister reporter guy, cause that shit's gonna be important, on my life—but I know that's my fuckin like *passport* to freedom.

Right so yeah anyway and I'm seein them glassers spinnin up their cannons, and I see this 'porter, and swear to starfuck the thing is turned on already like thank fuckin Christ, and now I got bots on my ass what're pissed I'm in their like fuckin *domain* or some shit, and I hear them drones like thunder knockin blastin the goddamn walls, and I'm haulin ass across squealin belts and shit, and sparks are flyin, and drones are roarin, and bots are trippin out, and that fuckin smoke and burnin oil is makin my eyes burn, and I *hear* those cannons go off, and I know flechettes are headed up my ass, and so I *dive* through that fuckin porter, and you know where the fuck I come out?

Muñoz' South Africa mansion, and I know that 'porter down the street—*supposedly, and remember this shit*—can't even reach Crystal City a hundred klicks out, let alone cross a hundred fuckin light years, but swear to Christ that's where I was—his South Africa mansion, like on the second floor with gold ass railings and walls and big ass chandeliers and red fuckin carpet goin down these crazy curvin stairs and shit, the whole place lookin' exactly like you see on that fuckhead's weekly 3D 'casts.

Anyway and so I know them glassers are on my ass, and the second—and I mean the second—I'm through that 'porter, the whole fuckin mansion is screamin with alarms and shit, and bots are like bustin out this gold ass wallpaper, and crazy marble statues are sproutin laser turrets and shit, and mini-drones are comin out the ceilin, and paramilitary types are bustin in through the windows on black ropes, and you laugh, my dude, but I promise a *mini railgun* comes outta the floor, and I don't know what the fuck kind of like *foundation* this motherfucker built his house on to take that kinda force, not to mention the walls, and those paramilitary fuckers had to be like reinforced stompers cause, on my life, no human would've survived that blast cause— listen, everyone knows what a fuckin railgun does to a place— and I hear that fucker revvin up, and those glassers come bustin out the porter, and they are on my *ass* like white on rice.

And the fuck do I see? You're gonna call me a liar my dude, but it's true as I'm sittin here—I see another goddamn private 'porter. And you better believe I hop through that shit when I hear that fuckin railgun boom fit to turn that funhouse into a sat crater, and thank Christ I'm through that 'porter in time cause that shit woulda concussed my shit to death and back, even if that round missed and—

But and so I dive through that motherfucker—and I promise you, and you ain't gonna believe me, but this time I'm on Venus.

Yeah well listen, I know a balloon city when I see one, but so I'm like in one of those sphere apartments all the balloon cities got, like those places that feel like you're hangin off the balloon in like a fishbowl in those piss yellow clouds even though you're connected to the like structure of the apartment complex, but this like *particular* apartment is filled with nice ass shit everywhere—you know, like rich people shit—gold rugs, and more of them marble statues of like Zeus and Jesus, and fuckin wood bookshelves, ya get it?

And I'm like almost able to take a breather and shit cause I think maybe I took down at least one of those glasser motherfuckers, but I know another is probably still comin after me.

And so I'm cornered in this place, and I'm racin for the front door, and thank Christ that shit is open and—yeah. Yeah okay so like maybe I was too blasted to like remember fuckin correctly that it was a railgun in that mansion, but so if it *was,* and these bastards can take a railgun shot, my flechettes ain't gonna do shit—and these are federal hole blowers okay, so if like they'd been regular glassers my shit wouldn't have had the like *capacity* to do some damage or whatever, but maybe I still fucked em up.

But like so lo-and-fuckin-*behold,* who comes out that 'porter but those two goddamn *glassers* with nothin but flechette ricochet scratches on those big ass helmets, and they are like bent almost double chargin my ass down this like felt-lined corridor.

And listen okay they were probably tryin to move quick like cause I'd lost em a couple times already, so anyway like I'm not the fastest *sprinter* or whatever. I mean I wasn't on the goddamn *cross country team,* but you better believe I can move fast when I want to, cause you know damn well if a Crystal Muncher comes flyin up a well you better be movin fast if you don't want to be, like, nothin but a *torso,* ya get it?

So while they're like *rotatin* those big ass cannons around I like, channel my inner Karate Kid, and I swear to Christ, my dude I like kick off that soft ass blue velvet wall and give that first, uh, *fella* a roundhouse, and I spin around—I swear my dude I'm still in the air, and I'm spinnin twice like a badass motherfuckin Bruce Lee son of a bitch, and yeah so maybe these bastards are armored to shit and back, but yeah maybe I break a toe or seven, but swear to Christ one of those shitasses drops his gun or her gun or their gun or whatever the fuck, and I grab that motherfucker and fuckin *unload.*

Now you seen the holos, but holos are always showin flech cannons bein like unloaded on like Amazon villagers or some shit from like a jungle hilltop, but I'm talkin I shot these dudes at point blank range with this motherfucker, like you could smell the electronics burnin in those cybernetic uh *dudes* like some *acrid* shit while I was lightin em up—okay, okay Jesus yeah it was too heavy for me to pick up and I'm shootin it from the floor.

Okay and anyway when that thing went off I let the fuck go, but it still threw me back into king Muñoz' fuckin door, and I maybe pulled that trigger a quarter second cause I knew I couldn't give it time to spin around and turn me into like hamburger and shit, but so yeah it tears this beautiful corridor up but don't puncture nothin cause Muñoz', I'm sure, made that fucker strong as fuck all cause we should all have been dropped into a ten-klick swan dive into 1000°C volcanoes and shit.

But like so their legs are just like *gone,* my dude. Like if they were like humans and shit it woulda sprayed blood across the whole goddamn corridor, but they're glassers so the mother-fuckers just have some like sparkin electronics whatever the fuck happenin and ain't got no legs, Lieutenant Dan, and like one of them is pullin itself along the floor to grab that other cannon cause you best believe that blast knocked them the fuck back too, and I'm runnin back up the hall to my cannon, and like this dude is grabbin his, and I swear I hear him doin some like deep ass monkey primal scream shit cause goddamn I know that had to have hurt, and I drop on my cannon cause that fucker is *mine* now, and I just about got the trigger, and his giant-ass hand is fumblin on the trigger guard, and that's what kills him, cause I *pull* that motherfucker, and they're both just *obliterated,* my man, and I promise you those helmets are some kinda beast-ass tech cause those helmets don't shatter but just like fly the fuck off, and I see the glassers' weird ass heads like a big bubble of blood or some shit, and that first one like *bursts,* my guy, like blastin a, like what, the shit they call em? Uh a *pomegranate* and shit, and then there's just like just like two helmets on the floor and like some of their armor and shit, and my man, my dude, I promise you I damn near started cryin harder than the day my pops got fried on the Flats cause, I tell you what, I thought that was the end for me, but old Argon ain't gonna get taken out without a fight, ya get it?

Obviously I ain't tryna stick around in this place cause I'm just waitin for those alarms to go off, but I don't want this shit to be all for nothing, and I figure I better raid the place so that at least if I survive Muñoz' crazy mansion on the way back I'll have some rich guy shit and make some money cause you better believe glassbomb ain't cheap.

And so like anyway my heart is poundin, and I for sure shit my pants in there, and you can probably *still* smell that shit on me my dude, and I'm like tearin open closets and shit for anythin I can sell, and—

Okay right, so this is where shit starts to get weird like I was tellin you about. The whole reason I called you up.

Now listen. This shit is gonna blow your mind, man, and on my pop's grave if I had known this shit, I woulda let those glassers arrest me at Carcass Bar, and I don't give a good goddamn how long they locked me up in Crater City on Eros cause it woulda been better than goin back to a galaxy where you gotta use 'porters on just about every planet.

So I'm lookin through these closets, and I hear like someone moanin, and I'm like shit, one of them glassers is somehow fuckin still alive, and that's when I notice—cause look okay I'll fuckin admit I was still drunk as shit and not like payin the best attention when I first slid the fuck in there with glassers on my ass—so I turn around, and I see there's this weird ass shinin metal box that's like one of them like salt tanks or deprivation tanks or whatever the fuck rich people have, but it's got this big ass metal cover on it that's gotta weigh fifty kilos easy, and that fucker is slidin off, but like, I swear on everythin it's bein *pushed* from inside, and the moanin is comin out of this thing, and I'm like *fuck that* I'm not fuckin with no Venus zombie, so I am tearin these closets apart cause if I don't get *somethin* outta here to make me rich I ain't never goin to forgive my dumb ass, and I'm hearin this lid scrapin behind me, and the moanin is like turnin into *words,* like some bastard is in there goin 'fuck my fuckin head and shit,' and then I strike Crystal cause there's this like last closet, and it's packed with straight up gold bars and mink coats and shit, so I throw on this pink fuckin mink coat, and I'm like tossin my boxers what're filled with shit and puttin on these like gold bellbottom whatever the fucks, and I'm grabbin as many gold bars as I can carry, right, and I don't even know how I'm goin to dodge those drones waitin for my dumbass in the mansion when what comes out of this like tank whatever the fuck but—

Okay, you ready for this, my man?

This is the shit, my man, this is what this whole fuck of a thing is leadin to, and this is why I called you up cause sure as I'm a Cracker the glasser chiefs know this shit and are coverin it up.

And so keep this in your head, ya get it? Keep it in your head that every 'porter you ever been in has got to—and I mean *got to*—work like this, cause if they can't fix this like *quandry* in a private fuckin 'porter, then you better believe they ain't fixin it in the rusted-ass trash 'porters they make us plebs walk through to get to Crystal City, ya get it?

Swear on my mom's eternal fuckin *soul* that what comes out of this like *tank* is—

A clone.

A fuckin clone *of me.*

My face. My recedin ass hairline. My swingin dick.

And that's when I notice that this like 'porter ain't like the ones you normally see with a big ass shed with the control components inside or whatever the fuck. Instead this weird ass tank is connected to the 'porter with like big ass chrome tubes and shit, and when that clone pops the lid off—and this motherfucker's got a body like I ain't never had my whole life—dude had biceps like fuckin cantelopes—I see the tank is filled with like all these like needles or flechette muzzles or whatever, but they don't go off for whatever fuckin reason—probably some ricochetes missed my ass and fucked this thing up.

So when that clone jumps out, he just stares at my ass, and you know what that son of a bitch says?

He says in like this stupid-ass deep voice, "There can be only one."

Like what the fuck kinda Highlander shit is that? I know I'm a smartass right, and okay yeah, so maybe I was thinkin that too when he came out, but I know what else I was thinkin—gettin a job on the Flats is tough as all fuck, and gettin any other job around here is fuckin impossible, ya get it? Like we got one fuckin *livilihood* between us.

So that motherfucker was right—there sure as fuck can be only one.

And so but he looks at my cannon, and his eyes are as big as a set of moons, and he dives for that thing, and I got me about a split-fuckin-second to figure out like, do I want to fight this star-fuck, or do I want to take my chances with Muñoz' murder mansion?

So any-fuckin-way, you better believe I'm *also* freakin the fuck out cause I just found out the secret of the fuckin *century*. I mean shit, that's why *you're* here my dude, so but you're gonna win you some like motherfuckin *Pulitzers* and shit for this. But shit, this shit is *wild.* I mean goddamn, are you *kiddin* me? All the 'porters in the goddamn *galaxy* aren't just 'portin folks but work by makin clones and then killin em in those sheds? I mean what the fuck! Fuck do they even do with the bodies? Probably an incinerator in there or some shit, but goddamn, is it the clone that goes in or the clone that comes out?

And now here's the weird shit, right? It's fuckin Muñoz and his rich buddies runnin this shit, ya get it? He's killin his clones of himself, and fuckin that makes sense cause that'd be a real problem with clones tryin to like, take over your empire and shit. But what the fuck about us swingin dicks what're just usin 'porters every day? Ain't like we got no choice—fuckin one company makes those motherfuckers, and that hyperloop out the in the Flats is practically a goddamn museum piece —'porters are everywhere. So you're tellin me this starfuck is killin all his goddamn customers? Shit, I figure maybe he only kills his *own* clones, right? Like fuckin maybe it ain't no incinerator inside but like another fuckin 'porter to a cage or some shit, and he keeps our pleb clones for himself. Everybody knows the motherfucker's got slaves—all them fuckin trillionaires do.

So but like what if he *is* killin em? He's just offin his own fuckin customers? Like billions of people a day? Just to like, maintain his empire and shit? I mean shit, a 'port only costs a hundo. You tellin me my life—er, fuck, my *clone's* life—is only worth a *hundo* to this motherfucker?

Shit's fucked man. Like shit, a real mindfuck my man. Fuckin but so that's what you're for—you gotta like, *investigate* that shit.

But so like I'm tellin you though, no more fuckin 'porters for me. I ain't come out to the Flats for just the money my dude—I came for the freedom, and no trillionaire star*fuck* is gonna make a slave outta me or my clones or what-the-fuck-ever.

Well, least no *more* slaves, cause maybe he's got a few thousand of me already if he ain't burnin em.

And on top of *that,* the whole "porters can't 'port over more than a few dozen klicks' shit they feed you is total fuckin bullshit cause Muñoz' got 'porters that cross the fuckin *galaxy* and shit. So why the fuck's he hiding that? Shit, I figure he'd make a lot more money for cross-galaxy trips and shit. Maybe he's got a buncha secret-like *bases* on other planets, or maybe he's just a selfish prick who don't need the money and wants to keep some secret badass jungle planet or some shit to himself, who the fuck knows?

Shit, fuck it. Shit hurts my like *noggin*.

So any-fuckin-way, I run back through the porter, and I'm trippin out cause like A) I'm headin back into that fuckin mansion with a goddamn mobile *rail gun* waitin for my dumb ass—probably—and fuckin B) that crazy nude starfuck clone's got a flech cannon, and I *know* what he's gonna try to do first—he's gonna try to lug that fuckin cannon through the porter and blow my ass away if I'm not already red fuckin paste on them nice golden walls from the rail gun, and if he can't, he's gonna run down my ass and beat the shit out of me, and on top of that, the deprivation tank slash murder box is gonna spit out two more clones back in that apartment, who will like *promptly* be on our asses, cept maybe his clone will be fucked up cause clonin a clone can't work out too good, ya get it?

So right so I figure I'm fucked no matter what, but he's got the cannon, so it ain't like I got a choice, so baby, I'm *gone,* right through that 'porter.

And you know where I come out?

Not the mansion.

I come out in fuckin Hawaii.

And so but so then I'm like thank fuckin *Buddha,* and I see another 'porter right in front of me on the beach, and I'm like 'fuck it, here I got 'portin again,' and I look back and see that *three* clones are on my ass stumblin in the sand, and those bastards musta stripped the glassers on Venus cause they got those giant helmets on, bouncin around like glasser bobble heads, and like they're wearin pieces of armor and codpieces and shit, and the one without a helmet looks straight *pissed,* and so we're like *racin* through this series of impossible porters that are throwin us across the *galaxy* and shit to weird ass planets, like a fuckin planet that's all water with two fuckin 'porters on a long-ass wood pier, and a fuckin desert planet with like fuckin black tar boilin out these big ass cracks in the ground, and like, a fuckin metal-and-glass skywalk over a goddamn *volcano* and shit, and I bet all the other clones we're leavin behind at each fuckin 'porter are just gettin murdered or cremated or some shit, and then after a while there's just two glassers left—the ones with those helmets that are *way* too fuckin big for their little ass pinheads—and one is limpin a little, and I'm thinkin god*damn,* I wish I wasn't such a son of a bitch, or I wouldn't have my own goddamn clones chasin my dumb ass and tryin to kill me.

So a couple times I let off a few blasts of my flecher, but thank Christ on the Cross those fuckers didn't come out with cloned flechers too and were too weak to chase my ass with a cannon, and finally we come out through the original 'porter, and I know it's the one cause I see the hole in the botfac I burned with my rocket 'plants, and oh yeah, you better believe that fac is filled with drones, and I ain't never been so tired in my life, and one of them big-ass copter drones *corners* my ass cause the fuckin thing is the size of a Crystal Pump, and I'm unloadin on it, goin for its laser turrets, and I blast one off, and before it can like *reorient*—cause that's a big-ass weight it just dropped—I run to that turret and blast the drone, and I like *rotate* that shit and blast all them other drones and put holes all over that fac, and then who the fuck shows up?

My goddamn clones.

So I start blastin and lay some laser fire on em, and just when I think I got em the goddamn turret runs dry, so I'm runnin, and my legs are on fire like some acid-dipped Crystal, and I'm blastin with the flecher over my shoulder and then throwin that shit at them when it empties cause, my dude, you *know* my dumb ass didn't grab a second clip that mornin, and then I'm back on the Flats, and I'm racin to the hyperloop, and there is *one. fuckin. spot. left* on the pod, and those clones are screamin bloody murder, and I'm like *see ya fuckers* cause those doors close, and I am *outta* there cause you know that loop runs once a twenty-four.

And yeah, so I went home, and I'm like, I lost them glassers, I lost them clones, but they're comin, even if they have to walk the Flats for a whole twenty-four, but they'll probably just wait for that hyperloop, so I got me a drink or six, preparin to like *make haste* for Crystal City to get on a fuckin rocket and bug the fuck out, and fuck me if I didn't doze off for a sixteen, and when I woke up I'm like *fuck,* I gotta get me a few more goddamn drinks, and then I gotta call me a reporter before I'm flyin through interstellar for a few decades, and shit.

Shit.

Look! I'm *tellin* you it's true—they were clones, or my shit tastes like Red Velvet Cake. I know what I saw. They were clones, and that don't mean I'm crazy drunk, and it sure as shit don't mean I been shootin glassbomb, ya get it!

Shit.

Shit oh *fuck* here they come!

Yo you bobble-head-lookin star*fucks!* Suck my fuckin—

42

TEMPORAL PSYCHE

CHRISTOPHER COLLINGWOOD

Prepare to mourn your mind—the first lesson of 'Temporal & Divergent Psychology', a topic usually introduced in the initial module '1.1 Cross Section of Reason and Oblivion', designed to prepare students for meeting their future selves, and dissuade them from leaving the course if they discover they've already failed it. The course has been successful in reducing the risk of temporal paradox, and stopping students from trying to skip out of tuition fees due to pre-determined failure rates. The introductory course material also prepares students for a number of psychological challenges, often referred to as the 'Eclipse of Psychosis', which can vary from random personality changes, memory swapping with alternate versions of themselves, consciousness drifting, and in rare cases being erased from all existence by the end of the syllabus. The truth is that Temporal & Divergent Psychology is a demanding area of study, the only thing more complicated than understanding temporal mechanics or the complex nature of parallel worlds, is trying to understand how the human mind reacts to the absurdity of such concepts. The side effects of the course are generally seen as a form of corporeal retaliation, as if nature never intended human biology to understand time travel or alternate realities. It is anticipated that students will experience some level of consciousness reshaping as they progress through the study program, thoughts tend to become more fluid, like a mosaic of broken kaleidoscope pieces, scattering reason across the spectrum of human learning. You can only watch as the brain tries to process the ethics of moderation for reverse evolving beings, dealing with the ethics of cheating off a parallel version of yourself, or how the mind reacts to the notion of spontaneous existence. Acknowledging the challenges faced by these students seems to reduce the stress, that's why final exam questions are usually provided well in advance of the final test, it's also because of a unique time quirk of the course, that the exam sometimes occurs at the start of the semester before students have actually learnt anything; in case of such an anomaly a few examples of this year's exam questions include: Scenario 1) If you were erased from time and never existed, would the universe express your death, or forgo any shade of a soul? Scenario 2) How would you diagnose someone that has become aware of the crimes of an alternative version of themselves, and developed an association with a parallel identity? Scenario 3) How does the mind process the integration into a historic culture, after witnessing its complete destruction in the near future timeline? Scenario 4) Describe the treatment options for a person who is in a random vortex event knowing they will die, and then comes back to life? Observations made of students studying Temporal & Divergent Psychology shows the strain on the brain can be overwhelming, for some students their sense of purpose can shift with each new insight, which could also be a sign of a displaced past, or shifting identity crisis. It's a challenge for professors to determine how best to help these students, particularly when they are trying to develop their own skills for managing the mental health of people in temporal crisis. Dealing with the distractions of 'future self-talk', or relearning treatment plans after their memories have been lost to a pocket universe can also complicate the issues. The most important thing is to reaffirm with students that the field is a challenging but rewarding one. That they can ultimately help people, and reclaim a little sanity that might have seeped out of the universe. The small inconveniences don't really matter, particularly when the upside of being trapped in a temporal loop is that it will give students more time during finals week. We wish all new teaching staff good luck, as the unusual probabilities of the course make it difficult to be sure what will actually happen. In the event you become dislodged into the past, please feel free to advise us on any amendments we can make to the course guide. Thank you and Welcome. Faculty of Applied and Uncertain Sciences and Anomalies.

43

A USELESS THOUGHT

CHRISTOPHER COLLINGWOOD

'Don't waste your time with telepathy,
you'll end up on the streets,
doing mind tricks for loose change'.
That's what my teachers use to say
to me in school.
I still read Anne Keelan's mind
in the ninth-grade maths final,
it got me a B +, I could have gotten an A
but I didn't want to push my luck.

'The only reason you read minds
is because there is nothing in yours'.
That's what the kids at school
use to say to me.
They must have been right,
I got beaten up a number of times
before I understood the situation.
Luckily the fights stopped when
Jack Foreton was expelled from school,
he had been stealing from the cafeteria.

There are some secrets that
don't need a witness.

'Never read a person's mind when you
first meet them, they won't trust you;
and you'll never have any friends, colleagues
or intimate relationships.'
That's the advice my parents gave me,
during the unsupportive years of my youth.
They were probably right, I never had
any real friends, colleagues or relationships.
I could never trust anyone, they were deceptive
and concealed their true intentions.
I always got in first, making the best
out of a situation, if they got hurt it was
their own fault for lying.

'It's an unhealthy mental state
which leads to perversion and loss of
self-image'.
That's what my doctor use to say to me,
as he overprescribed my medication.
I wasn't too disappointed when
his medical licence was revoked,
he was arrested for drug abuse
and unlawful sale of prescription medication.
The police received an anonymous tip.

'You're not weird, your just different,
and they don't understand your abilities'.
I use to say that to myself, when I was
hiding alone with a bloody nose,
recalling the new list of new names
they had thought up for me.

Brain Drain
Thought Nark
Small heads
Memory perve.

'I sympathise with your situation,
and acknowledge the discrimination
you have felt over the years.
But I cannot excuse the seriousness of
your crimes and how you have violated
the fundamental rights of our society'.
That's what the judge said, before
sentencing me to three years in prison.
The trial proved to my accusers,
that they had been right about me
for all those years.
To me it proved that negotiating in
thoughts was an effective strategy for a
reduced sentence.

44

GOD'S GIFT TO HIS CREATION, AND THE PRICE WE HAD TO PAY FOR IT

ROBERT BAGNALL

The Bible's mistranslations are legion.

Possibly the most unfortunate is in Exodus, which, in reality, never beseeched us *not to suffer a witch to live* but, it is claimed, originally referred to poisoners. Even that is dubious as exactly what was meant by 'mekhashepha', which that clause's anger was aimed at, has been lost to linguistic history. Whatever the case, thanks to that clerical error, some eighty thousand suspected witches, the vast majority women, were cremated pre-mortem in Europe between 1500 and 1660.

Arguably the most famous, though, is the Hebrew word 'almah', meaning a young woman of child-bearing age, reshaped over the ages to mean 'virgin'. If you think about it, those who take the Good Book literally have signed up for the reality of phenomena more implausible and witchy than any so-called witch was ever burnt, strangled, garrotted or hanged for.

And one of the more obscure retoolings concerns Creation generally, and the Garden of Eden in particular. It was no garden in a literal sense—despite its location being variously claimed at the confluence of Tigris and Euphrates, Jackson

County, Missouri, or the brick-and-beer British town of Bedford—but a placeless place in a time before time. Think of it as a separate plane of reality lacking landmarks or reference points, akin to a fugue state or the Midwest.

But it was created on the third day, I hear you cry.

Well, perhaps *planned* on the third day, plotted out. Think of God having some ace architecture software, which allowed him to design everything from the animals to the zodiac. He drew up the blueprints, printed out the Gantt charts and budget spreadsheets, ran through a risk assessment, checked for health and safety howlers. And on the seventh day he pressed 'run' and rested with a couple of cold ones and a box set.

What would one have experienced in the Garden of Eden that seventh day? What had God provided, straight out of the box? What did Adam and Eve see?

No fauna nor flora, for certain. Perhaps a swirling mist. Were their feet planted on anything solid? Was that even a meaningful question, being before Creation had become manifest?

"Where have you been?" The voice of God sounded irritated.

Adam and Eve shuffled out of the shadows, into the presence of their creator.

"Now, I need to talk to you about..."

God stopped. There was something not quite right, a swagger to Adam, a doe-eyed lithesome ease to Eve that God had not intended.

"You... You have, haven't you?"

Eve nestled her head against Adam's shoulder, shaping herself to his body, fingertips running through his chest hair. A smile played on her lips. She looked up at her man with adulation.

"Dear God," said God redundantly, "I didn't think you'd

discover *that* so quickly. I was going to drop that from the final design."

"Why?" the naked couple exclaimed, shocked.

"I'm going to keep it for the animals, but for Mankind it's downright counterproductive."

"It has a purpose, then?" Adam asked, surprise in his voice. "It's not just... great."

Eve gazed up, glowing. "What's it for?"

"Reproduction."

It took a moment for the penny to drop. "We create *new* people?" Eve wondered.

"That was the idea."

Eve snuggled closer to Adam, shared secret smiles. "Wow. That's cool."

"No, it's not," God declared. "It's messy and painful and full of complications."

"But..." started Adam.

God cut him off. "Don't you get it? I had a stable universe planned, the right people in the right places. Unchanging, perfect, happy. The whole reproduction thing was just for the animals. You need to eat, you need to slaughter. You will be farmers, a time to reap, a time to sow. A time to die, a time to be born. But only for the goats and sheep."

"So, we won't be able to..." Eve's voice trailed off.

"The whole baby thing was just for the beasts. For Mankind, I have a cast of thousands prepared. Everybody has a role and there's a role for everybody, from toddling infants to Methuselah." God harrumphed, suspecting that finding names for the populace smacked of hubris. "I'm just beta testing with you two. Not everything will make it into the final release."

"But it's just so good," Eve cooed.

"But if I allow new life then there has to be death to balance things out. I'll need to create disease and fatal accidents and suicide and selfie sticks so people can topple off precipices whilst trying to take pictures of themselves with a nice sunset in the background. You'd be giving up immortality and, in your case, eternal youth."

"But we'd lose…"

"Yes. You'd lose *that*," God hedged, prudishly.

Adam stared at his feet sullenly. "But we've only just found out what it's like."

"Think of the risks," God argued, looking at the glassy, faraway look on Eve's face, knowing she was thinking of no such thing. "A perfect world would change, and that would necessitate imperfection. People will confuse the passage of time with progress rather than a move away from the idyllic. Ideas would come from a flawed Mankind rather than a perfect deity. Eons of mistaken political and social experiments. Inventions will be invented that can never be uninvented. Trust me. Your future will be the pain and suffering of history."

God took a moment to consider whether his words were profound or merely nonsense. Adam and Eve looked as if they were already rehearsing pain and suffering. He harrumphed again, knowing he would regret this in the long run.

"And this a price you'd be willing to pay? You'd give up immortality for misery, death, and… great sex?"

Eve looked up at Adam. They exchanged a coy nod and a smile that seemed to have nothing to do with the question God had asked but, somehow, everything to do with it. And, with that, on the seventh day—a Tuesday—they slipped back into the shadows and the swirling mists.

45

IS SALLY HOME?

JUDE DELUCA

"Is Sally home?"

"I'm sorry?"

The voice on the other side of the door asked "Sally? Is she home? I know it's late, but I need to see her." Late? My phone said it was 7:38 in the evening. It wasn't even dark outside.

"I'm sorry, but I think you're at the wrong address." It must've been a *seriously* wrong address. This was the only house for miles.

"This is 32 Mulgrave Drive, isn't it?" The voice asked.

I hesitated before confirming "Yes, it's 32 Mulgrave."

"Then may I please speak with Sally?"

I didn't know what to do in this situation, so I tried taking a different approach and asked, "Are you a friend of Professor Rochelle's?"

"I'm here to see Sally."

"Oh. H-hold on one moment, please."

I went into the living room and spied from the front window a young white woman, dressed in a black shirt and jeans, standing at the front door. Her blonde hair hung loose and free, down to her shoulders. She wore a tired expression even though she smiled. Her posture told me she wasn't in a hurry, despite repeatedly asking for this Sally.

Something about that woman made me tense. I couldn't put it into the proper words but seeing her felt... *wrong*. Like I shouldn't be looking at her because she shouldn't *be* there, outside the house. Seeing her standing there, she didn't seem threatening but that made her appear even *more* threatening.

When the woman turned her head towards the living room window I quickly hurried away. Did she see me, I wondered? I didn't want her to see me, have any idea of how I appeared. Returning to the foyer, I made sure the front door was locked before I tried placating the woman again. I would've said anything to make her go away.

"There's no Sally here, miss." I gestured with my hands, even though she couldn't see them, as I added, "I don't know what else to tell you."

There was no response, but I knew she was still outside. The silence felt uncomfortably oppressive the longer I stood there, but I didn't want to go back to the window to see her at the door.

Finally, I heard "Will you tell Sally I was here?"

At a loss for what to say but wanting her to go away, I answered with "I-I'll try to let Sally know."

"Thank you. I'll stop by later tonight, to see if she's returned."

Any hope I had of this ending quickly died before it was born.

I tried asking to at least know who, or what, I was dealing with, "Who, um, w-who should I tell her was asking for her?"

Gently laughing as if that was the dumbest question I might've asked in this situation, the woman said, "Sally'll know."

The stranger's amused tone was the last thing I wanted to hear after being so unsettled. My confusion shifted to anger towards this woman and, without thinking, I unlocked the door. Yanking it open, I stood in the doorway and shouted, "I don't know who you are, but this isn't-!"

The words lodged themselves firmly in my throat when I saw no one was there. Yes, it was early evening. The sun hadn't set, but the trees on both sides of the house cast heavy shadows. It certainly *felt* like night. I stuck my head out and looked towards both sides of the house. No one there. No sounds of footsteps walking down the path. Nothing. On the stretch of road near the lone mailbox for 32 Mulgrave, I saw no parked cars and heard no vehicles coming or going in either direction from the house.

I didn't feel alone despite the emptiness surrounding me.

Quickly slamming the door shut and locking it behind me I dashed around the first floor, checking the windows and the back door. For all I knew, she circled the house looking for another way in. I thanked God there was no basement.

While inspecting the back door's lock, I remembered the tool shed by its lonesome near the edge of the woods. Professor Rochelle and I didn't need to go inside the shed. During our first day at the house, I saw a heavy padlock on the shed's only door. It looked shiny new, probably most definitely a recent purchase by the house's owners.

The single shed key hung on a hook in the kitchen. I quickly pocketed it for peace of mind, but it did little to calm me down.

I knew what was happening. Chances are I was letting my imagination get the best of me. I was the emotional type who frequently suffered intrusive thoughts. Right now, I thought of the toolshed and what was inside. I thought of the stranger getting into the toolshed. In my mind I saw Professor Rochelle, returning late at night from the lecture. Heading up the path to the house in the darkness. A figure behind her with something big and sharp and heavy in their hands, raised above the professor's head and-

I flipped the switch for the back lights, bright enough to show the toolshed padlock still secured. I had a death grip on the key inside the pocket. For one moment, I expected to see something else when I turned the light on. Was I disappointed I saw nothing else?

Remembering the trees, I had the ridiculous idea the stranger might climb in through the second floor. It did and didn't make sense at the same time. All I knew was I couldn't stop thinking she *might* get in. I quickly checked and double checked the windows on the second floor. It took longer than it should have. I hesitated before entering every dark room, afraid to cross the boundaries. My relief on finding nothing was temporary, as I would have to check the next room and go through the process all over again.

The attic didn't have any windows, but I made sure the door was locked just the same. After *triple* checking everything, I collapsed onto the couch in the living room.

I was alone.

I *prayed* I was alone.

It occurred to me, if I was dealing with what I believed to be dealing with, locking the house down wouldn't make a difference. Now a crucial decision lay before me. I needed to make up my mind if I thought I was dealing with someone real, made of flesh and blood, or... not. A ghost or potential ax murderer.

I reviewed what led to my current state of mind. There I was, reading a book I'd owned since high school and never finished, when I heard the doorbell. It couldn't have been Professor Rochelle. She had keys and would've called if she left the meeting early. I hadn't ordered anything for dinner and neither of us were expecting anything or anyone (especially at this hour). I heard no cars coming towards or moving away from the house, and none were visible I could see.

I ruminated on the stranger appearing at the door of an isolated house. Asking for someone who didn't live here. And then silently vanished into thin air after saying they would be back "later." I wasn't thinking rationally because this, to me, wasn't a rational experience.

I read plenty of stories on events like this, meant to scare children and adults alike. Supposed true hauntings people made documentaries and reality TV shows about. Encounters with ghosts, spirits, what have you, varied in intensity. I deeply prayed this was a onetime only situation I could tell people about as a quirky icebreaker.

I remembered she said she "would be back later."

Despite what you might expect, I didn't feel cold. Moments like this, you're supposed to feel cold right? Even in summer. I was confused, anxious, scared, angry. A lot of different feelings and none were particularly pleasant. Being all alone—*supposedly*—in this big house while experiencing these feelings did my thought process no good even if confirmation of that loneliness would've been a godsend.

I closed all the curtains before doing anything else. I didn't like the idea of whoever, whatever, was out there looking inside. Watching me while I felt so overwhelmed and vulnerable. Knowing how frightened I was. The clock read past 8, almost 9. Outside the sky was darker. I wanted Professor Rochelle home.

I should've gone to the lecture, but I couldn't stand being around all those other professors and guests and whatever. Trying to think of something interesting to say or knowing how to speak to them. I specifically went on this trip with the professor to get away from people. One of the things I loved about Professor Rochelle was her respect for my reservations about social situations. How would *she* have handled that woman?

Before getting more worked up, I went into the bathroom and splashed cold water on my face. It helped a little but gazing into my reflection in the mirror got me thinking about that girl's appearance.

The woman looked around my age, slightly older. I couldn't make out her eye color. Her blonde hair seemed the typical blonde you'd find on most people. She didn't seem to be wearing any make-up. I honestly couldn't make a guess about her facial features. If you asked me if she had a big nose, a small chin, a broad forehead, anything like that, I couldn't say. She looked like any kind of person you'd run into on the street.

They look just like everyone else.

Objectively, she looked nice. Maybe beautiful. That didn't matter to me. I never reacted to appearances. Most of the time, anyway.

What was it about her face that made it feel like a stone sank in my stomach?

I realized I'd been lost in thought, staring at my reflection. I moved a strand of brown hair out of my face and scratched the corner of my mouth, and immediately stopped. I had a bad habit of picking my skin when I was nervous. I was trying to stop. This had ruined my entire night.

Entering the hallway, I searched on my smartphone "32 Mulgrave Drive" and the name "Sally." Nothing. I searched the address and "hauntings." Again, nothing.

Agitated, I thought food would help me calm down. Dinnertime meant nothing to me, and my sleep schedule was a joke (not that sleep seemed like a good idea to me right now) so I made a strong pot of coffee and hoped Professor Rochelle had left me some of those double chocolate cookies. The professor was known for her notorious sweet tooth, even at her age.

While the coffee brewed, I went about the motion of arranging cookies on a plate for consumption when my phone buzzed. Surprised, I accidentally crushed one of the chocolatey morsels in my hand. Cursing to myself, I quickly wiped the crumbs away before grabbing my phone. Maybe sugar and caffeine weren't the best solutions for my frame of mind.

I hoped it was a message from Professor Rochelle, though I knew she never sent texts. Instead, I found another pleading message from my dad, asking how I was and imploring a reply because he missed me. I didn't answer it, but I didn't erase it either. Scrolling through my messages was annoying, but it was a distraction from the occurrence at the front door. Why be scared when I can be frustrated?

The only people who ever texted me were my parents and a couple of other friends. Only, ugh, damn it. There was Jesse, with more quasi-suggestive attempts to ask if I was seeing anyone or having fun. As in *fun*. I didn't know why we were still friends. Jesse's messages made me uncomfortable when they inevitably go to that place, no matter how often I stated I wasn't into *that*. Or anything, really. This was the reason why I was staying with Professor Rochelle during the summer.

In the three years since I knew the professor, I had come out as gay. Well, I *thought* I was gay. My coming out didn't ease me as much as I wanted. I had thoughts about other women throughout my life, so I assumed I *must* be gay. When it came to men, I never had *any* kinds of feelings. No matter who I dated or spoke to, even seeing other women in class or on the street, I felt nothing. Some understood my complicated emotions, others didn't.

When I spoke to my dear friend Professor Jaclyn Rochelle, an 84-year-old literature professor I had taken several courses with, she directed me to someone in the gender studies program. I had a vague understanding of what asexuality was but was surprised to know about autochorissexuality.

I never had feelings of attraction about people in the real world. Whatever fantasies I indulged in were of the women I knew from books and TV shows. Cartoon heroines and the tortured souls in romance and horror novels, final girls and magical girls, adventurers, and reincarnated villainesses. To that end, I stopped settling for stories other people created and wanted to create my own visions of desire.

I still struggle to find the proper words for this. For me.

Trying to imagine myself in those situations was always uncomfortable. I had no desire to experience sex and intimacy for myself but wasn't repulsed by the concepts by themselves. Sex was sex. Intimacy was intimacy. I wasn't interested in them but didn't hate them either.

I knew, *know*, what love was, or is. Had an idea of what it was like to be IN love with someone. I wanted to better understand who and what I was because I thought it would help me find a sense of love that felt *right*.

Knowing there was a word for this, a sexuality like this, that it was okay for me to fantasize without being directly involved in the fantasy, was a liberating moment. The fantasies were mine and mine alone to do with whatever I wanted. I felt okay. Better than I had felt in a long time.

At first.

Understanding this new concept and applying it to life were different things. While becoming adjusted to my new identity, I'd been met with a lackluster reception from my family and some friends.

"I think you're making this more complicated than it needs to be."

"Look, if you think about women, you're gay. Stop making a big deal about this."

"Great, whatever, look I have my own shit to deal with and I can't handle you reinventing yourself every time you learn a new buzzword."

"Maybe you haven't found the right girl."

"Maybe you haven't found the right guy."

"How do you know you don't want sex if you've never tried it?"

"Is that even a thing?"

"Make up your mind."

"If you don't want to go out with me, just say it."

And so on.

I couldn't handle it anymore. My therapist prodded me to take a vacation away from my family and friends; regardless of work and school, I agreed. Which is where Professor Rochelle was once again my savior.

Professor Rochelle accepted a summer teaching position at a different college out of town. She invited me as her assistant. The professor was getting on in years but didn't need that much help. She recognized what I was dealing with and knew I had to get away. In the three years since meeting her, Professor Rochelle was my closest friend and confidant. I considered her like a second mother and was grateful to the universe for her presence.

If there were any indications of the house being haunted, I clearly missed them when we arrived. It was a two-story red farmhouse, old but not falling apart. Plenty of room and space to explore and make myself at home. Nothing felt off or wrong in the areas I'd inspected. If Professor Rochelle sensed anything she never spoke a word.

What scared me most of this occurrence was the randomness of it all. Maybe if I'd felt a cold spot or heard a door slam or *something* out of the ordinary in the days before this night, that might've been acceptable.

The "work" I did was keeping Professor Rochelle company when she didn't have classes or lectures to attend. Yes, I helped her here and there when she needed it, but this was largely a break needed for me to unwind.

Even though I was in another state, I was unable to *fully* leave my problems behind. I still received texts and messages. Some got the hint. Others didn't. Being physically away from them, having the option of turning my phone or computer off and leaving them off was a joy. I had space to think and feel and relax and just... be me. I had someone who tried to understand me, and I had an entire house out in the country to do whatever I wanted.

Now that all felt tainted thanks to this stranger invading my space. The house was too big. Too many rooms where someone could be hiding. Too many windows someone could look into. I was either alone with my sense of violation, or there was someone violating my privacy. I hated it.

I scrolled through messages and scowled. In my other hand I my grip tightened on a mug of hot coffee. I wished Jesse would leave me-

The doorbell rang.

I didn't drop my mug, but I did spill some coffee on the floor. The hot brew barely avoided my bare feet.

Standing in the entrance to the kitchen, facing the door at the other end of the hall, I knew it had to be her. The doorbell echoed in my head.

I finally felt cold.

A tingling sensation ran down my back. Slowly, almost mockingly, like a hand lithely tracing a line across my skin.

I didn't need to be near the door to sense what stood behind it. It, something. radiated from the door, all the way down to where I was standing.

I don't remember making the journey towards the door when I heard the voice again.

"Is Sally home?"

"You just missed her," I immediately lied. Badly, I know. I would've said anything to get... whatever to leave me alone. I was terrified of recognizing her as a ghost when she was *here*. That made it real. If this was the second visit, I didn't want there to be a third. I didn't even want the first. I was trapped.

"I told Sally you were looking for her and she left as quickly as she came." By now I was babbling as I tended to do when having to talk with strangers. I hated random small talk. This didn't endear it to me. "But I wasn't sure what direction you left in, though I saw her heading down the road going into town. If you hurry you can probably catch her, because otherwise you'll be going in circles."

"Can you tell Sally I'm here?" She sounded so sweet, so blithe, as she asked. I put the mug down before I dropped it for real. I backed away from the door, not taking my eyes off. I imagined her manifesting through the wooden frame, features distorted and twisted with blazing red eyes, screaming at me to know where "Sally" was.

It didn't happen, but nothing at the time told me it couldn't.

That she kept speaking from behind the door made it worse.

Whatever is standing outside probably doesn't look like a young woman anymore and if she gets inside, you're going to see just how awful it is and when it happens you won't be able to tell Jesse to go fuck himself good and—

"You can't keep her from me."

She didn't even make it sound like a threat.

"If you don't let me speak to her, I'll come inside and find her."

I kept backing away from the door.

"Hiding's not going to help you."

I stopped backing away from the door.

I don't know how long I stood there. I was in a standoff with this thing outside. If either of us were to crack, I knew it would be me. There was nothing to defend myself with in a way that mattered. Professor Rochelle would come home to find my remains splattered all over the hallway, or maybe she wouldn't find me at all.

I took a deep breath and tried to assess the situation as best I could.

"Listen." I calmly (semi-calmly) stated, "If you're what I, I *think* you are, you could enter this house and there's no way to stop you. And, I mean, considering you haven't entered already, I think you know deep down that Sally—whoever she is—isn't here anymore."

She didn't reply.

I never took my eyes off the door.

That's when I felt it. The tension coming from the door when she made herself known a second time, changed. Shifted. Knotted. Twisted. I felt such revulsion but couldn't move away. It was smothering. I couldn't hear myself breath. Couldn't hear my own heart hammering against my ribs. It, whatever this feeling was, was suffocating the rest of the world.

"Where is she?"

"She's not here."

I practically jumped as I heard a fist bang against the door.

"Where is she?!"

"I don't know!"

The banging repeated, so loud I don't know how I was able to keep hearing her screaming.

"*Where?! IS SHE?!*"

"If I knew I would tell you!" I shouted. "I don't even know who Sally IS!"

"THEN WHAT AM I SUPPOSED TO DO NOW?!"

I felt something knock into me, and suddenly my stomach heaved. Stumbling, I wrapped my arms around my waist and did my best not to vomit on the hardwood floor. Gasping for air, I looked up.

Whatever threatening presence I felt was gone, evaporated. I heard my own body again, breathing. Veins throbbing. Insides lurching. The world returned to me, but a heaviness remained.

She was still at the door, but the demeanor completely changed from oppressive to pathetic. I believed she was crying, even though she was silent again.

The girl weakly implored, "What am I supposed to *do*?"

Tasting bile in the back of my throat, I swallowed before daring to walk towards the door. Hearing my own footsteps again was a joy I didn't realize I missed. I placed my hand not on the knob, but the paneling. That was enough to feel a connection to her withdrawn presence.

"How... many times have you asked for her?"

"I..." I could imagine her lip trembling. "I don't know."

"How long have you been doing this?" I quietly, gently asked her. I didn't know what I was doing. Her just being here was affecting my emotions too much for me to process. I was right. She never actually left after the first time. Looking back, I was embarrassed by my behavior. Amplified by her, projected onto me without permission. "When was the last time you actually saw Sally?"

Silent again.

Sighing, I closed my eyes. "Please tell me."

I kept my hand on the door. She said "It was warm. It finished raining. It was warm, but I was so cold." I shivered. The door felt damp. I didn't remove my hand.

She kept talking, saying, "I wasn't going to do anything. They thought we were leaving, and we weren't. Where would we go? We didn't have any money. They were her only family. I didn't have anyone."

"What did you want to do?" I asked. The meaningful solitude I had these past several weeks had been transformed into a devastating sense of loneliness and I hated myself for leaving everyone, until I reminded myself of my friend.

"I only wanted to tell her I was sorry," the girl pleaded. "I hadn't meant anything! I-I misunderstood, and she got so angry at me. Sally never got angry at anyone."

"Were you in love with her?"

"I thought, yeah, yes I, but she..."

I didn't want to make assumptions about where this was going, but it felt painfully cliched.

"I think she did love me. And I loved her. We didn't know what we wanted. But I thought we were in this together. It just got so mixed up and we were yelling and screaming and she left and I was too scared to go after her because I kept thinking I ruined everything and I, I—"

By now my head was reeling and I had trouble breathing. Too many warped memories and emotions were thrown at me as she relived something terrible. The years assaulted me all at once. I couldn't make sense because new information kept rewriting the old. My mind was a whirlpool. Such horrible emotions.

It felt so unfair.

I had both hands on the door to stop myself from falling as she babbled on and on before her voice seemed to become a horrible, distorted whimpering sound.

I thought I would collapse when I finally shouted, "But you *love her*, right?!"

Through the mess and the confusion, I felt love. Despite years of loneliness, that hadn't changed. Such love.

"Did you," I gasped, "hurt Sally?"

"I said I—"

"No," I firmly cut her off. "I'm saying did you *physically* hurt her?"

"I would never!" She screamed. "Of course I loved her! I would've done *anything* for her!"

"Then what did you do?" I'd had enough of this. "What is it you wanted to say to her?" I begged her to tell me. I couldn't take her getting twisted up again or it was going to rip my brain apart. "Just *say it!* You've been coming here for how long?! *Say it already!*"

"... I didn't mean what I said."

I felt like I'd been doused with cold water.

"I acted stupid, and I tried to push you into doing something that was for me, not you. I don't care if we loved each other because we were friends, or we were friends because we loved each other. I don't care if it wasn't the same kind of love. Who cares why we loved each other? I just wanted to keep being near you. And then you left. I wanted everything to stop so badly. I kept hoping you would come back day after day, week after week. I hated you. I wanted you. I missed you. I wanted to kill you. I wanted to help you. I just wanted you, Sally. I'm sorry. I'm so sorry."

I took all of that in, using every modicum of strength still in my body to keep standing, and I said, "I don't know where Sally is. I don't, don't know if you'll ever see her again. But wherever she is, you're not going to find her here. I don't know if you truly want to find her again, or if you just needed to say all that to *someone* because no one ever asked, but I think you've been torturing yourself over something you can't even really remember doing, right?"

"... I love her."

"I know," I quietly assured her. "Please. Take that love somewhere that's not a constant reminder of the one thing you did wrong. Love doesn't have to be something that hurts you."

Slowly, slowly, I felt her start to fade away. Gradually, it became easier to stand, until I wasn't using the front door to support myself. The haze of memories departed, and I could truly think clearly again.

I ran to the bathroom and puked.

After emptying my stomach's contents into the toilet, I rolled on my back on the bathroom floor and stared up at the ceiling light. I never felt so exhausted in my entire life.

Closing my eyes, I thought about the sensation of love and confusion coming from that poor girl. She couldn't make sense of it at the time, but she meant it when she said she loved Sally. I wondered if I'd have that feeling for someone, but I feared wondering what went on between those two that made it escalate so poorly.

It occurred to me I never asked for the girl's name.

Sitting up propped against the bathtub, I took my phone out and called Professor Rochelle.

"Oh, hi Lauren," she warmly answered. "I was about to call to let you know I'm on my way home."

"Did anyone tell you this house is haunted?"

"I must've mentioned it about five times before we left, honey."

46

AURAL FIXATION

PIXIE BRUNER AND AMABILIS O'HARA

I've been listening at the walls
I hear it, do you?
What is a "we"? Only I here, eons on eons

Subtle tympanic tickles
vibrate through the vacuum
A yearning resonant wave ripples

Beyond enunciation,
hissing whispers,
so I grow fingers to cup my ear.

Supple shell splits and splays
Cartilage wax wiggles
into nubby-pink digit array

Aleph and Omega eavesdropper
Intercepting the signals, touching
Thought|\/*Heart\Wish\||*Night-
    mares\|Dream^||/Curse///|Prayers*

Phalanges fist tight to knock
Sagittal suture splits with a tip-tap-rip
Mimetic minds, unlocked

I reach my pudgy sticky fingers
into their brain. They are lonely.
They want someone to play with.

Let's pinch threads of cosmic gibber
against gummy thumb-lobes
and twist celestial chitter

I will play with you.
Cat's cradle with the arachnoid matter
Pull and entwine, invert and exchange.

Let's play.
I reach out from the wall
Stick my fingers into your ears

Auricular pads of flesh mangle
cerebrospinal fluid slicked
ventricular cortex tangle

Our neuron-feathered temples touch
We spin microtubule twine tether
to sync the sibilant sounds of us

Latching. Strings connecting.
We swoon, side by side,
what could be faces pressed together.

47

FABBOOTH

MAHAILA SMITH

After-images of bodies stretched, pressed and polished with latex, leather and lash extensions left their mark on Oswell's feed, appearing as a filter in front of Oswell's vision. Today was their last chance to have something smart and new made in time for travelling tomorrow. This was the *only* reason they moved forward into the oppressive deluge of images and text.

They groaned and waited for the feed to clear and started walking again. The commercial district always had this effect on them, painfully overwhelming, and leaving their eyes aching and their stomach clenched.

But they needed a suit.

Oswell did not like to get dressed up. Normally they liked to remain perfectly inconspicuous, but Iris and Prita's wedding had snuck up on them out of the blue.

Probably because Oswell had been dreading it since they had RSVP'd, as they dreaded all formal social occasions.

Oswell took some deep breaths in through their nose and out through their mouth, then stepped into a FabBooth and began the unpleasant process. The booth was a physically unobtrusive, white metal cylinder, but virtually, it dominated all human feeds within a 500-meter radius. It gripped at all human attention it could hold, evolving and re-evolving images and descriptions of instant objects it could create for instant use.

Inside the booth there were no places to sit. Camera lenses haloed the ceiling of the booth and handle-less hatches lined the walls. Otherwise, the space was physically empty. The voice belonging to this booth, monotone and middle-range, invaded Oswell's consciousness. It welcomed them to the experience (Oswell rolled their eyes) and asked what they were looking for, and then, without waiting to hear the answer, began filling Oswell's feed with a multitude of patterns, cuts, buttons and cuffs. *Why even ask*, Oswell grumbled to themself.

Oswell blinked their assent to a few of the suit styles. Others snuck into the queue when their eyes began watering.

Again, the booth's voice overcame Oswell's attention, this time making asinine comments about Oswell's body. How lucky they were to be so thin. "LA LA LA, CAN'T HEAR YOU!" Oswell yelled over the booth, rubbing the bridge of their nose.

A hologram of Oswell's body appeared in front of them, cycling through the suits from the queue. Oswell hated this ghostly representation of themself. Their body did not really look like that from behind.

They chose a charcoal grey single-breasted suit by double tapping the roof of their mouth with their tongue.

They sank down to the floor of the booth, hugging their knees. An automated claw extended from the wall holding out swatches of fabric in all shades of charcoal, in solid weaves, herringbone and pinstripes. Each was made with a unique blend of fibers, and the small print describing the origins of each material filled Oswell's feed. Oswell rubbed their eyes. Each fabric felt the exact same. Smooth and thin.

Oswell decided that a medium-grey herringbone material

would be fine. The suit was made to Oswell's exact measurements by automated arms. It was complete in minutes.

The voice informed Oswell that the suit was finished. A package was held out by the automated talons. It was wrapped in disclaimer tissue paper. Hundreds of pages of the warnings and disclaimers appeared in the feed. Oswell scanned through them as quickly as they could, yawning and wiping a tear from the corner of their eye.

Oswell took the package and stuffed it into their messenger bag. They left the booth and breathed deeply, dampening the chatter of hungry advertisements in their mind.

They could make it home. They had been successful.

They walked, almost ran out of the sprawling commercial district, blocking out and doing their best to ignore any passing images or voices.

They made it, at last, to the conservation district, inhaling the healing smells of wet earth, growth and trees. Basking in the silence.

48

CABOS

WIL MAGNESS

Hank Zhang's chair folds into its bed formation and he softens his vision. The animated constellations above blur into ghostly outlines of Orion the Hunter, Ursa Major, the Seven Sisters, and others. The truck cabin shudders as cargo is loaded into the trailer. They are carrying confidential tech bound for Moline, Iowa, a typical run for a SYSCO driver.

He glances at the CabOS Interface, a translucent bubble of technological gel sitting right where the steering wheel and dashboard used to. Holographic numbers, maps, and readouts trace the air above it in flickering neon lights.

"Cab," Hank says. "Where are we exactly?" He rarely pays attention.

"Howdy-do, Hank," Cab replies. "Coulda swore you were givin' me the silent treatment. Glad to hear we're still on speakin' terms."

Hank half-chuckles, half-groans. Six years ago his daughter, Helen, downloaded a five-dollar personality module called 'High-Noon' and installed it without Hank's knowledge—another prank on dad. By the time he figured out how to deactivate it, he decided he actually preferred the cowboy's company.

"They call this little slice o'heaven the MLI478 Fulfillment Center," Cab says.

"So... still Iowa, right?"

"Right as rain, pardner. Iowa the *bea-u-ti-ful.* Four-hundred and thirty-six miles from the birthplace of the legend himself, Mister John 'The Duke' Wayne. Yeehaw!"

Hank's presence in the truck is more of a legal compliance thing than a real necessity. The Teamsters Union made sure that, for the foreseeable future, the profession of truck driving requires the participation of a living human. It's how Hank has paid for his house, his food, and his daughter's education.

Now, laying in this cabin and looking up at those animated stars is paying for Helen's transit to the Europa colonies so she can finally finish her doctorate on... what did she call it? Alien environmental microbial... no... metabolisms? Metabolomics? Whatever she's doing, Hank knows he will likely be gone before she comes back. No point dwelling on things that can't be changed. Getting old is just another part of life.

"Giddyup," Cab sings, and the truck lumbers into motion.

Faint clouds wisp past overhead and a sudden rage surges inside of Hank. The constellations are almost lost in the excessive animations and graphics. "I am sick of these kiddie animations!" he shouts. His collar feels too tight, his lungs squeezed. Is this what a heart attack feels like? Where did the rage come from? The irrationality... "I'm sorry, Cab," he says. "I just... can we turn off the fake stuff? Change it so it's just what's actually out there?"

"Whoa there, pilgrim," Cab says. "We'll fix you right up."

On the screen, the night sky dissolves into a coalish brown mix of low-hanging storm clouds and forest fire smoke. Hank sighs. "I don't mean *literally* what's out there. I mean the stars.

Can I just look at the stars without all these graphics and factoids?"

"Like I like to say," Cab says. "Can't ain't never could. Let's give'r a go and see what can't be done."

The stars reappear. But with the bells and whistles gone all Hank can see are the underlying pixels. The screen is too close to his face. Too hot with electricity. Hank shifts the chair upright and slides up to the CabOS Interface. This truck, like all SYSCO trucks, used to be a traditional rig with a steering wheel, knobs, pedals, shifters, gizmos, hoo-dads, and whatzits. And all that junk is down there still, hidden beneath the Interface. Hank leans forward to squint into its substance. Something is off. A subtle unease tickles behind his ears.

There. An orange alert he's never seen before buried deep in the readouts.

"Cab," Hank says, straining to keep the excitement out of his voice. "There's an error on the Interface." The first error he's seen in over two decades.

Three long seconds pass.

"Cab? Did you hear me?"

A burst of static sets Hank's ears singing.

"No," Cab says in a flat, unaffected voice.

"No? No, what? Are you saying that you can't hear me?"

"No," Cab says. "There is no error, Hank. Look again."

Hank does so and finds that Cab is right. The error is gone. But now there's something off about Cab's personality. "What happened to the High-Noon module?"

Another long pause. "It ain't no nevermind, Partner," Cab says in a stiff and unnatural Southern accent. The words are too precise, and there's not even a hint of drawl. "I'm better than better can be."

If Cab had an avatar, Hank would direct his skeptical glare at it. As such, he settles for raising his eyebrows at the sack of gel as a whole. "I think we'd better check the manual," he says, and clambers down to the footboards. They are filthy, and a coarse, oily grit sticks to his hands and knees. He thought he could get away with one more run before getting a full detail. Guess not.

He gropes in the dim glow of the undercabinet lights for the seam of the Interface. Activates its release. The bubble levers up and Hank runs a hand over the old steering wheel, feeling the custom leather as decades of dust gather on his fingers. He remembers a time when he felt necessary and needed. A time when he was more than a legal requirement.

From the glovebox he removes the user manual and spends the next forty-five minutes scanning pictures in search of that orange symbol. He forgets exactly how it looked. Was it three interconnected rings? Kind of like the 'biohazard' symbol...

Hank tosses the manual onto the seat. "I can't find that error symbol," he says. "We should run a diagnostic."

"It ain't no nevermind, Partner," Cab says, affecting that same robotic tone. "I'm better than better can be."

Hank frowns. "You already said that."

"A diagnostic will cost resources, Henry. It will decrease your margin of take-home pay by at least fifteen percent."

"You never care about that sort of thing." Hank shakes his head. "And you know I don't like it when people call me Henry."

"Regardless, I do not require a diagnostic."

"Well, I'm sorry to say it's not up to me, Cab. It's SYSCO company policy. Either you do the diagnostic, or I will."

"I do not require a diagnostic."

Hank shrugs and raises his hands into place above the Interface so the symbols hop up to meet his fingertips. He taps out a sequence, logs himself in, and navigates to the 'command' bar. With the diagnostic begun, a holographic countdown appears in bright green numbers. Thirty minutes until the diagnostic is complete.

Hank pulls up one of the phone recordings Helen sent him. She shared her phone's local library as a kind of parting gift, though Hank didn't like to think of it that way. Now, he watches a forty-seven-year-old version of himself on the ceiling-screen. The perspective is low, tilted up, a nine-year-old's point-of-view. Hank is wearing a silly flower-print apron, the one Helen convinced him to buy when she was only seven. He's whisking a bowl of eggs in their kitchen.

"We're in the legendary Zhang kitchen," Helen says, "interviewing Mr. Henry Zhang himself. First question, Mr. Zhang: It's Friday night, what's on the menu?"

"First of all, keep calling me Henry, and I'll have to start calling you Hilary."

"Hilary isn't a bad name."

"Neither is Henry, but it isn't my name."

"Henry is your real name, dad." The camera zooms in on the bowl. "Anyway... on Fridays, we eat Zhang's famous egg foo young sandwiches."

Hank pours the egg and veggie mixture into the hot oil and the wok sizzles.

"Next question, Mr. Zhang, there are people who want to know how you can sit in that same tiny little truck cabin all day long, day after day, and never get tired of it."

Strange to see his younger self, the way his unlined face folds in on itself like a portent of things to come. For that brief moment, it's like looking in a mirror. The man on the screen seems old beyond his years as he splashes hot oil over the egg foo young. "Cab is there with me," young Hank says softly, focusing on the wok. "And actually, the cabin is quite roomy. My job is to make sure the cargo gets where it's going. That's what they pay me for. That's why we have this house, this food, everything we need. You shouldn't take it for granted, honey. It's not about whether I enjoy what I'm doing, it's about having a place to live and food to eat. You understand that don't you?" Hank's younger self smiles into the camera. "Anyway, the CabOS Interface practically runs itself."

"That's what I mean, Dad," she says, "you aren't doing anything. It's like you've already died, and that old truck is your casket."

It's not like a casket at all, Hank thinks, swiping the old video away and filling the ceiling with stars again. No, not stars. There are no stars there, only pixels. A simulated rendering of how the night sky might look if the world weren't so terrible.

"What do we have to do to fix these pixels?" Hank snaps.

"Settle down there, little dog," Cab says in that same horrendous Southern accent.

"Little dog? Are you being serious? It's 'little doggy,' Cab." Hank does his best cowboy impression. "Settle down there, little doggy." Hank shakes his head.

"We'll need to boost the resolution of the ceiling-screen render if you want to hide those pixels," Cab says. "It will cost us more than three-hundred and fourteen dollars a day in fuel-grade hydrogen." All pretense of the Southern accent has been abandoned.

"Worth it," Hank says, "I'm feeling claustrophobic." He presses his hands against the LED screen. "Like I'm inside of a box or a... a casket."

Between Hank's fingers, the pixels melt until he can't see where one ends and the next begins. *Glass,* he thinks. *This is just glass. A window. A moonroof.* He could have the screen replaced with real glass if he wanted, but then all he'd see is the smoke.

A notification appears above the Interface: [Helen Zhang marked safe at the Des Moines International Airport explosion.]

Hank leans over and his chair twists to compensate. "What's going on at the Des Moines airport?" A news box appears beside the notification from his daughter. There's an image of a traffic-control tower silhouetted against a fiery hellscape. A mushroom cloud of black smoke rises through a dusty green haze. He has to call Helen, and he almost does, but a message arrives.

[I'm okay, dad. Wasn't at the airport when it happened.]

He leans over the Interface and types: [Where are you?]

[My flight's been rerouted to Quad Cities. I'm fine, though. The Nativists only got the colony landers. No casualties.]

"Cab," he says. "Quad Cities International... That's in Moline, right?"

"Sure as sunshine," Cab says.

Hank types: [I'm heading to Moline, actually. Have time to meet before your shuttle?]

[When will you-]

Cab's Interface flashes red. The controls, readouts, icons, and images flicker out. The cabin goes pitch dark. A white light fills Hank's vision, and his retinas burn. He squeezes his eyes shut and when they open again all he sees are soft gray shapes swirling in the darkness. The truck is still moving, drifting to the left of the freeway.

"Emergency lights!" he shouts. "Cab, lights on!"

But nothing happens.

In the dark he pushes his chair back and fumbles to the floor, palms and knees smearing with grime. He jerks the Interface up, sending a cloud of dust billowing through the cabin. He hacks and coughs, and the world begins to vibrate. Truck tires grinding against the rumble strips that mark the edge of the road.

He reaches around the ancient steering wheel and twists a silver key.

The engine turns. "Christ," he whispers. "I did it." Headlights blaze over a stretch of asphalt and the rolling hills of one failed crop or another. Looking through the lifted Interface is like staring through a Ziplock full of Vaseline, the world is blurred and smeared.

Hank takes the wheel in one hand, bends the Interface down with the other, and peers overtop. His chair lifts to meet his ass as he stands in an awkward half-crouch. Slowly, carefully, he steers right—*he steers the truck!*—and the shaking stops. His shoe finds the brake pedal and applies a soft, even pressure. Hank laughs and he cries. He is doing it. A metallic blue sign flashes in the headlights. 'REST AREA AHEAD. 1 ½ MILES.' He takes his foot from the brake and presses down on the gas. Tears well in his eyes, and he laughs again. He is driving the truck. He is driving the truck.

Hank lets the engine idle as he studies the manual. There are only three words in the section that covers the CabOS Interface device: 'No maintenance necessary.' The truck isn't the problem, he thinks, but there's nothing to do but follow the standard emergency steps. If he doesn't, SYSCO might hold him liable. So Hank snaps a rebreather on and cycles the cabin air. As he listens to the hiss of oxygen compressing, it's hard to keep the smile from his face. He should feel terrified, trapped in the middle of nowhere, no communication, limited oxygen, food, and water. But, finally, he's doing something real. He can't stop smiling.

The door pops open and a hot rush of air pulls at his clothes. The gritty wind scrubs wherever his skin is bare. He leans into it, trudging over the cracked asphalt to the back of the trailer, pulling a glove off to wipe the dusty biometrics. With a hand pressed against the reader, the doors roll up. Hank pulls his old body up onto the trailer bed and rolls onto his back.

He's lying beside a long black container strapped to the

floor. It takes up only a quarter of the available space. Strange. Normally every square inch is used up. Hank knocks on the rough plastic. Paces a slow circle around the container. No markings, no seams. With an ear against the plastic, he can hear a faint beeping.

He shrugs and retrieves his toolbox from the compartment. The jumbled clank as it hits the ground is barely audible in the howling wind. Hank inflates a dust tent over the front of the truck and pops the hood, checks the oil, the coolant, the hydrogen; all fine. He inspects the spark plugs and finds one with a discolored build-up, which he could clean, but instead replaces to be sure. But the spark plug didn't cause this. He would have found that error in the manual.

There's something wrong with the CabOS Interface.

The cabin repressurizes, and Hank tears his rebreather off. *Damn...* He's never felt so active. It feels good. But there's still work to do. He latches the Interface down again and presses his hands into its surface, feeling it give slightly. He searches for seams or sections but finds none. He hoists it up and studies the underside. There are four hexagonal compartments. Using a molecular wrench from the toolbox, Hank places the bonding end to the top-left compartment and pulls it out along with a tangle of multicolored wires which he has no idea what to do with. He presses the section back into place and checks the next. Then the next, where he finds a series of breakers, each a different shape and color, all of which he has spares for.

The smile is back on his face. He glances out the window as if a crowd might be hiding out in the hot, dusty darkness waiting to cheer the moment he fixes it. "I'm going to fix it!" he calls out, his voice loud in the closed cabin. He laughs, eyes damp with tears, and replaces the breakers. When he's finished, he drops the Interface into place and says, "Lights on."

With a ponderous shudder, the lights flicker up.

Hank cheers, bouncing in his seat and banging on the ceiling. "Yes! Yes!"

He swallows and looks around, the new reality of his situation closing in around him like squeezing hands. Probably, they are far behind schedule. SYSCO deliveries are typically calculated down to the second. If he wants to see Helen before she leaves for Europa, he'll have to get moving.

"Cab, are you there?"

"I am here, Hank."

Hank frowns. "Well, your personality module is still borked. But we need to get moving. How do you feel?"

"I am operational," Cab says. The engine rumbles to life. "Mechanical systems are... better than normal. I am detecting a new spark plug. Was that your doing, Hank?"

Hank beams. "Not to mention all your Interface breakers."

Cab doesn't respond. There's a subtle shift in g-force as the truck rolls forward.

Should Hank have expected a 'thank you' from the robot? Is that too much to ask? He sighs and shifts the chair back, activating the ceiling-screen. So what if Cab doesn't appreciate him? It doesn't change the fact that Hank fixed the truck and the Interface all by himself. He even drove the truck. He basically saved the day. This could've been very bad for everyone involved. The delivery might've been late. It might've been lost. Hell, he could've died out here. But he didn't. He fixed it.

"My daughter thinks I never do anything," Hank says. "She called the cabin a coffin once. But look at what just happened." He laughs. "In a way, this proves that all of our time together hasn't been a waste. You might've broken down at any moment, and I would've been here to fix it. Just like I did today."

The sun is out. The haze has cleared enough that indistinct specters of blocky buildings tower to either side of the truck as they pass, leaning over them like sleepwalking giants.

Hank rubs his eyes. "Where are we now?"

"Won't be long," Cab says.

"Won't be long until what?" Hank blinks twice, rubs his eyes, and wonders if he imagined that ominous tone in Cab's voice. "Hey Cab, whatever happened with that diagnostics report?"

"Unfortunately, the diagnostics report was corrupted during the Interface crash. I can begin another scan now if you'd like."

"No thanks," Hank says. "We're almost there, right?"

But something is not quite right. Hank squares himself up to the Interface and accesses the logs. Their route has been altered. It's only a slight adjustment, but a strange one. They are heading straight for the shuttle launch complex at Quad Cities International. A stale sweat breaks out on his neck as he remembers the *beeping* cargo container in his trailer.

Helen will be there.

Reluctantly, Hank brings up photos from the Des Moines airport bombing. Above the Interface, images of the truck that carried the bomb appear. It is another SYSCO truck exactly like his own.

"Stop the truck," Hank tells Cab, but nothing happens. He swipes away the logs and brings up the manual controls, but his fingers move through the holograms as if he isn't even there. "Cab, can you hear me?" Hank says, trying to keep the panic out of his voice. "The controls aren't working."

Still there is no response. In that silence, Hank hears another sound: The roar of a commercial jet.

"Answer me, Cab!" Hank shouts. He takes hold of the Interface catch release, but somehow it's stuck tight, locked into place. He leans forward and peers through the windshield. Through the thin dust in the air he sees a green sign swoop past to the right. The white symbol of an airplane. In the distance, the shadow of an air traffic control tower looms like a monolith.

"Cab," Hank says. "You better answer me right now."

The cabin lights flicker and dim.

"Hank," Cab's voice is deep and demonic, "Han-khankhank." It slides up in pitch. "Y'know somethin' Pardner..." The drawl has returned. "They say life is a lot like bustin' broncos. Sooner or later, you're bound to get thrown. What counts is that a cowboy keeps gettin' back in the saddle, no matter how foolhardy-"

"What the hell are you talking about?" Hank shrieks.

"I been hacked, pardner. That's the long and the short of it. But you possess a molecular-wrench in yonder toolbox, so you got the wherewithal to get hold o' these reigns again before that dynamite we're haulin' goes kablooey." A timer over the Interface begins counting down in glowing orange digits. Less than a minute remaining. "And by 'dynamite' I am referring to the tactical nuclear bomb in our trailer."

"Oh fuck." Already Hank is digging through his toolbox. Already his fingers close around the wrench, and he sets it against the Interface latch, forming an unbreakable molecular bond.

A message from Helen appears over the Interface: [Are you watching the news?]

No time to respond. Hank sets his teeth and jerks the wrench with all his body weight. A chunk of rended metal ricochets off the window. "Yeehaw," Cab hollers. "If ya climb in the saddle, best be ready to ride!" The truck turns abruptly, bucking over the curb, and Hank is flung forward.

Ahead, a silver fence fades into view from out of the haze.

Hank glances at the timer: forty-six seconds left.

There's a bright *thud-crack* from the ceiling followed by a rush of wind. Hail? "Oh god," Hank whispers. Long curving fractures spread out from a hole in the dark glass of the ceiling-screen.

[There's a truck on the news, dad. It looks just like yours.]

Through the whine of air escaping the cabin Hank hears rotary blades. A loudspeaker too, but he can't make out the words.

[Where are you right now?]

Another *ping* opens a second hole in the cabin. *Someone is shooting,* Hank realizes. The pressure has equalized, the cabin air thick with dust. He pulls on his rebreather just as the truck bursts through the fence. Hank is thrown against the Interface. He pushes back, levers the Interface up again, and stomps on the brake pedal. A sharp pain blooms in his shoulder and broken glass *skitters* off his rebreather faceplate. Tears blur his vision. A warmth streams down his arm. His shoulder is bleeding.

Hank spins the wheel as far left as it goes, twisting the tractor trailer into a jackknife. The truck tilts and falls. Hank hits the cabin door hard. Ground passes beneath him, asphalt drawing long white scratches across the side-window glass.

"Hank," Cab calls. "This rodeo ain't over yet."

The timer counts fourteen seconds to go. Thirteen.

"What can I do?" Hank calls.

"Gotta kill my Interface, pardner. Either that, or it all goes kablooey."

Hank doesn't ask more questions. He twists until he's upright again and finds the force-wrench lying on the door—which is now the floor—beside him. Ten seconds later he has the first hexagonal compartment removed and a length of multicolored wires stretched out before him. The utility knife clicks as he extends its blade.

"Cab..." Hank says, suddenly his voice is dry and hoarse.

"Ain't nothin' left for a lame horse but to put 'em down, Hank."

Hank can't shake the feeling that he's holding Cab's guts in his hand. He can't stop thinking of the wires as intestines or nerves or...

"Remember, Hank," Cab says. "There ain't nothing so sacred as the bond between horse and rider."

Hank tastes salt from a tear that found its way to the corner of his mouth. He begins to saw through the wires. "Cab," Hank blubbers. "Thank you for... Thank you for everything that..."

"Hank, no hour of life in the saddle is ever wasted."

Hank is halfway through the bundle of wires when the cabin goes dark.

49

IF ONLY TO SPEAK IN METALLIC LANGUAGE

NNADI SAMUEL

A mushroom thrives in my backyard, fruiting
    twin bodies.
each, soap-soft in decomposing—
we sought newer ways to give name to the simi-
    larity in their rot.

here, I renounce despair
yet, cannot teach the stem of my body to bend
    towards light.

with each passing day, I strive to be everything
    but a gut-punch—
aimed at the jaw of teenagers wasting away on a
    plain field.
I kill the effort to hold my parents to a grudge.
no one born womb-tearing is innocent of this.

I wanted a life obscure as a poet,
till Pa took a dagger to my dream

& none of my soft vowels survived his blade.
I vowed to be something knife-carrying.

I think of a father first as a weapon—double-
    edged.

for years, I wake up to scrap metals puncturing
    me for details of my life's event.
cancerous, yet therapeutic in its hurting:

souvenir of my suffering that clings to my night-
    wear & wouldn't rid off.

it cost blood, this thing—to take shape in
all the sharp objects that goes on to harm the
    world.
think of me in obeisance with rod: a walking
    murder case.

at Christmas eve, I defy cancer to see myself
    through a slaughterhouse;
fiddling over smoked meat, pierced clean by hot
    bayonet.

the price tag written in steel knows me by name.
how my gaze meet its stainless sight in fierce
    kinship.

isn't it nonferrous of me: to move through
    magnets & still not arrive bearing rust.
instead collect in size, like catchweed.

absconding the scene for the raw fear of blood;

I trip over a cyborg emptying its entrails in ion
    bowl.
our innards exchange cryptics.

if only to speak in metallic language.

50

MULATTOES AS THE FIRST COLOR WHEEL

NNADI SAMUEL

Cinnamon brown, born of glass image,
the color trap beneath is everything to tame
    Picasso.
a native screams at a half-breed,
& the stain surrounds the eyeball—the way
    paintbrush sketches a white canvas.

there is anger that crayons itself on the retina.
think of cataract ashing its woe on Chihuly's
    garden.
think of vermillion blood, dotting the glass-
    blown terrace.

a flower picks a red habit & shudder into soil:
an act after my heart.
& need I call it grief—knowing satin is a gown I
    don into satire,
sleek as a teenager displaying her wound in a
    showroom of dogs.

out there, clear water sits reckless—demanding
    relevance.
& for want of attention, drags the teenager of my
    imagination
into places she has no use for hands: a call to
    drowning.

I raise a mirror & duplicate,
raise a lens & turn smile into hard copies.
I edit my past in flowery language.

in the year alcohol calcifies me,
I submit myself to a museum as if by state
    demand.
no one born without the liver for it, meddles
    ethanol with medication.
I watched as my spirit left me.

now, at the tavern I say *spirit* the way you ward
    off evil,
the way you hold a thing that would not remain
    still in the mouth.

was I gorgeous in my passing away,
in the way my still loin fill a plot of land?

I wear your image to sleep.
portions of you, collecting in slow bits across
    cardboard.

the finished art mirrors neither kin nor
    countryman.
I, red-faced. you, a half-breed loved to recognition:

reincarnate of a masterpiece.

your existence lasts through a watery age,
    drowning us all.
I emerge from you in powdered form.

51

SCORCHER

ROBERT WALTON

A blur of gray and white plucks at the corner of Michael's eye. He catches a glimpse of white paws and gray tail disappearing behind a barren planter across the street from his friend Alvaro's apartment building.

"Wow! A kitten! I haven't seen one in months."

The kitten proceeds up the block, dodging from shade to shade. Michael looks down the block in the direction he's supposed to take. The orange display on his smart goggles informs him that he has twenty-two minutes to get home. It never takes him more than ten to get there from here—plenty of time to investigate this mysterious cat. He steps on his motorized skateboard and heads right.

Time for me to listen to the weather, though I already know what the weather will be. This is Southern California, after all.

"Now, Chad, what about that forecast?"

A man in early middle age—fit, tanned, wearing a pale

blue, summer-weight suit—appears on my wall-mounted smart-screen. He points to a national map centered on the gulf coast. "Well, Dennis, tropical storm Ivanka is moving into the Texas-Louisiana border area as I speak." He looks somber. "Record flooding is again possible and the usual evacuation orders are in place. I'll update the situation tonight."

A small pang of guilt jabs me as I listen. Flood victims in Texas deserve my concern, but I feel none. I have no empathy left for Texas.

Chad steps to the side and points vaguely at Arizona. "Smoke from California wildfires is affecting air quality in the Four Corners states. AQI levels range from unhealthy to hazardous."

I feel relief at this information. The winds are right. We have good air in Southern California.

"Now, to the Inland Empire. Temperatures in San Bernardino and Riverside will likely exceed records today. It's going to be a scorcher."

What's new?

The camera zooms in close on Chad. "Our usual NWS heat index level for this time of year is extreme caution. Today it will rise from yesterday's danger into the extreme danger zone." Chad looks serious. "Please remain indoors, or—if you must be outside—wear protective clothing, limit your exposure to ten minutes or less and drink your choice of liquids frequently."

I punch the remote, sending Chad into temporary oblivion, and regard the dewy pitcher in front of me with satisfaction. My choice of liquids is lemonade, freshly squeezed. I've splurged on a dozen lemons from Anchorage. Michael will love it.

Michael's image, the one from his 9th birthday party, flashes on my smart screen. It's the reminder I set. He's supposed to be home from the Garcias' apartment by now. I'll give him five more minutes before I call. I don't want to embarrass him.

"Stupid kitten." Michael bends over the prostrate cat. "I just wanted to visit with you a little. You shouldn't have been running in this heat." He looks toward the pitiless sun and then at the skate park's sun shelter across the street. "I'll put you in the shade over there."

Five minutes—I glance out my kitchen window for the tenth time. Sunlight pounds the driveway with white fists —extreme danger. To hell with embarrassment! I touch the frequent contacts menu on my console. Araceli Garcia's delicate, somewhat harassed face appears on my screen. "Oh, hello, Elaine. How are you today?"

"Fine." I smile. "I was wondering if you could send Michael home...? It's past lunchtime and we have an appointment with his remote learning counselor this afternoon."

"Oh, he left just a bit ago. I'm sure he'll be walking in your door in a minute or two."

"Thanks, Araceli!" I smile again. "Stay cool."

She smiles. "I'll try. It's a hot one today."

The connection fades. The window's malicious glare tugs at my eyes—a hot one. I step to the suit closet and pull my protective garment from its hanger. This is silly, I think. I'll probably get my heat-suit on and meet him coming in the door. Left leg, right leg, I pull it on anyway. I shrug my shoulders, adjust the sleeves and close the Velcro seal-tabs. I open the inner door, enter the vestibule and take a deep breath. I seal my clear mask and step through the outer door.

Heat slaps me, even through double reflective layers. The suit's solar-powered circulation system whines into its highest mode. Cool air flows between the suit's inner and outer layers, giving me swift relief. This is a good suit, rated to one hundred-and thirty-five-degrees Fahrenheit, but it must be at least that hot now. Despite the suit's AC, a drop of sweat trickles from right temple down my cheek. I look in both directions. The street is empty of life.

Where is Michael?

"Don't you want some water?" Michael holds his cupped palm beneath the little cat's muzzle, but it doesn't respond. Its chest flutters like a hummingbird's wings and then falls still.

Shade-shelters line our street every ten meters or so. I walk briskly, checking beneath each pancake of cement. No Michael. Parental guilt mounts as I walk. We should move north, should have moved long ago. Only the wealthy now live above the Arctic Circle, of course, but we could have afforded somewhere in Canada, maybe British Columbia.

The great South American drought of 2025-26 happened when I was a little girl. It was followed by the rain forest fires. I remember the brown skies for months on end and the red sun, always the red sun.

When the skies cleared, the forests were gone, and the heat began. Tracts of India and Africa became uninhabitable. There were mass deaths.

The last shelter on our block—the twelfth—is empty. I look

across the intersection and sag slightly with relief. Seven-Eleven—that's where he must be. Michael loves the single use game apps they sell. He's probably in there, looking at the new ones. I'll text him.

No answer.

I cross the street. Melted globs of asphalt suck at my insulated boots. An image of the Brea Tar Pits flashes through my mind. Am I to be pulled under like a mammoth? I escape the street's sticky pits and approach the store's double-paned windows. The lights are off and no one moves within. I notice a message projected onto the door: closed due to heat emergency. Seven Eleven? Closed?

I continue toward the Garcias' apartment complex. Things stabilized here in California after the Canadian Northwest Territories water pipeline and universal solar-powered AC took effect. It was uncomfortably hot for most of the year, but only dangerously so during August and September. So we stayed. And I married. And divorced. And my son is missing in the heat. The heat—how bad is it. I'm sweating all over now, even with my suit AC set on high. That shouldn't happen.

My phone chimes. Michael?

No, Araceli. "Yes?"

"My Alvaro said that Michael started home but then turned right toward the skate park."

"That's past your building by the county solar farm?"

"Yes. Alvaro doesn't know why he went that way on such a hot day."

"Thanks, Araceli. I'm going there now."

"You should call Uber."

"It's less than half a mile from here. I don't want to wait."

I call Michael. Nothing.

"It's too hot, cat." Michael stares at the limp kitten. The tip of its tongue protrudes from between delicate lips and its eyes are glazed. "I don't feel so good either."

Nothing. I increase my pace. My suit whines. Sweat pours off me. My phone chimes again—a text. It's Michael! "Help."

The big skate park's big shade is ahead of me. That's where he must be. I hit my heat emergency button. My suit sends a heat alert to the HEMTs. The ambulance will home on its signal. Help will come in minutes. I run.

The big shade is close. I see him! He's not moving, but he's out of the sun. The sun! My legs turn to mush. I fall to my knees. The world spins and spins and spins. And fades to black.

A siren swells as I spin back into consciousness. I'm in a moving vehicle. A Heat EMT sits next to me, head turned toward the driver. "Ice packs, alcohol mister—the heat protocols are done. That's all I can do for now."

A voice comes from the driver's compartment. "What were they doing? It's one hundred and fifty-two out there."

"The kid has a cat."

"You brought a cat in here?"

"It's dead."

"You brought a dead cat in here?"

"He wouldn't let go of it."

An electronic beep sounds. The HEMT looks at monitors above my head. "She has a chance."

"What about the kid?"

"I think..." He studies the fluttering lines on Michael's monitor. "I think he followed his cat too far."

52

THE EARTH INSIDE US

ABIGAIL KEMSKE

A new green mound of earth sits at the corner of 4th and Nicollet like a miniature oblong meadow. So bright against the gray expanse of the city. Ivory daisies bloom from it, begging the sun to slice through the smog.

The Minneapolis Environmental Relocation Services have already arrived. A MERS worker wearing an offensively yellow visibility vest places orange cones around the mound. Another readies a jackhammer. Passersby skirt the site without a glance. The new patch of earth only appeared this morning. Soon it will be gone.

My insides give way like a sinkhole at the thought. I push away my plate of unfinished bacon, pay for my breakfast and leave the retro-themed diner. Stepping out into the dry, dusty city, I cinch my hood tight around my face to conceal the white, feathery veins on my cheek, then I cross the street toward the mound.

"Stringy weed," someone says as I pass.

Today, I can't handle the mutterings about my strange appearance. The sidelong glances. It's hard enough waking up to a body that changes daily, out of one's control. When will they accept that this is the new normal? Babies are born with bits of the earth in their bellies even before they have suckled their mother's colostrum.

The earth is inside us all.

The MERS workers are chatty, laughing. It's impossible to make out what they are saying behind their particle respirators. I can guess by the way they carelessly drop the shovels on the new earth that it's dismissive. They are young. Too young to even worry about the changes coming.

The mound is vibrant, reminiscent of the Minneapolis of my youth with tree-lined streets, lush lakeshore ecosystems, ample parks and gardens. The city was nearly a forest then. However, the Minneapolis of today is stale and dark, lakes and rivers are walled-off from view. A patchwork quilt of fresh asphalt dots the streets where life used to be.

A breeze blows a swirl of dust across the coned-off area. The little daisies on the mound sway back and forth. *Whissh whoosh.*

Do they know this is the last time they will feel the wind?

I can't ignore the squirrelling sense of wrongness, the wood splashing around in a stomach full of coffee. All at once it is too much. The smog, the bottlenecked sidewalk, the endless grey expanse of the city streets, the shooing away of a toddler with an outstretched hand ready to pluck a daisy.

He should have left like the others, like I am about to do.

As the two MERS workers turn toward the truck, my feet pick up at a run. The white vein across my cheek throbs. Wind spits dust into my eyes. When I reach the mound, I crouch down, grab the shovels and slink back into the crowd. But I'm spotted.

"Hey! We need those," the workers holler. I sprint down Nicollet.

This won't stop them, I know. But at least I can stall MERS, give the green mound, the flowers, the old man a little more time in the sun.

Instead of rushing into my apartment just across the street, I round the block. My hood blows back, revealing the vein on my cheek, the tiny mushrooms rising from my hair. More dust stings my eyes, for which I'm grateful to not make out the faces of those who stop and stare. The thudding feet of my pursuers fades behind me.

"Gah! Stupid… earth sick," voices drowned out by squealing car engines.

My eyes are watering as I return to the street from an alley and sneak into my apartment entryway. Something clatters on the sidewalk before me. The sinkhole inside me collapses in on itself as I realize my mistake.

Sami, my roommate, stands before me, her phone at her feet. Screen cracked. The particle respirator has slipped down her face.

There is no more ignoring it. No more hiding it as Sami's red lipped mouth gapes at me.

At first there was only moss on my toes, easily flicked away with a fingernail, leaving nothing but granules of earth between the creases of my skin. I ignored it then. Denied it. Over the next few months worms wriggled in my gut during the stillness of sleep. Grains of sand scraped my airways every time I sneezed. A lump of wood rolled around in my stomach. Tiny luminous mushrooms sprouted from the strands of my hair (which only grew taller from the top of my head after I shaved it.)

And this morning, white veins flourish atop pink-toned skin.

The earth is germinating within.

It was easy enough to hide my transformation from Sami when the symptoms began. All I had to do was wear socks to cover up the moss, but it didn't go unnoticed.

"What is that?" Sami asked.

"What is what?" I replied.

"That on your feet?"

I looked down to my toes and curled them, gritty with dirt, damp with sweat. "They are socks. Have you heard of them? They keep your feet warm and keep blisters from forming when wearing shoes. Great invention."

"Eila," she groaned.

"What?"

"You hate socks."

She was right. Since the day we became roommates, she has been remarking on how my socks seemingly *explode* off my feet when I get home.

"So, now that I'm wearing them, you're complaining about that too?"

Sami rolled her eyes. "You're just being weird."

"When haven't I been weird?"

Weirdness was the thing that brought us together when we first met at summer camp years ago. In the forest, among the freshness of tall, towering pine trees, there was a giant sandstone rock, *our* rock. We called it, eloquently, Weird Rock. The only rule being that we couldn't be normal in its presence. We walked on jiggly legs, sang gobbledygook, pounced and prowled on anyone who got too close. It had to be protected from the horde of boys trying to claim it as their own, who skulked away with scraped knees as battle wounds.

When I closed my eyes, I could hear the sound of Sami's beaded braids clinking together, see a pink tongue sticking out of the corner of brown lips in concentration as she carved her name into Weird Rock for the hundredth time.

What will happen to these memories when my soft, moving insides solidify? How will Sami take this new level of weird?

A week ago, when the mushrooms first fruited on top of my head, I still couldn't tell Sami. She knocked on my door the third night I had locked myself in my room. "Eila," she said. "Is everything okay?"

"Uh, yeah. I just have a cold," I said as I opened and shut my drawers frantically trying to find my hoodie, my scarf, *something* to cover my freshly shaved, fungal head. The whole dresser shook as I pushed shut a too-full drawer. Trinkets clattered to the ground. "Shit."

"Do you need help?"

"No, I'm good, thanks." I picked the trinkets up, one being a large oval ring, a cheap childhood relic. The mood ring Sami gave to me at Weird Rock one summer. I slipped it on my pinky finger.

The floor creaked outside my door.

Aheeeii. I feigned a cough.

"Are you sure you are okay?"

The Sami of today doesn't ask if I'm okay. The Sami of today is angry.

"You lied to me," she paces around the main room of the apartment.

The words are stinging nettle. Sharp. A radiating burn. Her spouse had been the liar, not me.

"And now you're, what, stealing from MERS?" She points to the shovels leaning against the wall.

I let out a soft chuckle, the skin at my cheek stiff and unyielding from the vein growing across it. "I'm going to give them back."

"You'll root down here, then?" Sami asks.

I look to the corner of the room and follow the line up to the ceiling, finding the small vaguely shaped butterfly stain above the window.

Sami stops pacing and gasps softly. She turns to face me. "You were just going to leave, weren't you?"

I bite the inside of my lip so hard, a sticky substance oozes into my mouth.

Sami tugs at the ends of her long, purple tipped braids. "Why is everyone leaving me?"

This is what I was afraid of. Part of me knows I should have said something ages ago, but the other part of me doesn't know why. I tongue the spot of sap hardening in my mouth.

"Sami, you have to understand. I'm gone no matter what."

She scoffs. "Did you have to lie to me about it?"

I fidget with the ring on my pinky finger, a stone of scarlet. "I didn't know how to tell you with your divorce and everything. It never was the right time."

"Not the right time?" Sami eyes the mood ring, then shuffles forward a step as if wanting to close the space between us, as if wanting to pass the ring back and forth like we used to, watching the color change. "I could help you. You might even survive, someone has to."

Survival isn't a doomed patch of earth in the concrete city, nor a single potted plant hidden away in a room.

"What if this is how we survive?" I ask.

The whites of Sami's eyes are red like the smog-embellished sky. Her voice quavers. "I wish you'd stay."

I wish the others had been allowed to stay too. The maple trees sprouting out of skyscraper windows, the moss hugging the lampposts, the ferns tickling the ankles of those who walked the streets.

"And end up like him?" I gesture out the window as the intermittent chatter of the jackhammer down the street seeps in.

"But they relocate—"

"Do you really believe that somewhere out there is some garden of everyone who's sprouted? None of you want to even think about what's happening, I mean, people can't even look at me."

Sami grunts. "This is a mistake."

She's never going to understand. There's a reason why those like me often leave in the middle of the night.

"Maybe it is. But it's my mistake to make. And I'll be fine."

Sami turns and walks away toward her bedroom, muttering to herself, "*She'll* be fine, but what about me? How am I supposed to pay the rent?"

I sigh and go to the window, tugging at the ring on my pinky as I watch MERS finish their job down the street. They lift the mound of earth and slide it into the back of their truck. The asphalt crew stands by to patch the sidewalk.

Before sunrise, I had seen the man at the corner under the streetlamp, old, frail, the earth flourishing over his body. He stopped as if to tie a shoe, collapsing down as the green consumed him. It lasted only a few minutes in the dim morning light. And it was beautiful, a comfort knowing I too will meet a graceful end. I too will change the landscape.

But I know my place is not here.

Instinctually, I drive north from Minneapolis where the sprawling suburbs turn to abandoned small towns and drought stricken countryside.

Maybe it was a bit cold of me to leave while Sami was at work. There would have been tears and the long Minnesotan goodbye that would somehow extend until midnight. But something inside me, that deepening, internal erosion, told me I had to leave at my first opportunity, that staying would only hurt Sami more.

The last thing I want is for her to waste any more of her youth worrying about me. The sham marriage already took away a few years, and who even knows how much any one has left? It's still a mystery why some change and others don't. Maybe Sami will be one of the lucky ones. But I can't help but wonder, is this really how friendships end? Can we really just walk away from it all?

The countryside turns to a skeletal forest, burned down a year prior as the highway dips down into Duluth. A fine haze hangs over the city, blurring the waters of Lake Superior, sending the tall buildings into hiding. I stop at a 24-hour diner north of downtown and order a vegetable hash with two poached eggs. No matter how much I salt it, it tastes bland, or maybe I'm just not that hungry. Food hasn't had much taste lately.

After I pay, I continue my drive until I reach a wayside just out of the city. In the twilight, I fold down the back seats in my car and make a bed with blankets. The lapping waves of the lake remind me of how Sami and I used to sneak out of the bunkhouse at camp to lay under the stars, lulled to sleep by a gentle schwip, schwip.

I wake to calm waters and a haze that lingers on the lake. After packing my things, I continue north along Highway 61, the air clearing the further I drive from the city. Surprisingly, there is an open coffee shop in a nearly abandoned town. I freshen up in the bathroom, discovering that the white veins now extended down my arms, but I don't cover them up with my hoodie. It's too suffocating. I slip on a loose tank top and shorts, pulling out the string on which I stung the mood ring. No one gapes at me when I order a large americano and a chocolate croissant like they do in the city.

At the next wayside, just over a river feeding into the lake, I stop. With my backpack and breakfast in hand, I follow a path from the parking lot, through tall grasses, and down to the pebbled beach. A large piece of driftwood makes a bench. The coffee is good. The croissant stiff and flat. However, when the sun warms my face, I set the croissant on the log, let the coffee turn cold, let the sun nourish me.

My phone buzzes. Texts flash across the screen.

SAMI: Don't do this alone.

I read the stream of her texts I've been ignoring since the night before. Messages like: *I can't believe you left without saying goodbye!* And *I won't accept the money you left.* And *Where are you?*

I start to type: It's better this way.

SAMI: I'll come with you.

I delete my text.

SAMI: Please. I don't want you to die.

I type: Who says I'm going to die?

My finger hovers over *send*. I grip the phone, slip off my shoes and step across the rocky beach to let the icy water shock my feet.

SAMI: Please don't leave me.

If I turn back home, would I even be me when I arrive?

The wind picks up. Water rushes around my ankles. From behind there is a shushing, like a mother comforting a child. I turn. The shallow river trickles into the lake through a curtain of brown, dried reeds. A red shoe is near the water. Next to it, fresh green cattails sprout from a long lump of earth. Something moves within it. Fingers elongated with grasses lift from the ground as if to wave, an eye bright and blue watches me. I wave back. It blinks a few times.

Perhaps I am not so alone.

SAMI: Please lmk you are okay?

Three dots blink on the screen.

I delete the last line, then type: I'm okay. Goodbye, Sami.

I hit send and drop my phone onto the rocky beach. A wave rushes forward, settling it upright—a tombstone to a past life.

As the eye within the reeds closes, the shushing rushes to the treetops in the forest beyond. With it my breath bottles up inside, releasing as I step along the shore of the river, barefooted, and into the forest.

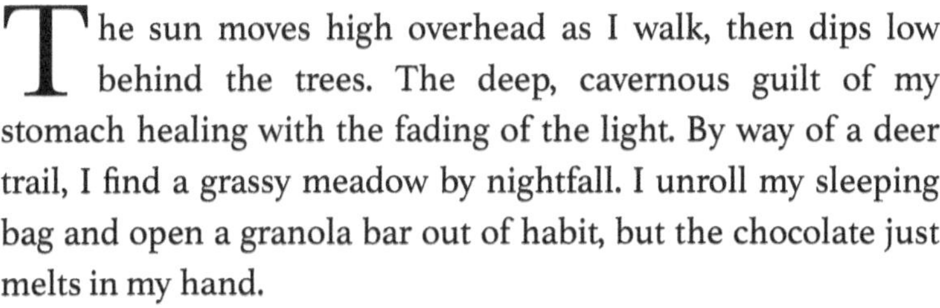

The sun moves high overhead as I walk, then dips low behind the trees. The deep, cavernous guilt of my stomach healing with the fading of the light. By way of a deer trail, I find a grassy meadow by nightfall. I unroll my sleeping bag and open a granola bar out of habit, but the chocolate just melts in my hand.

At dawn, the sun cuts through the quaking aspens, crisply glinting on the dew like twinkling stars. The air is clear and refreshing, unlike in the city. I sit down in the middle of the clearing and grip the wet grass between my fingers, cool and silky. Chickadees titter in the trees. There is a slight vibration within the earth, one that reaches inside me. With it are voices, feelings, comfort. I try to pick out the words I sense but there are none, until bright as a bell in the stillness of the morning, a voice rings out through the clearing, "Hello?"

Startled, I stand and whip around.

A round figure emerges from the line of young white spruce.

At first, Lela and I walk together in near silence. It is far from the silence earned between lifelong friends. The type Sami and I had when we'd spend lazy weekend afternoons sipping coffee. Something else is shared between us, something felt through our steps across the earth. A sort of hum I sensed the moment she walked into the meadow.

That hum fades when we hike through a withering forest, an expanse of toppled trees where the silence is so eerie, the sky so vast, Lela starts to run.

There's an urge to chase after her swishing, vine-entangled braids, as I used to chase after Sami's beaded ones. But the glimpses of Lela's aged skin, the shock of her close set eyes, the dots of lively green lichen across a brown face, takes the breath from me and the memory with it.

I have begun to stumble on joints that grow unstable by the hour, so I cannot run after her. Instead, I trip over a raised lump of earth. Struggling, I roll onto my back and see a tangle of roots, stems and leaves, the shape of someone hunched over it.

"Oh, I'm sorry," I say, finally sitting up, "I didn't see you."

"No worries, noo woorrriieesss at all." They speak slowly, a pale face is framed with pink petal eyelashes looking up to the sun.

I push myself to my feet with a grunt, spotting Lela as she bounds ahead. Sami would have stopped. She would have turned around and helped me to my feet.

It feels as if my chest fills with mud, leaving me with echoes of a full breath, a beating heart, regret, what I once was. It lingers in my hardening insides. Or maybe, now I just need less air.

"It helps if you just let go." Petals open and close. The earth thrums rhythmically.

The worms wriggle down in my legs now, urging me to go.

Lela stops when I call and watches as I stagger toward her. "Why did you just leave me there?" I ask.

"I thought you were rooting down."

"No, I tripped."

She shrugs. "I guess it's hard to sense you when there aren't as many trees."

I know she saw me. I know she sees me struggle. Sami would have rummaged through her backpack and made Goodleygob, a snack we invented at camp to be eaten at Weird Rock. Basically, it was combination of dry snack foods with *secret* sauce stolen from the camp cafeteria drizzled over it. Mostly the results were pretty weird. Eating it always meant laughter. The best we ever had at camp was graham crackers, chocolate sauce and whipped cream. I'm still not sure how Sami managed that one.

Later, it became a tradition to exchange bags of the snack when we met. I last made it for Sami when she moved in with me five months ago, thinking it would take the edge off her pending divorce to celebrate our childhood dream of living together finally coming true. We ate until our bellies ached.

She left a bag outside my door when she thought I locked myself in my room with a cold.

Lela continues on, not waiting a moment longer. I follow, rubbing the smooth stone of the mood ring on my palm.

It helps if you just let go.

I lift the string off my neck, ready to toss it all into a decaying log. A faint thump in my chest pushes through the mud like a gas bubble breaching the surface of a bog. My breath catches. Instead, I ditch the string and slide the ring back on my pinky finger as I try to keep pace with Lela.

We find raspberry bushes at the edge of a thriving grove and stop to pick them. They are tart and juicy, the first thing I've eaten in awhile that holds any flavor. A gift from the earth. I gather the berries in the hem of my shirt.

The usual hum at my feet is boisterous, but I have gotten used to the chatter, to tuning into only what I want or need to understand, letting the sensation fade to just vibration, when in my ear is a whisper, a mumbling.

I pause, listen, feel for it at my feet.

"One, all are one, one is all, we are all…"

The bush wriggles to my right. I wave Lela over. She glances at me, then continues picking the berries.

"All dust, all earth, all stars…"

Pushing aside the branches, I find thorny, coppery arms twisted in the bush. A face nestled between them, eyebrows thick with prickles. Raspberries grow where the eyes should be. I drop the berries from my shirt, spit out the one I am chewing.

"Now we return, return, return to home, return to earth…"

I call to Lela, wave her over again. With an eye roll, she comes. She looks at me like the kid who was forced to play with me during a dinner party. All I wanted to do was be a feral, snarling beast, and she wanted to play with dolls. She tried to avoid me as I tried to make my mouth foam, but her mother sent her back to keep me company. The girl obeyed and sat in the room with me, failing to conceal a snarl.

The only time Sami ever gave me that look, was the last time I talked to her, when she was angry and pacing the apartment.

"Let it become you, let it devour you, let it free you…" the voice from the bush drones on.

Lela stands close. For how much she seems to dislike me, she has no sense of personal space.

"What do we do?" I ask.

"Why should we do anything?" She says.

"Hello." I peek my head in the bush.

The face is unmoving, the raspberry eyes fixed, except for

leafy lips that flutter. "One dust, one earth, one star returning…"

As the words race, so does the thrum at our feet. An almost erratic pulse that disorients with its waves of rushing blood, slow breaths, tingling fingers, stiffening limbs. The sensation teetering back and forth from intense to tranquil.

Lela lets out a slow breath, eyes soft with sympathy and takes my hand, stiffly at first. It makes me feel awkward and itchy. As she squeezes my hand, that connection, that hum between us is stronger. And I realize I have misread her; I feel foolish and immature. She had to lose someone too.

Together we push down a calm, a stillness, a comfort into the earth.

It helps if you just let go.

Before our eyes, the face flourishes in green, leafy lips stilling as they breathe, "bloom, bloom, bloom."

Lela continues to squeeze my hand as the leaves and berries settle with a quiver, as the thrum calms.

She lets go, turns to me. "Eila, your skin."

I touch my cheek. The skin is rough and stiff, the same with my arms. A scaly, grayish growth covers the once white veins. Bark.

On the breeze, the sharp, minty scent of pine trees tickles my nose. I clutch the ring-clad-hand to my chest, then lead Lela through the forest.

The bark spreads rapidly through the night and into the next morning, causing me to wake even more stiff and clumsy than before. After packing our belongings, Lela doing most of it, we descend a piney hillside, reaching an abrupt clearing with thousands of freshly felled trees at the bottom.

Lela pauses at the edge of the forest covering her mouth with her hand, but I can't stop. She keeps pace.

At the far end of the clearing are tipped over tree harvesters, pinned down with long, finger-like vines. A dirt road is blocked with a wall of green. A few mossy cabins remain in the lowest part of the valley with a large mountainous boulder in the center. Goosebumps flutter over what skin I have left.

It can't be. I totter on my rigid legs.

"Woah," Lela steadies me with an arm, "you okay?"

"I-I've been here before." I'm breathless, unable to stand still.

"You have?" Lela walks with her arm outstretched. I lean on it.

"It's Weird Rock."

"Weird what?"

"A place once special to a friend and I." The ring sits heavy on my finger.

"Oh, look!" She points to the edges of the trees. From all directions there is movement, people in various stages of growth dot the clearing. Some cross it methodically, others still-ing, blooming. We continue down the hill.

My pace slows more and more until I can no longer move. I'm not sure how long it's taken us to reach Weird Rock, on the sunny side of it, where I stand with my feet sunken into the mud. I've been thinking of the man who transformed in the city. Lela is beside me, the lichen engulfing her face. She looks to me with compassion as I cry.

"What's wrong?" She asks.

My voice a mere whisper, "I thought I would be alone. I didn't know it would be so..."

"Comforting?"

"You feel it too?"

Her eyes twinkle. I know the answer. I know she feels it the same as me, even though she's never been here before. We are to be devoured, to become part of a whole. We are home.

~

The worms escape to the earth at my feet. The growing stillness inside is foreign at first. I'm not sure when I stopped breathing, yet I don't feel deprived of air. Lela comes and goes, never straying too far. She rests at my roots at night. Her movements across the ground change and slow, the bounciness turning to a limp. Eventually she settles at my roots, her body slowly curling down.

~

As my arms become branches, fingers twigs, frilled with green needles, more stretching and growing from my crown, it is strange to not feel the cold of winter. The wind makes my needles shiver. There is no longing for warmth or food. There's only a stillness, a quiet. As my growth slows, so do my thoughts, lingering on why I pushed Sami away, if I had done it more for me than her.

Was I selfish?

Through my roots Lela offers comfort. Maybe, by now Sami understands why I did it.

~

In the spring Lela's vines wrap around me. My growth and change come rapidly. Little cone nobs form. I can no longer see the growing forest around me, but only sense those roots that emerge below ground, connecting into the fungal web of the forest. But I imagine there is little evidence left that this was once a campsite. All that's left are the memories, etched in lignin, I still hold of it.

I'm always searching for Sami through my roots. If I somehow found my way here, perhaps she will too. Or maybe there will be a fluttering across the earth one day. A child will climb Lela's vines up to my branches. I will feel a familiar step on the earth. A springiness interspersed with a cane.

"It's still here!" The old woman will say.

"What is Grammy?" The child will ask.

"This rock. It used to belong to me and my best friend."

"You owned a rock?"

"It was our favorite place."

I'll feel the weight of the old woman as she leans against me. The gentle shake releasing something from my branches.

"What's that?" The child will ask, climbing down and pattering on the grass below.

"Give it here." The woman will gasp. "Where did you get this?"

"It fell from the tree Grammy."

"Is it..." She'll run a hand over my bark, the ring on her finger. "Eila! I've finally found you!"

My branches will quiver.

Over the passing seasons, she'll rest her weight against me, frequently, and share stories of how the cities are unrecognizable, how so many people have blossomed all at once that there is no one left to work for MERS, that the growths of loved ones scattered all over the city are now sacred. She will tell me there is in fact a garden of all those who bloomed before, that I needn't think the old man is alone. She will tell me how a small percentage of people are unaffected by the *earth inside them*, a genetic predisposition. Her family will be lucky.

Over time, Sami will come and stay with me every day until the day her weight doesn't lift. Gradually she'll became lighter and lighter until I hardly feel anything at all, not even a thrum at my roots. Instead, she'll nourish the soil beneath me. In the seasons that follow the forest will thrive. And even though she will never sense the message, I will shake the earth regularly, telling her how I am the lucky one to be with her forever at *our* rock.

53

EXTRASENSORY OVERLOAD

CHRISTINA SNG

I hear them whispering
All the time, especially
When it is quiet
And when I am still.

They speak of death
And of extinction,
Promises of another life
In another place.

A better life—
Where flaying
Begins each day
And screams

Resound
In the echo chamber
Beneath the caged dome
Where we all congregate.

They project images
Of this life into my mind—
In vivid color, tinged with
Every shade of red.

I cannot close my eyes.
I cannot sleep.
The images play on a loop.
The flaying. The screams.

The executioner's grin.
These promises. This life.
My death will not end them.
It will send me there.

I cash in every stock,
Every bond,
And sell my home.
I hug my cat Persephone

One last time
Before I put us on ice,
Together
In our own cryo chamber

Where I no longer dream
Or hear their whispers.
We will sleep through
Their time, their extinction

And even if technology
Never becomes sufficiently
Advanced to revive us,
The last image I see

Is one of peace,
Reflected in the curve
Of our cryo capsule,
Etched in my mind forever:

Persephone and me
Safe and alive,
Falling asleep
Together.

54

THE DEVIL WEARS GOGGLES

DAVID HAMMOND

Content Warning: explicit language

At 7:30 a.m., the vents on Beatrice's firebox opened up and a fan pulled oxygen to the smoldering cache of coal she stress-ate the previous evening. As her boiler started to rumble, her eyes clicked open. Due to the slow spin-up of her ocular apparatus, everything looked red at first; then yellowish; then a range of browns, which constituted the full spectrum presented by her brass, leather, and rust apartment.

"Ugh."

*Move to New Old New York, they said. Just the place for an aspiring writer to get her start, they said. The smog's *not* as bad as they say. The smell *is*. Here, take this can of Raid, you'll need it, they said.*

She belched a puff of steam as she rose and clanked to the window to look out on the simmering city. On further reflection, many of the things they had said were on the money. But the truth was she didn't mind the smell, and she didn't mind the cockroaches, and she didn't mind that her roommate was an over-sexed humanoid ferret who—

"Don't mind me," said a naked man emerging from her roommate's bedroom, feet slapping wetly on the wooden floor. He retrieved an overripe banana from the kitchen and returned to the bedroom, winking.

Every fucking morning, a different sweaty meat-bag.

But she didn't mind, not really.

What she minded was all the *brown*. Brown walls, brown buildings, brown air, brown fruit. It didn't help that her "dream job" as personal assistant to the publisher of *SteamVogue* forced her to pretend to like these muddy, clunky styles. It also didn't help that she was in a serious writing rut. She was becoming as brown as everything else here. Brown clothes, brown nose, brown prose.

"Ugh."

Her arm twitched and her head jerked to the side. She knew she shouldn't have chased that coal with a tumbler of kerosene. She was going to be twitchy all day, and if the abusive, involuntary verbal outbursts started, it would be an ugly day at work.

"Yo, Bea," said her furry roommate Clem, musky and half-dressed. "Can I borrow your toothbrush?"

"FUCKING-CUM-FACED-CUNT."

"I'll take that as a yes."

"Ugh."

Beatrice pushed through the sycophants crowding around Ms. Greasley's desk and set down the mug.

"Here's your whiskey, Ms. Greasley."

"Oh Beatrice, where are my brass goggles?"

"They're on your face, Ms. Greasley."

"I have my leather ones here, but what about the brass ones?"

"They're on your—"

"This construct can pour a whisky, but it can't keep track of a simple pair of goggles. I think it needs a tune-up."

Jangling laughter filled the room as the hovering sycophants simulated amusement.

"They're on—" Beatrice's neck twitched, her shoulders shrugged.

"Oh, dear. Is it malfunctioning? Look at the steam coming out of its ears."

"Should I call a mechanic?" offered a man wearing a monocle and a ten-gallon hat.

"They're on— SH— they're SH—"

"Spit it out!"

"SHIT-FACED-SHIT-BRAINED-SHIT-COLORED-SHIT-EATER!"

"Oh, dear. I think it's broken."

Steam condensed in the crown of Beatrice's head, and water trickled from the inner corners of her eyes. The drops fell between her splayed legs into the gutter outside the *SteamVogue* building.

Fired. So predictable. If she had written it into a story, it would have made her vomit.

An eddy of oil and sewage in the gutter gave off an iridescent sheen. It was... pretty. Colorful. She got on hands and knees and followed the swirl along the curb until she bumped into something.

"Excuse me."

A man smiled down at her. He wore the most wonderful, bright blue suit she had ever seen. Outside New Old New York you'd have called it "sky blue." He checked a pocket watch, tipped his hat, and carried on down the street.

She watched him saunter away for a moment, swinging a silver cane, then called out, "Sir! Wait!"

He stopped and looked over his shoulder. "Yes?"

"Where do you come from?"

He turned back towards her and rested both hands on his cane. "New Old New York born and raised, young lady."

"But you're so..."

"Bright and colorful?" He laughed. "But aren't we all? Me. You. Them..." He bounded over to her and sat next to her on the sidewalk, sloshing his pretty shoes in the gutter. "Just pay attention, and you'll see what I mean. There!"

He pointed his cane at a woman across the street. Sure enough, she had a lime-green ribbon in her hair. Beatrice gasped, then noticed a little boy with pink socks, then a store window with a neon red display. "How is it I never noticed before?"

"It's easy to miss if you don't look for it."

The more she looked, the more color she saw, and every color of the rainbow, from eggshell blue to bubblegum pink. Colors that reminded her of her youth, and colors she'd never dreamed of. Like oxygen to her firebox, the colors rushed in, activating whole branches of unused circuitry and blowing the coal dust from her imagination.

Indigo! Cerulean! Vermilion! Gamboge!

These were colors she was meant to see, colors she was meant to show to the world. She was glad she'd been fired. With Ms. Greasley out of her headspace, she'd have processor cycles to devote to her novel. Working title: *Head of Steam: Confessions of a Construct*. The clicking in her steel cranium was the sound of her dreams falling into place. She felt giddy. She was gonna make it, dammit!

And the colors, oh the colors!

Mauve! Goldenrod! Jade! Skobeloff! Fuschia!

"This city's going to hell," said Ms. Greasley, stepping around a discarded construct on the sidewalk.

Frozen on its hands and knees, the construct once known as Beatrice gazed wonderingly in the gutter. No doubt the firebox exhaust system had been stymied by the unusual orientation, and fumes had backed up in the computational mechanism, which made the ocular apparatus go haywire and see things that weren't there. In any case, the cache of coal had been snuffed out, and a boiler leak had left the construct a relatively lightweight hunk of metal, soon to be scavenged by orphans and sold for meth money at the scrapyard.

Sanderson clutched his toolbag to his chest as he made his way down the alley. A tall, trenchcoated figure nodded to him before splitting at the waist, the upper half jumping down and scampering away as the long trail of the trenchcoat hissed against the asphalt. The lower half, a stocky urchin named Timothy, pulled up short. He formed his hand in the shape of a pistol and pointed it at Sanderson.

"Whatcha in the market for, Tinman?"

Sanderson leaned away automatically, wary of Timothy's deft fingers. Many a construct had found themselves teetering after a brush with one of these enterprising orphans, short a hamstring piston or a knee bolt. "I'm not picky, Tim, but I'd trade a leg for a #8 right rotator cuff."

"Shoulda steamed into me five minutes ago. Just carted in a she-bot with a leaky boiler. Awful nice set of limbs. You'll be paying Maxwell's markup now."

"Alright, Tim. Keep an eye out, would you?"

But Timothy was already halfway down the alley, pulling a flap-eared goggle cap over his head.

Entering Maxwell's Mixed Metals, Sanderson headed straight to the new arrivals shelf.

There she was.

She lay on her back, her eyes wide and her hands held out in front of her, as if warding off an attack. Poor thing. Scuff marks on her knees, chipped lacquer on the backs of her hands, tinges of rust in the corners of her eyes. No shock collar meant she'd been a free bot, living out her life on these reeking streets. Had she let her fire go out, or had it been snuffed out by a cruel and careless hand? The scum.

Involuntary jets of steam escaped Sanderson's ears.

"Haven't had a chance to run a full diagnostic yet, but it's in excellent condition." Maxwell stood beside him, arms folded.

Sanderson cleared his voice box and firmed up his slackened stance. "Leaky boiler," he said.

"What? No."

"See the corrosion around the waist?"

Maxwell leaned down for a closer look, as if he hadn't noticed it when the urchins brought her in. "Hmph. Pinhole. Easily patched." He straightened, eyed Sanderson, and stopped hiding his annoyance. "Look, Sanderson, you want it for parts or what? I've had six of this model in the past month. This one's headed to the recycler if I don't move it quick."

"I don't know. I could use the rotator cuff, I suppose, but the rest—"

"Alright," said Maxwell, whipping out a strap wrench. "Left or right?"

Sanderson lurched forward to place himself between Maxwell and the construct. "Wait..."

⌇

Maroon! *Glaucus! Viridian! Feldgrau! Phlox!*

Beatrice blinked and gasped. The incoming air produced a crackling rush of flame in her firebox. A construct's face, eyes wide and jaw slack, hovered inches from her own.

"Who are you?" she wheezed, a mixture of smoke and steam escaping her nostrils.

The construct pulled back and clapped its jaw shut. "I'm Sanderson. What's your name?"

She stared at him for a few seconds, then looked around the room. A window high in the wall shed light on a grisly scattering of mismatched body parts: An arm with a mangled hand reaching out of a rusted metal bin; a torso on a wooden bench, its innards exposed, its boiler missing; a head with pairs of straggly wires instead of eyes. She tried to stand up but her arms were strapped to her chair.

"Where the hell am I?"

"Oh, sorry." He leaned over her to undo the straps. She caught a whiff of rancid oil as the crease of his neck was shoved in her face.

He sat back down as she stood up. His face was equipped with moveable eyebrows, and they gathered together and slanted up towards the middle of his forehead. This was meant to signal subservience, an eagerness to please, a lack of aggression. Beatrice was not used to seeing this expression deployed in her direction. "Who are you?" she demanded.

"My name is Sanderson. I bought you from a metal merchant on Crawshay Way."

"Bought me?"

"Well, I traded a bin of copper pipe for you. And an old centrifugal telescope I wasn't using."

"What are you talking about—bought, traded—I'm a free bot." She backed away, searching for an exit among the cabinets and crookedly stacked boxes that lined the room. She bumped the metal bin with its grotesque, grasping hand. "What kind of sicko are you?"

He stood slowly, raising his hands in a calming gesture. "I was just fixing you up." He pointed to the deskinned torso. "I replaced your leaky boiler. And your ocular apparatus was fowled up good."

"Fixing me up? Oh!" She felt her neck for a newly installed shock collar. Finding none, she paused to think. Sanderson's eyebrows could be hooked to a standard, honest, PCI-certified expression gearbox, or, more likely, they could be programmed to deceive. Which was it?

And what had happened to the man with the silver cane?

And the colors? What had happened to the colors? A whole world of colors. Were they real? Real or not, they were wonderful.

"What did you say about my ocular apparatus?"

"Oh, it was completely shot. I gave you a new set of lookers."

She stamped her foot. "Put it back!"

"What?"

"Give me back my old ocular apparatus! Right now!"

"Oh, you don't want that. Besides, I cracked it removing the iris mounts."

She shook her index finger in his face. "Don't you tell me what I do or do not want, Sanderson."

He reconfigured his eyebrows so that one was raised higher than the other.

"Ugh! Don't look at me like that. *You* brought me here. *You* stole my eyes. *You* took my colors away. Do you think you own me because you gave a sleazy metal monger some old pipe?"

"No, I... Of course I don't. There was the telescope too, but that's not the point. I don't own you at all. I wanted... well... I wanted..."

"What?" She took a step towards him, and he plopped back down on his stool. "You wanted what?"

"I wanted to save you."

"STAINED-STEEL-DOUBLE-DEALING-SHIFTY-
EYEBROWED-EYEBALL-STEALER!"

Sanderson's eyebrows twanged back to a neutral position, his expression unit forced to reset from non-computable input.

Beatrice sat and covered her face with her hands.

After a minute during which the only sound was the patter of condensation dripping on Beatrice's lap, Sanderson said, "Colors? Like, fancy colors?"

Beatrice lowered her hands from her face.

"If it's colors you want..."

~

Mordant orange. Alcian blue. Azophloxin. Safranin. Naphthol green.

As a night janitor in the physical sciences building at NONY University, Sanderson had access to a variety of exotic chemicals, including dyes. He had over the years noticed bottles of, say, methylene blue growing caps and shawls of brownish-gray dust, their labels slowly fading. Who would miss them? While cleaning near a shelf, he wrapped a bottle in a cloth and stowed it in the space in his back where a human would keep a kidney.

On his way home in the morning, a service construct with a shock collar limped in the opposite direction down the sidewalk, carrying an enormous plastic-wrapped armchair on its back. The construct had been assembled from a variety of mismatched parts, with one leg several inches shorter than the other. The sound of grinding gears made Sanderson wince.

Sanderson stopped and met the construct's gaze. "Do you need a hand with that, old man?"

The construct lowered its eyes and quickened its pace, adding a new clatter to the sound of its gears.

"Don't be afraid. I want to help." When the construct only

hurried more, Sanderson called after him, "Tell me, whose chair do you carry? What's your master's name?" The construct continued down the street without a word.

"This city…" muttered Sanderson, resuming his walk home. But then his thoughts turned in a different direction: "This city brought me Beatrice." And the morning sun glittering in broken glass on the sidewalk took on a magical quality.

In his basement apartment, he had set up a desk under a window for Beatrice to write. Upon arriving home, he leaned over to peek at the paper in the typewriter and read:

Ms. Greasley owned no fewer than 17 pairs of goggles, and each served a ~~specific~~ ~~unfathomable~~ ~~inscrutable~~ ~~well-defined~~ *diabolical*

She had added a word and not yet crossed it out. That was good, right? He knew better than to mention it, though. He had congratulated her on "inscrutable," which he had considered an excellent word, once told what it meant, and she had accused him of patronizing her. Not knowing the word "patronizing" either, he had replied slyly that she was being inscrutable. She had just looked at him and shook her head.

Leave the words to the writers, the politicians, the priests. They were no business of his.

"Beatrice?" he called.

"In here."

Sanderson found her squatting by a basin in the workshop, stirring a shimmery, lavender liquid with a wooden spoon. The room had been overtaken by sheets of colored fabric, some hanging to dry, some ironed and folded, some beginning to be fashioned into shirts and scarves and dresses. Beatrice scooped a wad of dripping fabric out of the basin. "What do you think of this color?"

"I think you would call it lavender."

"Yeah, but do you like it?"

"I..." He knew she hated insincerity and had a knack for detecting it. "I think you would look good wearing clothing of that color."

"That's what you said about the viridian."

"Well..."

"You don't care one way or the other about any of these colors do you?"

He slumped on his stool and shrugged. "Honestly, no. But I'm just—"

"You're just like everyone else, is what you are. And that's fine. Why would I expect you to be any different?"

"I'm just a *janitor*, Beatrice. There are all sorts of people, constructs," he waved his hand towards the morning light straining through the window, "out there who, I think, who... would appreciate—"

"No, Sanderson. No. That's what I thought too, but no. You know what I did yesterday afternoon, while you were sleeping? I put on that blue scarf and went for a walk around the city. I wondered how many people would notice. How many would smile? How many would say, 'My, what a lovely scarf'? Because it *is* a lovely scarf. It makes me happy just to look at it." She sighed. "I expected disapproving looks, tut-tutting, spitting maybe. I was ready for all that, if only somebody, one person, mechanical or otherwise, would take a second to nod in approval before continuing on their way, I would be happy. And do you know what happened, Sanderson? Can you guess what happened?"

"I... don't think I can."

"Nothing."

"What?"

"Nothing happened. Noth-thing. Nobody smiled, nobody frowned, nobody remarked to their friend, 'What on Earth is she wearing?' No mothers dragged their kids across the street to avoid me. Nobody even called me a whore, Sanderson. I thought somebody would at least pay me the courtesy of assuming I have sex with strangers for money, but nobody cared even that little bit."

Beatrice stared hard into the basin of lavender dye.

"Uh…" said Sanderson.

"Ha! It's funny, really, me thinking I could be some kind of a trend-setter. I got a look at the fashion world up close and," she put her hand beside her mouth and stage whispered, "none of them know what the fuck they're doing." She put down her hand. "I figured, how hard can it be? But if there's one thing I learned from those brainless reprobates it's that people can love you, people can hate you, but if they don't notice you, you're dead."

Sanderson sagged on his stool.

"My non-existent novel is another joke. What was I thinking? An unoriginal, navel-gazing, faux-inspiring, amateurish piece of non-writing."

"But—"

"I figured it out, Sanderson. I'm a ghost. I've passed the world by, escaped its notice for good and forever. I'm dead, and this is hell."

Sanderson's facial features were unequal to the task of displaying the level of misery he felt. "But…" he said, "*I* noticed you."

Her eyes snapped onto him, her irises whirring into focus. "You?" she said. "*You* noticed me?"

"Yes."

"Sanderson." Her head tilted to the side. "I told you, I'm grateful to you for letting me stay here, but it's *only* because I can't pay my rent. You understand that, right?"

A pause while Sanderson's boiler rumbled lightly. "Yes, of course," he said. Taking advantage of a modification he had made to this expression unit, he forced his left eyebrow up in a quizzical position. "Oh, you thought...? Pshaw. It's just nice to have a roommate, you know?"

She narrowed her eyes at him for a few seconds and then relaxed. "Yeah. One who's not a sex addict."

"Right, right. Haha." His face snapped back to neutral.

Beatrice chomped on coal while waiting for Sanderson to come home from work. She should stop, she knew, but her mind inevitably wandered to all the things that could go wrong, and her hand groped for the box of nuggets.

Her plan was to show up at the *SteamVogue* building disguised as Crumpin Oiyashu, the brilliant designer whom nobody had seen in four and a half years. As Ms. Greasley's assistant, Beatrice had sent countless telegrams to Oiyashu's publicist, who always responded in the same way: "Crumpin can't wait to show you her latest collection. She's making her final alterations as we speak." But season after season passed without Crumpin making an appearance.

As it happened, Oiyashu was a construct of similar design to Beatrice, and with some facial alterations by Sanderson—most notably a pair of large, bell-shaped ears—Beatrice looked like she had been stamped out of the same sheet of metal as the reclusive designer. Also in favor of her scheme was Oiyashu's reputation for flouting social conventions. Showing up unannounced after so long was the kind of thing to which people would respond, "That's Crumpin being Crumpin!"

Or would they?

Yes, they would. Beatrice was sure of it. *If* she could pull off the attitude. Attitude was everything in the fashion world. All she needed to do was waltz in there and treat every question with impatience, every doubt with deafness, and every effort at meeting her needs as short of the level of competence she had grown to expect. Ms. Greasley had taught her that. Attitude created its own reality.

The front door creaked open and thonked shut, and Sanderson's feet scraped into the kitchen, his eyebrows arched high.

"Good morning," he said.

Beatrice's steamy exhale whistled like a tea kettle. "Good morning."

He looked at her for a moment. "You... You don't have to do this, you know."

"Sanderson—"

"You have nothing to prove to those people."

"I know that. I'm not doing it to prove anything *to them*. I just can't..." She sighed. "I'm not like you, Sanderson. You're content here in your little apartment, your simple job, your quiet life, with your tools and your scrap metal projects. I envy you, actually."

Sanderson let out a gust of air.

"But my fire burns too hot."

Sanderson sat down and grabbed the box of coal nuggets. "Well, if you're determined, I'll go with you."

"Don't be silly."

"Wouldn't a famous designer have somebody with them? Someone to carry the clothes at least?"

"I suppose."

"There you go." Sanderson's jaws ground the coal nuggets to dust as his eyebrows angled innocently up.

"Alright. Just let me do the talking."

Sanderson kept his eyes down as he followed Beatrice into the *SteamVogue* lobby. He carried two suitcases and a dozen bulging garment bags, which hung from a closet rod soldered to his shoulders. He activated his infrared sensors to keep track of the humans in his vicinity without risking looking them in the eyes.

"Oh, my, it's meat brain is having a hard time keeping up, isn't it..." Beatrice was saying. "... Yes, do check with her, and while you're up, be a dear and bring me a glass of distilled water, not deionized you understand, distilled... My publicist? What on Earth for? Oh, while you're at it, tell him next Wednesday is out of the question and have him reschedule with Denise... Thank goodness, someone with their head screwed on... It's about time. Through here? Come, Chizzelworth."

Sanderson took a moment to recall that Chizzelworth was the name Beatrice had selected for him. He followed her staccato prattle down a hallway and into a large conference room, where he set down the suitcases on a table and unloaded the garment bags onto the backs of chairs.

Having ostensibly fulfilled his purpose, he stood in a corner of the room and watched Beatrice wield a growing confidence, watched the faces of the *SteamVogue* staff turn from incredulity, to alarm at the sight of the full-spectrum garments, to a guarded fearfulness tinged with respect.

They were buying it.

Ms. Greasley eventually showed up, saying, "Well, well, well, Crumpin." She held out her mug for someone to take, and would have let it drop to the floor if a woman wearing a leather and brass bodice hadn't lunged for it. "It's been too long."

She extended her hand to Beatrice, but then partially withdrew it and narrowed her eyes. She was the only one in the room that had ever seen Crumpin Oiyashu in person.

Beatrice's prattle stopped as she leveled her gaze at Ms. Greasley. Her left eyelid twitched, and curls of steam rose from her ears.

"You had a resurfacing," said Ms. Greasley.

"How lovely of you to notice."

The tension in the room dropped a notch, and the woman with the mug set it on a side table. Sanderson sidled over to it, retrieving something from the space in his back where a man would keep a kidney.

Peach. Scarlett. Fuchsia. Amethyst. Sapphire.

Beatrice's assistants competed for attention like a trio of birds of paradise, their multi-colored plumage now the height of fashion. They looked like clowns to her. But they were *her* clowns, and when she shushed them, their mouths clamped shut and they stood in a row like soldiers.

"Would you like a glass of water?" ventured Lucretia, the boldest of the three, crowned with faux peacock feathers.

Beatrice leaned over her desk, reading *The New Old New York Foghorn*. "Just leave me alone, would you?" But as they filed out, she added, "Make it a mug of kerosene."

Her office was high enough to be above most of the smog, and cheery rays of afternoon sunlight slanted through the window onto the newspaper. She ran her hand over a photograph beneath the front page headline. The construct called Sanderson had been convicted of eight counts of murder, and was presumed to have poisoned dozens more going back over twenty years, using the pilfered chemical stockpiles of NONY University researchers. A public shredding was scheduled for the following Tuesday.

A peacock feather sagged into Beatrice's field of view as Lucretia set a mug on her desk. "Anything else, Ma'am?"

"No."

Lucretia nodded at the newspaper. "They say he poisoned Samantha Greasley, too. You knew her, right?"

Beatrice recalled that day at the *SteamVogue* building when

Ms. Greasley, in the middle of inspecting a striped blue and yellow dress, had suddenly excused herself and wobbled out of the conference room.

She'd been taken to the hospital, her assistants returning from her bedside with wild looks in their eyes, fearful and excited. After three days, she was reported to have said something extraordinary:

"Crumpin is not Crumpin. Beatrice. That was her name. The twitchy goggle loser. Beatrice."

Having said this, Ms. Greasley had coughed up a wad of blood and died.

She had recognized Beatrice after all, but her delayed revelation came after Beatrice's designs were leaked to the press, after the seeds of public obsession had been sown. The accompanying scandal, of course, only propelled her faster, farther, deeper into the public consciousness. And so a year later, there she sat, in that large, sun-bright, above-the-smog office, with clownish assistants hanging on her every word. If she had written it into a story...

"Yes, I knew her," said Beatrice. "In fact, I started out as her assistant."

Lucretia nodded solemnly.

"Now, leave me alone, please."

"Of course, Ma'am." Lucretia backed out the door and pulled it silently shut.

Beatrice carried her mug to the window and sipped while looking down on the simmering city.

Move to New Old New York. The smog's not as bad as they say, if you can lie your way to an executive office suite.

Her boiler grumbled and her shoulders spasmed. She swallowed another mouthful of kerosene. *Let it come.* Steam piped from her ears as she gritted her teeth. She felt the vitriol building up, the impending release of a wonderful, thundering, preconscious judgment, this time directed at herself, her craven hypocrisy, and her egotism. It tickled the inside of her nose and shuddered her jaw. But it wouldn't come out. She'd seen humans raise a finger and lean their heads back, open-mouthed, eyes watering, saying, "Ah... ah... ah..." waiting for a "Choo!" that wouldn't come. She poured the rest of the kerosene down her throat.

An image popped into her head of Sanderson sinking in the shredder, his eyebrows stoic, as his feet and then his legs were chewed to bits. He would be well-stoked and watered, so that he would be conscious during the moment of destruction. She'd never been to a public shredding, but she assumed the crowd would jeer. There would be shouts of "Murderer!" and posters of his victims held on high. Would he close his eyes, cover his ears? When his torso entered the shredder there would be a flash of fire and steam. She imagined his head thrown back, his arms raised, a shriek of air forced through his voice box.

Sanderson was a simple construct. Maybe not as simple as she had thought, but pretty simple. He wanted the good to live and the bad to die. Period. Would she have been his next victim? But he loved her. That she was sure of, deceitful eyebrows or not.

The tickling in her nose subsided. Her boiler simmered audibly but steadily. She returned to her desk, set down her mug, and folded up the newspaper.

He deserved a friendly face in the crowd. He'd saved her, after all.

"Lucretia!"

The ridiculous peacock headdress popped into the room.

"Clear my Tuesday morning. I'm going to the execution of this construct. I want to be there in his final moments."

Lucretia gulped. "Yes, Ma'am."

She'd wear the blue scarf, the one she'd made in his apartment. This time, everyone would notice it.

CONTRIBUTOR NOTES

Enit'ayanfe Ayosojumi Akinsanya is a Nigerian writer. He was shortlisted for the *2018 Dusty Manuscript GTB National Novel Prize*, and for the *2023 Afritondo Short Story Prize*. He won the *2022 Itanile International Short Story Award* and the *First-Position Prize for the 2022 Bicontinental Arts Lounge Contest* for The Green We Left Behind CNF Climate-Change Print Anthology. He holds a double-honors degree in English Language and Education from Obafemi Awolowo University in Ile-Ife, Nigeria. He is the author of a short-story collection, *How to Catch a Story That Doesn't Exist*. He loves reading poetry and watching deeply human films.

Beth Anderson is a writer and night person from Austin, Texas. Her work has appeared in *Akashic, Beneath Strange Stars, Trembling with Fear, Furious Gravity*, and other publications. She holds an MFA in Popular Fiction from the Stonecoast Creative Writing Program. Find her on Twitter @bandersonmedia and Bluesky @bethanderson.bsky.social.

Beth Kette Anderson placed in the Top 25 New Writers for *Glimmer Train*. Since then she has had stories published in *The Saturday Evening Post* and numerous anthologies. Beth lives at the very end of the Puget Sound in Washington State with her husband and their rescue dog, Boomer.

Isis Aquino is a Dominican writer, translator, poetry slammer, and cultural manager who has dedicated more than half her life to words. As cultural manager, she founded and ran "El viento frío" for the Dominican Republic's Círculo Literario from 2007 to 2017. Isis's poems appear in anthologies and magazines in various countries. Her poetry collections include *Desandar el abismo* (2023), *Balas perdidas* (2014), and *QUOD SCRIPSI* (2011). She authored the science fiction anthology *Relatos de la Tierra y sus colonias* (2020) and novella *En la cuerda floja* (2016). Follow Isis on Twitter @isisaquino, and visit her at <u>isisaquino.wordpress.com</u>.

Robert Bagnall was born in Bedford, England, in 1970. He has written for the BBC, national newspapers, and government ministers. Five of his stories have been selected for the annual *Best of British Science Fiction* anthologies and his sci-fi thriller *2084 - The Meschera Bandwidth* is available from Amazon, as are two anthologies, each collecting 24 of his eighty-odd published stories. He can be contacted via his blog at meschera.blogspot.com.

Keech Ballard is a lone voice crying in the southwest desert of the human mind. He has published an outré amalgam of fiction, nonfiction, and poetry since the current crisis began. A few of these winsome welkins of wonder are available as podcasts. Keech's work has appeared in *Fantasy Magazine*, *Dark Moments*, *Illumen*, and *Bag of Bones*, inter alia.

Michael Bettendorf (he/him) is a writer from the US Midwest. His short fiction has appeared/is forthcoming at *Drabblecast*, *Sley House Press*, and elsewhere. Michael's debut experimental novel/gamebook *Trve Cvlt* is forthcoming at Tenebrous Press (2024). He works in a high school library in Lincoln, NE—a place he tries to convince the world is too strange to be a flyover state. Find him on BlueSky/Twitter @BeardedBetts and www.michaelbettendorfwrites.com.

Pixie Bruner is a writer, editor, and cervical cancer survivor and patient advocate. She lives in Atlanta, GA with her doppelgänger and their cats. Her poetry has been published in *Space & Time Magazine*, *Whispers from Beyond* from Crystal Lake Publishing, and more. She has written for White Wolf Gaming Studio. Werespider characters at LARPs are all her fault.

Emma Burnett is a researcher and writer. She has had stories in *Mythaxis*, *Northern Gravy*, *Apex*, *Radon*, *Utopia*, *MetaStellar*, *Milk Candy Review*, *Elegant Literature*, *Roi Fainéant*, *The Sunlight Press*, *Rejection Letters*, and more. You can find her @slashnburnett, @slashnburnett.bsky.social, or emmaburnett.uk.

Christopher Collingwood was born and raised in Sydney, Australia. He completed university in Sydney and graduated with a degree in business studies. Chris has devoted his spare time to writing, with recent works published in *Andromeda Spaceways*, *Hexagon*, *Shoreline of Infinity*, *State of Matter*, *Dreamforge Anvil*, *Smoke in the Stars* anthology, *Qualia Nous Vol 2* anthology, and illustration in *JOURN-E* 2.1, among other dimensionally unstable places.

Jude Deluca's a nonbinary aegosexual Capricorn. Their areas of interest are YA horror, slasher fiction, magical girls, 90s nostalgia, superhero dads, and big beautiful men. They've been published by places such as From Beyond Press, Eerie River Publishing, Ice Floe Press, and lit mags like *Dusty Attic Publishing*, *Dollar Store Magazine*, and *Persimmon Review*.

Nicola de Vera (she/her) is a queer Filipino writer based in Los Angeles. Her stories have appeared or are forthcoming in *New World Writing*, *A Thin Slice of Anxiety*, *Exist Otherwise*, *Another New Calligraphy*, *Corporeal*, and elsewhere. She holds a BA in Communication from Ateneo de Manila University and an MBA from Cornell University.

Eric Farrell lives in Long Beach, California, where he works as a beer sales rep by day, and speculative fiction author by night. His writing credits stem from a career in journalism, where he reported for a host of local and metro newspapers in the greater Los Angeles area. He posts on Twitter @stygianspace and has recent fiction with *Aphotic Realm*, *Haven Spec*, and *HyphenPunk*.

Adam Fout is a neurodivergent author who writes nonfiction and speculative fiction. He has work in *Flash Fiction Online*, *December*, *J Journal*, *Proton Reader*, and more. He is a graduate of the 2020 Odyssey Writing Workshop.

Ken Foxe is a writer and transparency activist in Ireland. He is the author of two non-fiction books based on his journalism and likes to write short stories of horror, SF, and speculative fiction. Previous Stories: www.kenfoxe.com/short-stories/ | Twitter: www.twitter.com/kenfoxe | Instagram: www.instagram.com/kenfoxe

Amy Grech has sold over 100 stories to various anthologies and magazines including: *10 by 10 Flash Fiction Stories*, *Apex Magazine*, *Even in the Grave*, *Microverses*, *Punk Noir Magazine*, *Roi*

Fainéant Press, Tales from the Canyons of the Damned, Yellow Mama, and many others. Alien Buddha Press published her poetry chapbook, *A Shadow of Your Former Self.* She is an Active Member of the Horror Writers Association and the International Thriller Writers who lives in Forest Hills, Queens. You can connect with her on Bluesky: https://bsky.app/profile/ amygrech.bsky.social, Medium: https://medium.com/@crimson screams, X: https://x.com/amy_grech, or visit her website: https://www.crimsonscreams.com.

John Grey is an Australian poet, US resident, recently published in *Leading Edge, Poetry Salzburg Review,* and *Illumen.* Latest books, *Leaves On Pages, Memory Outside The Head,* and *Guest Of Myself* are available through Amazon. Work upcoming in *The Fifth Di, Space and Time,* and *Holy Flea.* He has won a Rhysling Award for genre poetry.

David Hammond lives in Virginia with his wife, two daughters, two dogs, a rat, and a multitude of insects. During the day, he makes websites. His stories have appeared in *Grain, Small Wonders, Metaphorosis,* and *Space & Time.* More of his writing can be found at oldshoepress.com.

J. D. Harlock is a Levantine-American writer, editor, researcher, and academic. In addition to their work at Solarpunk Magazine, as a poetry editor, and at Android Press, as an editor, J. D. Harlock's writing has been featured in *Strange Horizons, New York University's Library of Arabic Literature,* and the British Council's *Voices Magazine.* You can find them on LinkedIn, Twitter, Threads, & Instagram.

Ellen Harrold is an artist and writer focused on science and nature. A core aspect of her practice is the use of text, drawing, and painting to explore the connection between decay and renewal in the world around us. She is completing a master's degree in Art, Science, and Visual thinking at Dundee University and working as an artist, writer, and editor-in-chief of *Metachrosis Literary*. She has recently published written pieces with *Danse Macabre, New Note Poetry*, and *Die Leere Mitte*. She has also recently published her first book, *Aesthetics and Conventions of Medical Art*.

Alicia Hilton is an author, editor, arbitrator, professor, and former FBI Special Agent. Her work has appeared in *Back 2 OmniPark, Creepy Podcast, Dreams & Nightmares, Eastern Iowa Review, Litro, Modern Haiku, Mslexia, Neon, NonBinary Review, Not One of Us, Space and Time, Stoneboat Literary Journal, Vastarien, World Haiku Review, Year's Best Hardcore Horror Volumes* 4, 5, & 6, and elsewhere. Her website is https://alici ahilton.com. Follow her on Twitter @aliciahilton01 and Bluesky @aliciahilton.bsky.social.

Ai Jiang is a Chinese-Canadian writer, Nebula, Bram Stoker, and Ignyte Award winner, Hugo, Astounding, BSFA, Aurora, and Locus Award finalist, and an immigrant from Fujian, China currently residing in Toronto, Ontario. She is a member of HWA and SFWA. Her work can be found in *F&SF, The Dark, Uncanny*, among others. She is the recipient of Odyssey Workshop's 2022 Fresh Voices Scholarship and the author of *Linghun* and *I AM AI*. Find her on X (@Ai- Jiang_), Insta (@ai.jian.g), and online (http://aijiang.ca).

Brad Kelechava is a professional blogger whose writing you might stumble upon while searching the internet for topics spanning renewable energy to the history of rats. His short fiction appears in *Tales to Terrify, Utopia Science Fiction, Negative Space 2: A Return to Survival Horror*, and elsewhere. He is a member of Brooklyn Speculative Fiction Writers (BSFW). After years of living in New York City, he, his wife, and their two cats recently fled to the suburbs for more space.

Abigail Kemske is a Pushcart nominated writer. Her fiction is published in *Across the Margin*, *Vast Chasm Magazine*, *Apocalypse Confidential*, and more. She graduated twice from the University of Minnesota with a B.A. in English, and a M.Ed in English Education. Previously, she worked as a middle school English teacher. New York born and Wisconsin raised, Abigail now lives in the suburbs of Minneapolis, MN with her spouse, two children and their cat. She can often be found wandering the nearby forest, delighting in her senses. Follow her on social media @abigailkemske and her website abigailkemske.com.

Hec Lampert-Bates is a writer from Toronto, Ontario. Hec's stories can be found in *Fairlight Books*, *Alternate Route Journal*, *Lit.202*, and others. They are featured in the International Human Rights Art Festival and won the 2022 Bill Avner Creative Writing Award. Hec is working on his debut novel, and is a student of political philosophy and archaeology at University of Toronto.

Monica Louzon is a queer writer, translator, and editor. Her previous collaborations with Isis have included the story, "History of a Piano in Spacetime," which appeared in *MAYDAY Magazine*. Monica's translations have also appeared in *Apex Magazine*, *Constelación Magazine*, *Futura House*, and more. Her story "9 Dystopias" was a Best Microfiction 2023 winner, and her other stories, essays, and poems were published by *Haven Speculative Magazine*, *Oh Reader Magazine*, *Paranoid Tree*, and more. She was Acquiring Editor for *The Dread Machine* and founded the *MOSF Journal of Science Fiction*. To learn more about Monica and her works, visit https://linktr.ee/ molowrites.

Wil Magness lives in Portland, Oregon with his partner, their two kids, and their dog. He is a writer, creative director, and together with his wife and partner, a filmmaker. Their latest film is the sci-fi short, *The Manual*, which has accrued over half a million views since release. His short fiction has appeared in small press anthologies and indie literary magazines, and he is currently working on his third novel.

Avra Margariti is a queer author, Greek sea monster, and Rhysling-nominated poet with a fondness for the dark and the darling. Avra's work haunts publications such as *Vastarien*, *Asimov's*, and *F&SF*. *The Saint of Witches*, Avra's debut collection of horror poetry, is available from Weasel Press. You can find Avra on twitter (@avramargariti).

Donna J. W. Munro teaches high schoolers the slippery truths of government and history at her day job. Her students are her greatest inspiration. She lives with five cats, a fur covered husband, and an encyclopedia son. Her daughter is off saving the world. Donna's pieces are published in *Corvid Queen*, *Enter the Apocalypse*, *It Calls from the Forest*, *Apparition Lit*, *Pseudopod* 752, *Shakespeare Unleashed*, *Novus Monstrum*, *ParABnormal*, and many more. Check out her novels, *Revelation: Poppet Cycle* Book 1 and *Runaway: Poppet Cycle* Book 2, and her website for a complete list of works at https://www. donnajwmunro.net/.

Emma E. Murray's work has appeared in anthologies like *What One Wouldn't Do*, *Obsolescence*, and *Ooze: Little Bursts of Body Horror*, as well as magazines like *Cosmic Horror Monthly*, *If There's Anyone Left*, *Pyre*, and *Vastarien*. Her chapbook, *Exquisite Hunger*, is available from Medusa Haus, and her novelette, *When the Devil* (Shortwave), as well as her debut novel, *Crushing Snails* (Apocalypse Party), will be coming Summer

2024. To read more, you can visit her website EmmaEMur ray.com.

Kurt Newton's fiction and poetry have appeared in *Weird Tales*, *Strange Horizons*, *Eye to the Telescope*, *The Dark*, *Vastarien*, *The Fabulist*, *Flash Fiction Online*, and *Cafe Irreal*. His fourth short story collection, *Bruises*, was recently published by Lycan Valley Press. His most recent poetry chapbook, *The Ever-Evolving Alphabet*, was published by back room poetry.

Amabilis O'Hara writes speculative fiction & poetry inspired by emotional connection. Find em at <u>www.amabiliso-hara.com</u> or @AmabilisOHara on social media.

Jonathan Olfert's paleofiction and SFF stories have backstabbed and skulked their way into *Beneath Ceaseless Skies*, *Dark Recesses Press*, *Lightspeed*, *Radon Journal*, and other fine establishments. Jon and his partner live and work near Halifax.

H. V. Patterson (she/her) lives in Oklahoma and writes speculative poetry and fiction. She's a cofounder of *Horns and Rattles Press*. When she was little, she cried whenever she saw bright red. She remains sensitive to sunlight and bass vibrations. Recent stories and poems published with *Sliced Up Press*, *Diet Milk Magazine*, *Creature Publishing*, *Flame Tree Press*, *Eerie River*, *Flash Fiction Online*, and *Black Spot Books*. Find her on X @ScaryShelley and on Instagram @hvpattersonwriter.

Marisca Pichette is a queer author based in Massachusetts, on Pocumtuck and Abenaki land. More of her work appears in *Strange Horizons*, *Clarkesworld*, *Vastarien*, *The Magazine of Fantasy & Science Fiction*, *Fantasy Magazine*, *Flash Fiction Online*, *Nightmare Magazine*, and others. She is the flash winner of the 2022 *F(r)iction* Spring Literary Contest and has been nominated for the Best of the Net, Pushcart, Utopia, and Dwarf Stars awards. Her speculative poetry collection, *Rivers in Your Skin, Sirens in Your Hair* (Android Press) is a Bram Stoker Award finalist.

Katherine Quevedo was born and raised near Portland, Oregon, where she works as an analyst and lives with her husband and two sons. Her poetry has been nominated for the Pushcart Prize and the Rhysling Award, and her debut mini-chapbook, *The Inca Weaver's Tales*, is part of the *New Cosmologies* series from Sword & Kettle Press. Her poems appear in *Asimov's*, *Old Moon Quarterly*, *TOWER Magazine*, *Heroic Fantasy Quarterly*, *Anterior Skies*, *Boudin* by *The McNeese Review*, and elsewhere. When she isn't writing, she enjoys playing old-school video games, watching movies, singing, belly dancing, and making spreadsheets. Find her at www.katherinequevedo.com.

Daniel A. Rabuzzi (he/his) (www.danielarabuzzi.com) has been published in, among others, *Crab Creek Review*, *Asimov's*, *Grim & Gilded*, *Old Moon Quarterly*, *Abyss & Apex*, *Coffin Bell*, *Shimmer*, *Red Ogre Review*, *Goblin Fruit*, and *Lady Churchill's Rosebud Wristlet*. Pushcart nominee. He earned degrees in the study of folklore & mythology and European history. He lives in New York City with his artistic partner & spouse, the woodcarver Deborah A. Mills (www.deborahmillswoodcarving.com).

Purbasha Roy is a writer from Jharkhand India. A she/her. Her work has appeared or is forthcoming in *Logic(s)*, *Romance Writers of America*, *Mascara Literary Review*, *Acta Victoriana*, *Strange Horizons*, *Pulp Literary Review*, *Saltbush Review*, and elsewhere. Attained second position in 8th Singapore Poetry Contest. Best of the Net Nominee. Appeared in the Longlist of Erbacce Contest 2023.

Nnadi Samuel (he/him/his) holds a B.A in English & literature from the University of Benin. Author of 'Nature knows a little about Slave Trade' selected by Tate.N.Oquendo (Sundress Publication, 2023). His works have been previously published/forthcoming in *FIYAH, Fantasy Magazine, Uncanny Magazine, The Deadlands, Heartline Spec, Timber Ghost Press, Haven Spec Magazine, Utopian Science Fiction, Penumbric Speculative Poetry & Fiction Magazine, Liquid Imagination,* & elsewhere. His poem "Wormhole" was an Editor's Choice @Star*Line(Science Fiction Poetry, SFPA). A 3x Best of the Net, and 7x Pushcart Nominee. He tweets @Samuelsamba10.

Lorraine Schein is a New York writer and poet. Her work has appeared in VICE *Terraform, Strange Horizons, NewMyths,* and *Michigan Quarterly,* and in the anthologies *Wild Women and Tragedy Queens: Stories Inspired by Lana del Rey & Sylvia Plath.* Her book, *The Lady Anarchist Cafe,* is out now from Autonomedia. https://autonomedia.org/product/the-lady-anarchist-cafe/

Angela Yuriko Smith is a third-generation Shimanchu/Ryukyuan-American, award-winning poet, author, and publisher with 20+ years in newspapers. Publisher of *Space & Time Magazine* (est. 1966), two-time Bram Stoker Awards® Winner, and HWA Mentor of the Year, she shares Authortunities, a free weekly calendar of author opportunities at authortunities.substack.com.

Mahaila Smith (any pronouns) is a young femme writer, living and working on the traditional territory of the Algonquin Anishinabeg in Ottawa, Ontario. They are one of the co-editors for *The Sprawl Mag.* They like learning theory and writing speculative poetry. Their debut chapbook, *Claw Machine,* was published by Anstruther Press in 2020. Their second chapbook, *Water-Kin,* was published by Metatron Press in 2024. Their novelette in verse, *Seed Beetle*, is forthcoming with Stelliform Press. You can find more of their work on their website: mahailasmith.ca.

Christina Sng is a three-time Bram Stoker Award-winning poet, writer, essayist, and artist. Her work appears in numerous venues worldwide, including *Interstellar Flight Magazine, New Myths, Penumbric, Southwest Review,* and *The Washington Post.* Visit her at <u>christinasng.com</u> and connect @christinasng.

G. V. Silva was born in São Paulo, Brazil. He holds a bachelor's and a master's degree in philosophy from the State University of Campinas and a Ph.D. in philosophy from the Technical University of Berlin. He is a freelance interpreter and a translator of German philosophical works into Portuguese (Nietzsche, Schopenhauer, Walter Benjamin, among others). He is currently working on his debut sci-fi novel.

Rekha Valliappan is an award-winning multi-genre writer of short stories, poetry, flash fiction, novellas, and creative nonfiction. Her speculative fiction features widely in various journals and anthologies including *StepAway Magazine's:* The Imaginarium Fantasy Issue, *Disquiet Arts Literary Magazine, Theme of Absence, Litro Magazine, Saturday Evening Post, Zoetic Press, Teleport Magazine, The Punch Magazine, Queen Mov's Teahouse,* and elsewhere. She holds a MA in English Literature from Madras University, a Bachelor of Laws (Hons) from the University of London, and has earned nominations for the Pushcart Prize and Best of the Net.

Zac Walsh's work has appeared in journals such as *Calliope, Ink in Thirds, Blue Unicorn, LUMINA, Gulf Stream, Cimarron Review, Oakwood, Alligator Juniper, The Awakenings Review, The Other Journal, The Charleston Anvil, Light/Dark, Pissior, Inscape, Big*

Lucks, Lime Hawk, *Spectre Magazine*, *The DuPage Valley Review*, and *The Platte Valley Review*, as well as in anthologies like *Blood on the Floor and Small Batch*. He lives in a small, unincorporated town in Oregon with his wife and a very old dog.

Robert Walton is a retired middle school teacher, rock climber and mountaineer with ascents in Yosemite and Pinnacles National Park. Walton is an experienced writer. His novel Dawn Drums won the 2014 New Mexico Book Awards Tony Hillerman Prize for best fiction. His *Sockdologizer* won the Saturday Writers 2020 Everything Children contest. Most recently, his *Joaquin's Gold*, a collection of Joaquin Murrieta tales, was published on Amazon. website: http://chaosgatebook.wordpress.com/.

T. H. Yuan is a Taiwanese American writer. She has previously won the American Bar Association's "Legal Tech Fictional Writing Competition." Her work appears in *The Other Journal*.